Have a Great Summer

Have a Great Summer

FRANCESCA COCCHI

kensingtonbooks.com

KENSINGTON BOOKS are published by

Kensington Publishing Corp.
900 Third Avenue
New York, NY 10022

ISBN: 978-1-4967-6079-1 (ebook)
ISBN: 978-1-4967-6078-4

First Kensington Trade Paperback Printing: June 2026

10 9 8 7 6 5 4 3 2 1

Printed in the United States of America

The authorized representative in the EU for product safety and compliance
is eucomply OU, Parnu mnt 139b-14, Apt 123
Tallinn, Berlin 11317, hello@eucompliancepartner.com

To Matt, for crushing back

Chapter 1

Now

Everyone assumes the worst thing about living in a beach town year round is the off-season lull. The truth? It's those glorious summer days filled with constant reminders that other people are on vacation and you are not.

Take, for example, the fact that I—a twenty-nine-year-old woman—bike to work in the summer, not because I'm particularly nostalgic for the time when my baby blue beach cruiser was my only mode of transportation nor as part of my efforts to be environmentally conscious, but because parking is a nightmare. A year ago some benny (what Jersey Shore locals call the New Yorkers and North Jerseyans who flood our beaches every summer) discovered that no one checks the meters in my office's employee lot and spread the word like tourist gospel.

Or take the forty-three-minute line I waited in for lunch at my favorite bagel place today, packed between a group of college girls in bikinis that looked like they had been purchased on Instagram and a sunburnt dad bartering with a four-year-old (one more hour in the ocean in exchange for three bites of lunch—fine, how about two?). I scarfed down my toasted cinnamon raisin with cream cheese in two minutes, which left me exactly zero minutes to bike back to the office.

And while you're at it, take the Jeep I park my bike next to when I arrive at the city clerk's office a few hours later. It's a black Wrangler with the doors off, two sandy surfboards strapped to the roof. The kind of car that brags, *I'm off the clock. Jealous?*

As I lock my bike, I silently hope that the Jeep's driver is here to pay a parking ticket.

Inside, I wave to Linda. She smiles at me from behind the counter and holds up a finger, then disappears into the rows of filing cabinets to grab the documents we spoke about on the phone.

I'm here for a story—or, at this point, I suppose it's really just a pitch. A few weeks ago I'd heard rumblings that a buzzy Manhattan-based restaurant group was eyeing Brantley Beach for its next concept, so I'd emailed Linda, asking if she could keep an eye out for any leads. She'd called me this morning with an update: Sure enough, Diamond Group had applied for a local liquor license.

I scan the drab waiting room. There are only three other people here: Linda's coworker and the couple she's helping at the far end of the counter, their backs to me. The Jeep's owners, I assume. I listen for keywords, but instead of "parking violation" I catch "marriage license application." Figures.

I take a seat along the back wall and pull my laptop out of my bag, then balance it on my thighs so I can catch up on emails while I wait. The contents of my inbox remind me just how desperately I want the Diamond Group news to be true. If they really are opening a restaurant in town, Shore Life will want to cover it.

I'll want to cover it.

Partly because it has the potential to be an exciting food

story, with appeal beyond our usual Monmouth and Ocean counties audience. But mostly because it has nothing to do with weddings.

Because honestly? I'm starting to get sick of weddings.

My whole career up until now has revolved around them. After college, I landed a job as a severely (though predictably) underpaid editorial assistant at the biggest bridal magazine in the country, *Ever After.* I couldn't afford to live in New York City (even with the three potential roommates I'd found in a Facebook group, it would have been a stretch), so I opted to move back in with my parents and commute an hour and a half each way via train from the town where I grew up, smack-dab in the middle of the New Jersey coastline.

Ever After was my dream job. It didn't matter that the hours were long, or that my salary roughly translated to minimum wage (a hefty chunk of which went straight toward my student loans), or even that I wasn't writing as much as I'd hoped. I'd gotten a job in "the industry"—something I'd been warned by countless professors and friends' parents and parents' friends would be next to impossible these days.

And yet there I was, researching floral trends for the staff writers, fetching samples for photoshoots and transcribing interviews with famous planners, designers and (my favorite) chefs. The editor in chief was brilliant, creative and devastatingly chic, but also kind and supportive—so different from the Miranda Priestly incarnate I'd conjured when I'd first accepted the role. I managed her calendar with the steadfastness of a president's chief of staff. I wanted to be her. I fell in love with the job, the team, the city—and somewhere along the way, I fell in love with weddings, too.

Each morning I settled into my squishy plastic seat on NJ Transit, turned up my podcast and watched the shore give way to skyscrapers, content.

The problem with a dream job? Eventually, you wake up.

Two weeks after my one-year anniversary of working at *Ever After,* the publisher called an all-hands meeting. She announced we'd be decreasing our frequency from twelve issues a year to six, and that only half of the staff would be keeping their jobs. I wasn't one of them.

I spent the next month refreshing job boards on LinkedIn and Ed2010 to no avail: It was 2018, and it seemed like all of the big New York City publishers (and most of the small ones) were facing a similar fate. I sent LinkedIn messages to every writer and editor and stylist and photographer I'd crossed paths with during my first year as a working adult and set up phone calls with a few. Everyone promised to keep me top of mind for any openings or freelance opportunities. But something about the way they spoke warned me not to get my hopes up. I felt my connections to that world severing as quickly as they'd formed.

I breathed a sigh of relief when an editor from a local website called Shore Life emailed me about an opening for a lifestyle reporter, based right in my hometown. The company was shifting its budget and editorial strategy toward content designed to bring in either a new audience or ad dollars. And, as it turned out, weddings attracted both. No matter that I was twenty-three and unwed myself—my experience at *Ever After* meant I was the perfect candidate to become Shore Life's resident wedding expert, responsible for churning out dozens of digital stories per week: roundups of the season's biggest trends, local vendor spotlights and a big, monthly feature on a Jersey Shore wedding that would soon become my "Real Weddings" column.

I wasn't ready to give up on New York, but Shore Life felt like the perfect solution for the time being. I could save some money, build up my clips, then try again next year.

But instead of just one year, six passed. I'm still working at Shore Life, I'm still single—and I have major wedding fatigue.

I flood my editor's inbox with pitches for non-wedding stories, and she reluctantly approves about one a month to appease me. Which is why I really need that document Linda found to confirm my suspicions.

I glance toward the counter but she still hasn't returned. That's when I hear his voice.

"I'm sorry, Claire. I honestly just didn't think of it."

I know that voice. I haven't heard it in thirteen years, but that hardly matters—I'd never mistake who it belongs to. I freeze, my fingers hovering an inch above the keyboard, and shift my gaze to the left as subtly as possible, toward the couple. And now that the man has turned to face the impossibly beautiful blond woman next to him I can see that he is, in fact, who I think he is.

Sebastian Nikolaou. The subject of a big, embarrassing, years-long high school crush. And—though I doubt he even realizes it—the first and only guy to truly break my heart.

His hair is a little different—still thick and dark like I remember, but cut much shorter on the sides, with what remains of his once-wild curls combed into submission. The woman next to him is pretty tall, maybe five feet nine, but still he towers over her. His already olive skin has taken on a deep tan, like it always did this time of year. He wears a white knit polo, navy blue chinos that skim his mile-long legs and buttery leather loafers, an expensive-looking watch on his wrist. It's jarring to see him so dressed up, so adult-looking. He's thirty-one now, I realize. Whenever a flash of him appears in my mind—something that has happened more often than I'd care to admit over the years—he's always sixteen or seventeen and wearing either swim trunks (no shirt, no shoes) or a navy blue Bubba's shirt, khaki shorts and white Vans—his uniform for the two high school summers we worked together at his family's restaurant.

"Well, I really thought we'd get this done today," the woman says, a pinched look of desperation on her pretty face. She looks effortlessly chic, wearing a chambray blouse tucked into white linen trousers, her tiny waist cinched with a leather belt, and a pair of designer sandals. "It was hard enough for me to even get this week off. I don't think I'll be able to get out this way again until the wedding."

That's when I notice a sparkling diamond on her left ring finger, and I realize that I know who this woman is, too: She's Sebastian's fiancée, Claire. I mean, I don't *know* her know her, but I still follow Sebastian on social media, and I'm embarrassed to admit that I recognize her. He isn't very active on any platform, but on the rare occasions he has posted over the years, I've certainly taken notice. A tagged Facebook album of ever-so-slightly blurry photos of him with friends at a college party his freshman year at the University of California in Santa Barbara. A sepia-filtered Instagram feed post of a new surfboard in the sand, the Pacific in the background. A "Throwback Thursday" at Bubba's with his mom for her sixtieth birthday. And, yes, an engagement announcement, reposted to his Instagram Stories from a user named @ClaireC717.

I'd seen the photo right before bed one night this past fall, my traitorous Instagram algorithm serving it front and center the second I opened the app. It was taken on the beach, somewhere in Santa Barbara, I assumed—he'd stayed there after college, working in restaurant supply chain strategy, according to LinkedIn. I remember thinking it was a stunning photo that appeared to be taken from the vantage point of a drone. Something an influencer would post and the social lead at Shore Life or *Ever After* would DM for permission to share.

There was Sebastian, down on one knee, looking as devastatingly handsome as ever. His mouth slightly open as if he'd just let out a joyful laugh. His teeth a flash of bright white. The collar of his linen button-down blowing in the breeze. Claire was facing him, doubled over with her hands covering her mouth, shock playing on her blue eyes. (Does something about being proposed to render women physically incapable of resisting this pose? If I wrote for a less earnest outlet, I'd pitch an investigative report.) The caption read, EASIEST YES! I CAN'T WAIT TO BE YOUR WIFE, @SEBASTIAN_SURFS.

I'd tapped her profile, but it was private. A dead end. All I could see was a smiling profile photo of her and a bio that read UCSB CLASS OF 2016, followed by the Greek letters of a sorority.

"Shelly?" Sebastian says now, turning back to the woman behind the counter while Claire taps out a message on her phone. "What if you signed it for us—would that work?"

Shelly sighs, as if she's about to recite something she's told other people a thousand times. "Like it says on the site: No witness, no license. I'm already the notary." She taps her pen against a section of the papers between them for emphasis. "Can't do both."

Sebastian drags a hand down his face and rubs his chin, but then he nods, accepting this. He turns back to Claire.

"Who could we call?" Claire asks, looking up from her phone.

Sebastian raps his knuckles lightly on the counter. "Not my mom. She's closing the restaurant tonight, and she's really short-staffed since the high school kids aren't out of school for the summer yet."

"What about Andre? Or Theo?"

I clock the names of Sebastian's best friends from high school.

"Both working. And even if one of them could cut out early I doubt they'd get here by five." I glance at the time on my laptop: 4:47. "We'll just have to come back another time. I'll figure it out."

I can't see Claire's face very well now, but I imagine she does not look happy. She nods, quick and curt.

"Bring a friend or family member next time," Shelly says.

"Someone who really knows you—they're attesting to your intention to get married to each other." She hands the unfinished paperwork to Sebastian, smiling. "And unless you want to come back to see me a third time, make sure they bring ID."

I'm head down, rummaging through my bag for a pretend object to avoid being seen by Sebastian and Claire on their way out, when Linda's traitorous voice travels from the depths of the filing cabinets. "Ha! There you are." She emerges, waving a manila folder in my direction. "I'm so sorry, Angelina. Our intern must have refiled it this morning by mistake. His system is all madness, no method."

I offer Linda a tight smile and wait, like a hunted animal that knows it's been discovered and has nowhere to run.

"Lina Mariano." Heat burns my cheeks at the sound of my name coming out of his mouth: a fact, not a question.

I'm still sitting, frozen in place. I force myself to meet his eyes across the room. "Sebastian Nikolaou," I manage to croak out. His name is an incantation I've been afraid to utter for years, worried of the dark powers it might wield. "Hi."

He crosses the room, reaching me in a few long strides. I slide my bag and laptop onto the chair next to mine and stand, awkwardly. He's standing right in front of me, curved slightly, like a question mark, to address our height difference (I'm only five feet tall, and the Converse I keep under my desk and changed into for the ride here aren't helping me out). I tip my head back until I make contact with his eyes (they've always reminded me of green sea glass), an action that proves a lot more intimidating than it was a minute ago when he was all the way on the other side of the room.

Just as I'm wondering what will happen next, he bends down and hugs me.

I squeeze my eyes shut and hold my breath. Acts of self-preservation: My senses simply cannot take any more of him. I need to restrict access.

I pull away first and push my shoulders back, determined to look totally unfazed by this run-in. I quickly imagine what he's seeing right now. I blew out my hair this morning, so that's a plus, though I'm sure I could use a comb after biking here. I'm wearing a white blouse with a tie at the waist, my favorite Abercrombie jeans and the aforementioned Converse. I wish I'd taken the time to put on more makeup than tinted moisturizer and a few swipes of mascara, but overall, not bad.

"I can't believe I ran into you," he says, and the genuine smile that follows has my ego doing somersaults. "My mom will be so jealous when I tell her."

Now I'm the one smiling. I've run into Barbara "Bubba" Nikolaou, restaurant owner and beloved Brantley Beach community member, every now and then over the years, and she's always over the moon to see me (a mutual feeling). She still says I'm one of her favorite employees of all time. "How's Bubba doing?"

"Good, good. She's retiring, believe it or not. After this season."

He's right: I can't believe it. "Really? Wow—I mean, good for her, though! She certainly deserves it."

Just as I'm about to ask what will happen to the restaurant, Claire appears. Because I'm a tragic woman, I'd briefly forgotten about her.

"Lina, this is my fiancée, Claire Cunningham."

"Nice to meet you!" she says brightly, wrapping one manicured hand around Sebastian's bicep and extending the other to shake mine.

"Lina Mariano," I say as we shake.

"Lina Mariano. . ." she repeats, with some familiarity. Her big blue eyes shift as she tries to place me—identify my significance. I indulge myself for a second: Maybe Sebastian has told her all about me when he's feeling nostalgic.

But then she snaps her fingers. "Shore Life, right? I love your column! It's how I found all our wedding vendors. I know nothing about New Jersey, so you really saved me." She says "New Jersey" in that sort of mocking way people who have spent very little time in New Jersey but hate on it anyway always do.

"Don't think it will win me a Pulitzer, but it's fun," I say. I can practically hear my best friend, Maren, on my shoulder: *Would it kill you to cut the whole self-deprecation thing for, like, two seconds?* While I'm always flattered to meet a reader in the wild, I'm also a little embarrassed. Sebastian probably had no idea that I cover the local wedding scene for a living—when I'd told him I wanted to be a writer all those years ago, this isn't exactly what I'd had in mind. "I'm glad you found it helpful," I add.

"You're always so modest, Lina," Sebastian says. "My mom told me every business up and down the Shore with a remotely wedding-related service would kill for you to feature them. And the ones you do cover can barely keep up with all the calls they get after."

See? Give yourself more credit, says shoulder-Maren, smugly. I relax a little.

"So how do you know Seb?" Claire asks.

I internally cringe at this nickname, which I've never heard before. Then I look to Sebastian for help, curious how he'll concisely sum up our relationship to one another.

Those green eyes consider me for a moment before he answers. "Lina and I worked at the restaurant together in high school. She's one of my mom's favorites."

The truth, if quite an oversimplified version of it.

"That's perfect!" Claire exclaims. When I knit my brows, confused, she adds: "You can be our witness!"

I catch the briefest flash of concern on Sebastian's face before he nods. "Do you mind, Lina? It should only take a minute."

I look from Sebastian to Claire and back again, wondering how I got into this situation.

Sebastian Nikolaou is getting married to someone who isn't me. And, apparently, I'm going to help him do it.

"Of course," I say, feeling my fragile little teenage heart break all over again. "I'd be happy to."

Chapter 2

Then
Fifteen Years Ago

I'd thought slinging hot dogs and slushies would be a pretty easy gig. Certainly better than sweating in the sun as a lifeguard or operating rickety rides at the boardwalk. But that first morning made me seriously doubt my own judgment.

It was the summer of 2009—for me, the one between eighth grade and high school—and I'd be working the snack bar window at Bubba's, the diner-slash-seafood-grill where the boardwalk begins in Brantley Beach. My best friend, Maren Murphy, had gotten her first summer job, too, sorting vintage clothing and accessories at the hip thrift store her aunt owned. At the time we felt like we'd waited a lifetime to finally become working women. I could practically smell the perfume-scented Hollister jeans I'd buy with my first paycheck.

The first red flag I ignored? My shifts started *early*—and even back then, I wasn't a morning person. Bubba's opened at 7:00 a.m. to serve lifeguards and boardwalk joggers, which meant I'd have to arrive at 6:30 sharp to brew coffee, slice bagels and fill the pastry case. I could kiss sleeping in goodbye. If I woke up at six, I'd have just enough time to brush my teeth, run a comb through my thick brown hair, throw on my uniform (a navy Bubba's polo, Bermuda khaki shorts, and the pair of nonslip white sneakers my mom and I had picked up at Payless) and bike to the restaurant.

But the bigger problem proved to be something—or should I say, someone—I couldn't have anticipated: Kevin Herman, the rising senior and snack bar veteran who, to his dismay, was responsible for training me.

Kevin Herman took working at the snack bar quite seriously. And it became clear, as that first day wore on, that my execution of each task he assigned me fell short of his expectations. I was too chatty with customers while on the register, too slow restocking the condiment station with packets of ketchup or honey mustard, too clumsy transferring plastic white baskets of chicken tenders and crinkle-cut fries from the kitchen window to the pickup counter.

Around 1:00 p.m. I learned I'd committed a rookie mistake of the gravest order: Apparently, I'd failed to sufficiently clean the soft-serve maker ahead of the lunchtime rush. When I flipped the switch on the big silver machine to dispense a twist, it began gurgling and shaking, then simply shut down. I handed a sunburnt eight-year-old a sorry excuse for a boardwalk cone, more of a dollop than a proper swirl, as Kevin watched, shaking his head with resigned disappointment.

Kevin ordered me to take over monitoring the kitchen window for him while he marched to the back office, presumably to call a technician and list my shortcomings to Bubba, the eponymous owner. I groaned, pressing my palms to my face.

One of the cooks called, "Order up!" from the kitchen, then deposited a row of baskets along the counter. My arms loaded with as many of them as I could carry, I turned toward the customer pickup window just as the door that connected the snack bar to the main dining room swung open.

And then I was on the floor, covered in French fries and ketchup.

"Shit," a boy's voice said. "Are you okay?"

I opened my eyes and saw only the ceiling at first. Then the voice's owner appeared in my field of vision, kneeling over me.

The first thing I noticed was that he was tall. Sure, I was lying on the ground, but even from that vantage point I could tell. The snack bar was tiny, and Kevin wasn't much bigger than me. This boy seemed like a giant in comparison. Each detail rendered him more like an entirely different species from the boys in my eighth-grade class. A defined jawline. The curve of a bicep peeking out from under his polo sleeve. He wore the same shirt as me, with khaki pants and white (now ketchup-stained) Vans. He raked a hand through his hair, which was the darkest shade of brown, overgrown and curly. He had thick eyebrows and long, dark lashes to match that contrasted with his striking green eyes.

He extended a big, tanned hand to me. I grabbed it and let him pull me to my feet in one effortless motion. I immediately wiped my hand on my shorts, praying he didn't notice how clammy it was.

"Did you hit your head or anything?" His dark brows knit with concern.

I smoothed my shirt, wincing at the glob of ketchup smack-dab in the middle of my chest. Then I tried to fix my hair a little. A fry fell to the ground. "Um, no. I think I'm fine? But this is my only uniform. . . ."

"We've got extra shirts in the back office. You can totally grab one."

"Thanks."

After a beat he asked, "Do you have a grilled cheese for table three?"

I opened my mouth to speak, but nothing came out so I shut it again.

"Sorry," he said, sensing my confusion. "It's probably your first day and you have no idea what I'm talking about. I'm Sebastian. Bubba's son."

"Bubba's your mom?" I asked, stupidly.

"To her disappointment." He said it with a smirk, like it was definitely a good-natured joke. When I didn't say anything, he asked, "You're Angela, right? My mom said she had someone new starting today."

"Angelina," I said, clearing my throat. Did all high school boys besides Kevin Herman make this much eye contact? "I go by Lina, though."

"Cool." He smiled, and I remember thinking that it was maybe the most beautiful smile I had ever seen. It animated his whole face.

A voice from the kitchen announced another order was up. Sebastian maneuvered past me to grab it.

"Thanks, Omar," he said, picking up the basket. He turned back to me and hooked a thumb over his shoulder, toward the swinging door. "I serve in the restaurant. Most of our menu comes from the main kitchen, but people can order off the snack bar menu, too—burgers, chicken fingers, that kind of stuff. The servers pick those orders up from here, so you'll see us throughout the day. I just started the afternoon shift."

"Copy," I said, trying to make my voice sound relaxed. "I'll be ready for you next time." (I seriously doubted this.)

He smiled again, then nodded over my shoulder. I traced his gaze to a family of five waiting at my register. Two of the kids were running circles around each other, and the third was crying. The dad waved a wad of cash in the air at me, a look of desperation in his eyes.

"Good luck with that," Sebastian said.

I laughed nervously. More of a cough, really.

"And Lina?" he called as he backed into the door to swing it open.

"Yeah?"

"Let me know if you need anything." He smiled again, and then he was gone.

I turned back to the register, thinking with that distinctly teenage combination of desire and dread that maybe this summer would wind up being even more eventful than I'd expected.

Chapter 3

Now

When I get back to my apartment that night, the first thing I do is march straight to my balcony and collapse onto the gently used West Elm love seat (my proudest Facebook Marketplace acquisition) that takes up most of it. The second thing I do is message Maren.

I click open our WhatsApp chat and start documenting the bizarre past hour of my life, leaving no detail spared. It's almost 6:00 p.m., which means it's nearly 11:00 in London. My best friend is probably fast asleep in her posh little European flat. She's going to wake up to quite the novel.

I tell her all about the Sebastian and Claire sighting. How he looked (hot as ever, but more grown up and with nicer clothes). How she looked (effortlessly chic, also hot). The nearly botched marriage license application. His plea for my help and my selfless agreement.

I physically cringe as I relive what happened next. Shelly arranged us in a line, Sebastian in the middle, then raced through the obligatory questions with one eye on the clock and, I can only imagine, happy hour on her mind. Did Sebastian attest that the details listed on the application were correct? Did Claire? They did. Did I confirm that I knew at least one person in the couple for at least six months, and that, to the best of my knowledge, their plans for marriage were accurate and genuine? Yes, yes and—a slightly shakier—yes. Shelly handed us a pen and the paperwork to pass around. Sebastian signed first, then Claire. I scribbled my name on the only remaining blank line, barely looking down. I couldn't wait to get out of there.

We handed the papers over to Shelly, who disappeared into the back office to process them. Claire threw her delicate arms around my neck and called me a godsend. Sebastian thanked me and made a joke about how I'd gotten him out of the doghouse. I felt a little sick, but I dutifully kept the small talk up until Shelly returned with not two but three legal envelopes with photocopies for each of us—a physical reminder of this truly wacky afternoon just in case I thought I had half a chance of forgetting about it. I waved goodbye to the happy couple and wished them luck with the wedding, and Sebastian actually told me to have a great summer, like he was signing my yearbook. I almost forgot to grab the folder I'd actually come there for from Linda on my way out.

I end the message with a melting face emoji and a broken heart emoji and hit SEND, then toss my phone onto my little outdoor coffee table and press a Home Goods throw pillow over my face.

As much as I want to grab my iPad and inhale some trashy reality TV to remind myself how much more dramatic my life could be, I know that what I should really do is finally take a look at what Linda found for me. I need to figure out if I have an actual non-wedding story to write when I get to work tomorrow. I'm finding it harder and harder to convincingly write about love lately and tomorrow I suspect it will be borderline impossible.

I pull the envelope out of my bag and slide the papers out. I catch the words MARRIAGE / CIVIL UNION APPLICATION printed across the top—jump scare—and quickly turn that stack face-down in my lap, then grab the correct envelope.

I know from the few dining stories I've written so far that obtaining a liquor license in New Jersey is more difficult than you might think. A Prohibition-era law still in effect allows each municipality only a finite number of licenses at any given time, which means that if you want to open a new place that serves alcohol, you have to purchase an existing license from another business. So at first I assume that the reason Bubba's restaurant is listed on the license is because a transfer like this is happening. Sebastian had said his mom is retiring after this season. Maybe she plans to close the restaurant altogether and has no use for the license anymore. But upon closer inspection, I notice that the address where Diamond Group will be operating the new license is Bubba's as well: 11 Ocean Avenue, Brantley Beach.

Diamond Group isn't just buying a liquor license from Bubba's. It's buying the whole restaurant.

My phone buzzes, and the screen lights up with a WhatsApp message: **OH. MY. GOD.**

I laugh. I should know that, when it comes to my best friend, sleep is no match for this kind of gossip. I pick up my phone and the screen changes to a picture of Maren and me in our awkward middle school glory. I swipe to accept her FaceTime.

"OH. MY. GOD." The top half of Maren's face fills my screen. It looks like she's in a dark room, holding her phone only an inch from her face. Her glacial-blue eyes are wide, her white-blond curls wild from sleep.

"You said that already."

"This is beyond cringe." I raise a brow, glaring at her. "Sorry! I know I probably shouldn't say that—but honestly, like, what are the *odds*?"

"Trust me, I know."

"You know, there *is* a bright side here."

"Do tell."

She smirks. "Sebastian Nikolaou finally got to see how hot you turned out."

"I'm sure he's kicking himself."

Maren nods earnestly. "I mean, he definitely should be."

I roll my eyes. This is silly. Sebastian Nikolaou is happily engaged. And even if he weren't, he'd made it crystal clear fourteen years ago that there was zero chance he'd ever want anything to happen between us again. And after how he handled everything, I felt the exact same way.

"The good news is I don't think I'll run into them again. His mom is retiring and I wondered for, like, a second if Sebastian might be taking over the restaurant, but it looks like she's selling it. And Claire doesn't seem to want to be here a second longer than she needs to for the wedding."

"Bubba's is closing? Jeez. Talk about the end of an era. My parents will be so bummed when I tell them that."

"Yeah. Mine, too." I've lost count of the invitations to join my parents for dinner at Bubba's I've declined over the years.

Maren yawns. "Go back to sleep," I say, shuffling the papers into their respective envelopes and tucking them back into my bag. "I'm glad I could entertain you for a little."

"Fiiiine. Hey! Two days."

I smile. Maren flies in for her annual summer visit this Friday. I'll have my best friend back for two whole months. "Two days. I can't wait."

We say our goodbyes and I love you's and hang up. I feel the familiar pang in my chest that always arrives after talking to Maren. She'd studied abroad in London and accepted a job as the assistant to a luxury fashion buyer there after college. Now she has her old boss's job and has become a full-on Londoner—complete with a slight accent she insists she must have picked up from living there so long. We both put in the effort required to keep a long-distance friendship going: daily messages and Instagram DMs (mostly memes that remind us of each other), weekly FaceTimes. But Friday can't come fast enough. I miss my best friend, and it won't really feel like summer until she's here.

I linger on the balcony for a few more minutes, pushing thoughts of Sebastian to the periphery so I can try to enjoy the cool evening breeze as I look out at the shoreline in the distance. I like to start and end my days here, a coffee in hand in the morning and a glass of wine or a mug of tea before bed. It's by far my favorite thing about my apartment, a one-bedroom I started renting a few years ago. I'd stayed with my parents for the first couple years after I was laid off, while I got my footing at Shore Life. I may not be living the city life I'd once dreamed of, but I'm proud of myself for earning enough to afford a place on my own. And I have to admit that I like living close enough to go home for Sunday dinners with my parents or meet my mom for a walk along the beach before work.

I head inside to make dinner. I'll see Maren on Friday, then my parents on Saturday. And for now, I have the cast of *Below Deck* to keep me company.

Chapter 4

Then
Fifteen Years Ago

Two important things happened to me that summer.

The first: I got much better at my job.

I got better at balancing armloads of fried food while maneuvering around the tiny snack bar station. I memorized coffee and bagel orders for lifeguards, police officers, badge checkers and other regulars. I figured out (by trial and many errors) the ideal ratio of crushed ice to soda from the fountain. And, to Kevin Herman's measured delight, I kept the soft-serve machine sparkling clean and functioning.

The second: I developed a huge crush on Sebastian Nikolaou.

I'd had crushes before, of course. Boys from class. Maren's aloof older cousin who stayed with her family over Christmas break one year. My sixth-grade math teacher. A long list of fictional characters from books and movies. But this was different—this was . . . all-consuming.

Whenever Omar or one of his cooks called out "Main!" as they dropped an order on the counter that separated the snack bar from the kitchen, I'd feel heat creep up my neck, because that meant the order was for a table in the main dining room and a server would be coming by to pick it up. Sebastian and I overlapped on three out of my four shifts, which meant that on Mondays, Thursdays and Saturdays he stopped by my station at least a dozen times for pickups. I'd grab the plastic basket of food from the counter before Kevin could (the first time I did this, he complimented me for taking initiative) and seamlessly hand it off to Sebastian just as he appeared, the door swinging closed behind him. He'd smile and thank me and I'd melt. Every time.

Those interactions alone made me more than happy to jump out of bed at 6:00 a.m.

For the first time I found myself wishing for rain in the summer, because rainy days meant fewer beachgoers, which meant fewer customers, which meant I'd have more time with Sebastian. On those slow days everyone helped out with prep in the kitchen, so I got to see Sebastian in his element: joking with the cooks, teasing his mom, making up games and challenges with the other servers and hostesses. About once a week Sebastian and I opened the restaurant together, and I'd memorize every word we exchanged so I could repeat them back to Maren accurately later. He was like a magnet, drawing me in.

And I quickly learned I wasn't the only one.

The restaurant was constantly whirring with rumors about Sebastian's love life. He was sixteen—a rising junior—which meant he had admirers in every grade. Carly, a freshman who worked the hostess stand that summer, reported that he met someone from her class for frozen yogurt at the mall one weekend, but upon further investigation it turned out to be a group thing—false lead. A junior waitress named Tina claimed a friend group recently broke up because all three girls were planning to ask Sebastian to prom. And according to a busser named Helen, he was seeing a girl from New York City whose family had a summer house down the Shore (though Helen admitted she didn't know anyone who had actually seen this girl).

Sebastian was, by definition, unattainable. Out of reach.

Unfortunately, that only seemed to make me (and everyone else) want him more.

Maren and I spent countless hours that summer meticulously dissecting every interaction I had with Sebastian. We'd endlessly analyze his tone, his word choice, his body language. By mentioning what time he liked to surf (sunrise, before it got too crowded), was he low-key inviting me to come watch? Did he actually need my help rolling silverware (each place setting got a fork, knife and spoon wrapped in a white napkin and secured with a navy paper band—a tedious process, but I found comfort in the repetition), or was he just trying to get more time with me? Maren sometimes took her lunch break at the snack bar, which gave her a front-row seat to at least four or five handoffs so that afterward she could gush along with me about Sebastian's arm muscles and the way he said, "Thanks, Mariano," when I handed him a basket of fried food.

When I think back to that summer I sometimes wonder if my obsession really had much to do with Sebastian at all. It was probably one of those classic "idea of him" situations. A puzzle for Maren and me to direct our restless energy toward decoding.

A crush can define a summer—or at least it can feel that way in the moment. But in retrospect I'm also able to remember plenty of things about June, July and August of 2009 that had nothing to do with Sebastian Nikolaou.

Like making dinner with my mom. She taught elementary school, but in another life she could have been a private chef, or maybe an Italian version of Martha Stewart with a Jersey accent. Her summers off were sacred. I tagged along to her favorite specialty shops and farmers markets while she leisurely browsed for ingredients we could turn into an elaborate meal. I held my own as her sous-chef, chopping and slicing and sautéing under her patient direction. We rotated between tried-and-true specialties (shrimp scampi with a crispy breadcrumb topping, a loaf of homemade, no-knead bread and a simple salad was my favorite menu as well as my dad's) and new ones we found on recipe sites or in vintage cookbooks my mom picked up from the used bookstore in town.

The three of us would have dinner on our small porch, glasses of wine for my parents and a homemade iced tea for me. Our two-bedroom house was more of a bungalow a few blocks from the beach; we didn't have a view, but we could smell the ocean and, on quiet nights, hear it, too. My parents are on the older side and had bought the house twenty years earlier for so cheap it sort of makes me want to throw up if I think about it for too long now.

Unlike Maren, who constantly quarreled with her parents about everything from her clothes to her artistic aspirations, I more than got along with my parents—in fact, I genuinely enjoyed their company. They seemed to have a good marriage. Not particularly remarkable or passionate, I supposed, but secure. Steady. Uncomplicated. Even at fourteen, I suspected that a volatility existed within me that made such a relationship unlikely for myself. But I admired theirs nonetheless.

I spent my days off and most evenings with Maren, doing the usual things that beach kids did. We parked our bikes at the boardwalk and slid under the silver railings to avoid paying for beach badges, then spent hours in the ocean, where we were safe from the badge checkers roaming the sand. I'd bike home with pruned fingers, my hair stiff with salt water. Other days we spread our towels at the edge of the jetty and watched high school kids surf and paddleboard, feverishly debating which boys were hottest and which girls had the best swimsuits. We'd pick up sandwiches from the snack bar (I got a discount, and I still wasn't sick of the crispy Buffalo chicken wrap). On paydays we'd pool some money for Twizzlers and a Slurpee from the 7-Eleven and eat on our favorite bench, which was somehow always in the shade, balancing the haul on our laps as we people-watched and gossiped and daydreamed about having money and careers and boyfriends, blissfully unaware of how special what we did have was.

At night we met friends from our class for beach bonfires and makeshift fireworks, all of us buzzing about the start of high school. It felt like an important summer, one filled with anticipation. The summer between our childhoods and the beginning of our real lives as high schoolers. When I look back on that summer I of course think about Sebastian, it being the one that I met him. But mostly I think about my parents and Maren and how safe and simple it all was. Even as I was living it, it felt bittersweet, an ending as much as it was a beginning.

Chapter 5

Now

The next morning, I get to the office early and submit a revised pitch for the Diamond Group story to my editor, a hardened newspaper editor turned digital click-chaser named Mandy Nguyen. Confirming that the team behind New York City's hottest restaurants has targeted Brantley Beach for their next venture would have been intriguing enough, but now I could reveal that they'd be replacing a local institution in the process. Mandy loves "a talker"—and I'm certain I have one on my hands with this story. On one hand, Diamond Group taking over Bubba's prime boardwalk location will, without a doubt, boost the local tourism economy. On the other, it's the latest of many examples of the old guard getting pushed out, whether locals like it or not.

While I wait for a response I file a quiz designed to help couples find their perfect signature cocktail recipe, then pivot to a first-person roundup of my takes on Pinterest's top floral trends. Petite centerpieces? I do. Branch bouquets? I definitely don't.

"Are you in early to break the news that fifty percent of

heterosexual marriages in the U.S. end in divorce?" asks David Torres, Shore Life's audience development manager and my work husband, as he takes his seat at the desk next to mine.

I swivel my chair and shoot him a snarky glare. "Thinking of saving that for my next column. Could be a very romantic kicker."

He stifles a laugh as he boots up his laptop and monitor.

"Actually," I say, "I was pitching a food story. I'll let you know when I hear back from Mandy. Might be good for the newsletter."

"Clicky?"

"See for yourself." I take the envelope from the clerk's office out of my bag and hand it to him.

"This better be good, because the new tip line we're doing on Instagram and Facebook is a total flop. If one more middle-aged lady named Susan slides into our DMs saying she swears she spotted Bruce Springsteen at the beach, I may quit and put my law degree to good use like my parents always dreamed I would." He holds up the papers in front of his face. "Wait, what is this?"

Shit. I definitely handed him the wrong envelope. "Long story," I say, snatching the papers back. "I'll tell you all about it at lunch." But as I go to tuck them into my bag I really look at the top page for the first time. And my stomach drops as I realize what I'm reading.

It's a marriage license application, but not the one I thought it was. Because Sebastian's information is listed in the section of Applicant A, but Applicant B isn't Claire Cunningham.

Applicant B is me.

"Holy fuck." I realize too late that I've said this out loud rather than in my head. Debbie from analytics shoots me an appalled look from across the room.

David scoots his chair closer to mine. He lowers his voice. "Lina, what's happening?"

I fail to formulate a coherent response. I pore over the page again, searching for Claire's name. I finally find it on the witness line.

According to this document, I'm getting married to Sebastian Nikolaou, and Claire had been *our* witness.

"I'm okay," I manage to squeak out to David, who is clearly worried and waiting for answers. "I'm just . . . processing." I look up from the papers to him. He raises one eyebrow, his expression shifting from one of concern to curiosity.

"I'm great at processing," he says. "Try me."

I double over and cradle my face in my hands as I speak, because I physically cannot handle seeing David's reaction to what I'm about to say. "Remember that guy from high school I told you about? I think it was a Thai day." David started working at Shore Life about a year after me. He correctly identified the New York Times Cooking recipe for the pesto he saw me taking out of the kitchen fridge and we've eaten lunch together nearly every day since, confiding in each other about everything from our gripes with Mandy to our relationships (his current status: happily engaged to his college sweetheart, Henry. Mine: nonexistent).

I hear David snap a finger. "Is this the Cali guy? Hot Greek surfing god who destroyed you and then vanished into thin air?"

I groan.

"Sorry, sorry. Continue."

I take a deep breath. "I ran into him and his fiancée while I was picking up something at the city clerk's office. They were applying for their marriage license and needed a witness, so I helped them."

"Okay . . . okay, I mean, not an ideal run-in for sure, but was he, like, a total dick or someth—"

"I signed the wrong line, David." I keep one hand on my face and extend the application to him with the other.

Pause. Then: "Holy fuck."

"Is everything *all right* over there?" My eyes are still closed, but I can tell this is Debbie. I shoot up, grabbing David by the arm and pulling him into the break room. We huddle next to the coffee maker.

"Daaaaamn," David trills. He looks like he's just gotten to the plot twist in a movie and can't quite believe what he's seeing. "This is some rom-com shit."

I shush him. "You're the one who went to law school," I hiss. "What does this mean? Am I *married* to Sebastian?"

David folds his arms across his chest, thinking. Then he sighs. "I need to read it again." He's still holding the first page, and I look over his shoulder as he reads. "No," he says finally, with lawyerly authority. "Not yet, anyway. Technically this means that the state of New Jersey has issued you an approved license to *get* married, but you'd still have to actually do the thing—have some sort of ceremony, get an officiant to sign it, all that jazz—to certify it. Too long; didn't read? This really isn't a big deal for *you*." He points at me with the paper for emphasis. "Embarrassing, sure, but legally meaningless at this point. It's kind of a big deal for Surfer Boy, though. He needs to get this shit fixed before the wedding. There's a seventy-two-hour waiting period to get a marriage license in Jersey. You have to tell him, because if he shows up to his ceremony with this there isn't going to be a wedding—not a legal one, anyway."

My stomach drops. I can think of nothing more embarrassing than having to find Sebastian and tell him that I botched his marriage documents. But actually I can: David's right, letting him find out on his own—on his *wedding* day—would be a million times more humiliating. What if he thought I sabotaged him and Claire on purpose? Or, at the very least, that some subconscious part of me was still obsessed with him and had taken control? The whole situation is mortifying.

I hear a loud throat-clear behind us and turn to find Mandy's latest assistant, a twenty-four-year-old with a master's degree in journalism named Jenny, who treats managing our boss's calendar like operating a news bureau. She reminds me of myself in my *Ever After* days, before I became jaded and cynical.

"Lina? Mandy wants to see you in her office." She's clutching a clipboard to her chest so protectively you'd think it contains confidential military tactics. It's probably Mandy's lunch order.

"Thanks, Jenny," I say with a tight smile. "I'll be right in."

Jenny waits for me to follow her. When I don't, she lets out a huff of disappointment and turns to leave. David moves to follow her.

"Where are you *going*?" I hiss.

"I have a call," he says, wincing at my wide-eyed look of abandonment. "We'll come up with a game plan at lunch, okay? Everything's going to be fine, I promise."

Once the two of them round the corner and disappear from sight, I take a series of deep breaths, attempting to temporarily expel the memory of this ridiculous situation with each exhale. Then I follow orders like the good soldier I am and head to Mandy's office.

"Lina, come in," says Mandy, gesturing for me to take a seat as I try to blink away the image of my name on the application. How could none of us have noticed the mistake?

"I was just reading your pitch."

Focus, Lina.

"What did you think?" I ask.

Mandy pushes her thick black reading glasses up the bridge of her nose as she considers my question. She's a short, stern woman with the no-nonsense attitude of someone who had started her career as a crime-beat reporter at a leading New Jersey newspaper, back when newsrooms were good ol' boys clubs. Ten years ago—after being passed over for assignments and promotions one too many times—she'd decided if you can't beat 'em, pitch 'em an idea for a sister site focused on lifestyle content. Something about that word, *lifestyle*, made men feel emasculated, but her publisher couldn't argue with Mandy's business case for the idea. Shore Life launched later that year, with Mandy as founding editor.

"It's good stuff," she says finally.

I fight the urge to squirm in my seat. "But. . . ?"

"It feels a little . . . dry. For us, at least. I'm sure the papers will cover. We'd need to figure out an angle we could own."

"I'm not sure we need to overthink the angle here," I say carefully. "Bubba's is a local institution. And Diamond Group is a giant in the industry right now—one with national name recognition. I think this deal will interest a lot of people. It will cause conversation, maybe even some controversy—"

"I heard Bubba's son is getting married at the restaurant at the end of the summer," Mandy interjects.

He might not be if I don't fix this mess, I think.

"I looked up the bride," Mandy continues. "She's got a solid Instagram following. She's even on TikTok. Apparently she's got quite the skin-care routine."

And then I *do* squirm, because I realize what Mandy's suggesting.

"Mandy, I can't . . ."

She cocks her head, curious. But what is there to say? That I can't cover this wedding because I used to be in love with the groom and his fiancée probably thinks I'm a crazy stalker who's trying to sabotage their marriage?

"I mean, I can imagine the wedding will be beautiful, and heavily sponsored," I try. "But I think there's a bigger story here."

"Lina." Mandy folds her hands on top of her desk. "'Real Weddings' is consistently one of our most-viewed pages on the site. You have a talent for writing about weddings—about love!—in a way that feels fresh week after week. In our last demographic survey, readers said they love your column because they find it accessible. The events that big national publications like *Ever After* feature are aspirational—way out of reach for ninety-nine percent of people. But the weddings you capture? They're *real*! Women up and down the coast devour it for tips from brides who came before them. You help them find their footing." Mandy's voice drops an octave to emphasize this next point. "Not to mention all the money we make from it through ads and affiliate links. This wedding is our angle."

"I've got my column planned through the summer," I say uselessly. When Mandy brings up revenue it means the discussion is over—she's made her decision. She stands and starts pacing across the room, excitement playing across her usually stoic face.

"We'll do a photo-heavy spread on the home page with a jump link to the full column. We've been courting Kleinfeld for a digital cover sponsorship for months and this may just seal the deal. Find the couple's contact info and email them today, will you? It's best you get involved as soon as possible so you can capture some lead-up details. Maybe you can even tag along on an appointment or two, get some behind-the-scenes quotes. Readers love to feel like they're really part of the planning process.

"And Lina?" She stops pacing and faces me. "I know we're overdue for a conversation about what's next for you here," she says gently, mistaking the dread that's surely written all over my face for nothing more than career frustration. "I assure you, I value you more than you know, and I see that you want to move on from weddings. Let's finish the summer strong, and then we'll talk about giving you more verticals to oversee. You have my word."

I make eye contact with David on my way out of Mandy's office and gesture toward the break room. He follows me there and gets to work making us flat whites with the fancy Breville espresso machine—a gift a local home goods store had sent to the office after I'd featured them in a short-lived social series called "Registry Rundown."

"Mandy killed the Bubba's pitch, and that's not the worst news," I say, hoping all the pulling and steaming will muffle my words and deter Debbie's wandering ears. "She wants me to do Sebastian and Claire's wedding for my column."

"*Shit*," he says, handing me my drink.

"I know. She dangled a promotion and more verticals to get me on board with the new plan."

"Mandy has been dangling that promotion for years. What makes you think she's not just stringing you along again?"

I throw a hand up. "She totally might be. But she thinks she can finally sell Kleinfeld on it, which would maybe give me some leverage. And it's not like I really have a choice, right? She's the boss."

"Maybe this is a good thing," David says, eyes on his drink like he's reading tea leaves.

"Are you even listening to me?"

"A great thing, even."

I throw back half of my flat white. I should have asked him to make me a triple for this conversation. "I'm dying to know how you can possibly spin this."

"First of all, it gives you an opportunity to make light of the whole witness . . . *snafu* and then quickly distract him from it. But more importantly, you say whatever happened between you and Surfer Boy was forever ago, but you're clearly not over it. In your mind he's still that hot, elusive guy from high school. Your first big crush. A guy who humiliated you and then disappeared from your life." I squeeze my eyes shut, shooing away mental images of the day I found out who Sebastian really was. What he really thought of me. "You've been able to, like, preserve him in your mind exactly the way you remember him back when you had feelings. But there's no way he's still that person. You said it yourself: He wound up being a dick to you in the end, and he's probably still a dick now."

I start to interrupt, but David holds up a finger and continues. "Spend a little time with him and his fiancée and you'll probably realize she's insufferable and he's just a regular guy—or, more likely, a total asshole who isn't worth your time. By the time you finish writing your column you might even feel bad for this girl! It sounds crazy, I know, but I think writing this article is going to finally give you some closure."

Or, I think, *what if I realize that he isn't an asshole at all?* What if I see how happy and successful and in love he is and it reminds me just how foolish I was to have ever thought for a second that I could have been part of his future? What if I realize that he turned out to be a great guy after all—just one who didn't want to be with me?

I like David's version a lot better, because it's the version that validates my understanding of what happened that summer.

I *need* David's version to be true.

"Trust me," I say, "I don't think about him in a good light. I did get closure—when I was fifteen and ignored my teenage hormones long enough to see that he didn't deserve the pedestal I'd built for him."

"Even better," David says. "Then this will just confirm what you already know. And give you more leverage with Mandy. You do this well enough and it might be the last wedding you ever have to write about."

I massage my temples, hoping David is right. Because I can't imagine surviving this assignment—this whole absurd situation—and winding up with nothing to show for it. Moving on from wedding writing might be the only thing that could make all this worth it.

"I've got another call," David says, checking his watch. "Just send an email—go through the bride so it doesn't feel so personal. Treat it like any other story."

I groan, waving him off. I take my time washing our cups

and wiping down the espresso machine. Then I notice the counters are a little grimy, so I sanitize those, too.

Once the break room is sparkling clean I know what I have to do.

I walk out the door, unlock my bike and ride toward the boardwalk.

Chapter 6

Now

"Good morning, ma'am," says the high school–age girl behind the hostess stand at Bubba's, a greeting that makes me feel ancient. She's wearing the same navy polo I did back in the day, but that's where the similarities between high school me and this Gen Zer end. She wears an array of miniature butterfly clips in her hair and her makeup is TikTok perfect. "Joining us for breakfast?"

I glance at her nametag. "Hi, Parker. I don't need a table, actually. Is Bubba here by chance?"

"She left about an hour ago. I can write down a message for her?" She flashes an Invisaligned smile at me, and I think with millennial pride about the mouthful of colorful braces I sported throughout middle school. My awkwardness was more of an era than a phase. Parker may have an expensive skin-care routine and subtle orthodontics, but hey—at least I'd built character.

"Sure, thanks," I say, fishing a business card out of my bag. "I just had a work question for her—well, for her son. And I wanted to see if she could pass my current email along to him."

"Sebastian? He's here!" Parker gestures over her shoulder. "He's unloading a delivery out back."

"Oh," I say, surprised. Weren't he and Claire supposed to be long gone, happily back in California? My plan was to email him about the "Real Weddings" opportunity and throw in a quick heads-up about the witness fiasco. *FYI—we're halfway married, ha-ha!* Something like that, but less unhinged. I'm in no way mentally prepared to have either conversation in person.

I'm about to ask Parker to just take down the message anyway, but her eyes have drifted to her phone. I sigh, resigned. This conversation is going to be awkward as hell no matter the format. No sense delaying the inevitable.

I maneuver past Parker and toward the exit to the employee parking lot with my head down, praying no one I still know at this place will spot me.

I push the door open (it's just as heavy as I remember) and find Sebastian outside, transferring crates of soft drinks from the back of a truck to a dolly. He looks so different from how he did when I saw him yesterday that I have to do a double take. The expensive-looking clothes have been replaced by a Bubba's T-shirt, athletic shorts and sneakers. His forehead is slick with sweat, his curls messy and matted. As he lifts another crate from the truck, cords of muscle ripple along his tanned arms. Fine—so maybe I do a triple take.

When he notices me, he straightens. He shades his eyes with one hand like a visor, squints in the sun. "Lina?"

"Hey," I manage.

"Hey. What are you doing here?"

"So funny story actually." I cannot manage proper verbal punctuation with this man. It's strange, standing in this parking lot with him. Familiar, too.

He leans against the truck, arms crossed. Which only serves to emphasize his muscles, I notice with annoyance. "Let's hear it." His mouth quirks, like he's trying not to smile. God knows why he thinks I'm here—and whatever that is won't be as ridiculous as the truth.

I reach into my bag for the envelope and brace myself to rip off the Band-Aid.

"More of a question," I say, chickening out. "I was wondering if you and Claire would be open to letting me feature you for my column."

"For your wedding column?"

I don't love the way he emphasizes the word *wedding*, like it's trivial. Or the half smirk still plastered on his face.

"It's my boss's idea," I clarify. "It wouldn't be a lot of extra work for you guys or anything. Just an interview. Maybe I could tag along on some appointments and take notes. You'd barely notice me."

I scan his face, trying to ascertain how he feels about this idea—the girl who harbored a humiliating teenage crush on him writing an article about his wedding to someone he actually wants to be with. He still looks mildly amused. It's starting to infuriate me.

"You know what? This is weird. I'm sorry. I should go."

I turn to leave, but he reaches me before I get to the door.

"Wait," he says. "We'll do it."

I turn to face him. We're standing much closer now. I have to tilt my head back to meet his eyes. "Really?"

"Yeah. Claire's obsessed with your column." His half smirk shifts to a genuine smile. "She probably would have told me to ask you anyway."

"All right, then. Great. I can coordinate everything with Claire, if that's easiest?"

"Oh, sure," he says, narrowing his eyes. "I'll give you her email."

There's a pause, neither of us saying anything. He seems to be waiting for me to say something else. I should leave—I will, in a minute. But first I give in to my curiosity.

"So, how long are you out here for?"

"Just this week was the plan," he says, glancing over his left shoulder toward the beach. "Claire had to fly back. I wanted to stay a little longer, help my mom out for a few days. But now that I'm here I'm realizing she could probably use more help than she let on." His expression shifts again, brows knit with stress or concern or a mix of both. "So to answer your question, I'm not sure how long I'll be here. For now I canceled my return flight." He smiles, but it doesn't quite reach his eyes the way it normally does (or did, rather).

I *really* should go. Instead I say, "I heard she's selling the restaurant."

He nods, confirming. "One last season."

I shake my head in disbelief. "I bet that was a hard decision for her. I never thought she'd retire, to be honest." I don't add, *let alone sell the restaurant to strangers.*

"Me either. It's the right thing, though." His voice is firm, like this is something he's said before.

Yesterday, when Sebastian had told me his mom was retiring, I'd briefly wondered if he'd take over the family business. But I should have known better. So much of what I thought I knew about Sebastian all those years ago turned out to be wrong, but if there was one thing he had been unwaveringly honest about it was his resolve to never end up stuck here like his mom. It was no accident that he chose a college, a career, a fiancée—an entire life—based on the opposite coast. Don't get me wrong: I'm sure it pained him to see his mom give up the business her life had revolved around. Just not enough to stop her.

"Well, I'm glad she has you here for a while. I'm sure it means so much to her. Tell her I say hello, will you?"

He nods. "For sure. She'll be jealous she wasn't here to hear you say it herself." I feel a pang of guilt, brief but sharp, as I think again of how many times I've passed on joining my parents for dinner at Bubba's over the years. How many staff reunion invitations I've declined. Today is the first time I've set foot in the restaurant in more than a decade, and the flood of emotions and memories I'm wading through now reminds me why.

Sebastian takes a step back toward the truck. My cue to finally get out of here.

"I'm glad you came by, Mariano," he calls out. "Maybe I'll see you around this summer. For the column and all that," he adds.

"See you around, Nikolaou," I say as I use all my strength to push through that damned door.

Chapter 7

Then
Fourteen Years Ago

"Okay. Which earrings?"

I was sitting on the floor of Maren's walk-in closet, surrounded by piles of rejected clothing and shoes. I considered her question, then pointed to the oversize silver hoop she held up to her right ear. She nodded in agreement, slipping on the hoops as she turned once more to her floor-length mirror to examine the final look. Her dress was a multicolor patchwork situation she'd sewn herself, sleeveless with a high neck and a tie at the waist. On anyone else it would look have looked drab and grandmotherly, but Maren somehow pulled it off.

In the last year, Maren had transformed before my eyes from an awkward, artsy middle schooler with a costume-like wardrobe into the girl standing before me. She still made her own clothes, but her style had begun to mature and evolve. In a school of girls whose idea of fitting in fashion-wise revolved around sameness (same short UGG boots, same Alex and Ani bracelet stacks jingling down their wrists, same Abercrombie skinny jeans), her insistence on difference was equal parts cool and frustrating to the more popular girls, who regarded her with resigned respect. She zipped her thrifted white go-go boots, then reached down and pulled me to my feet.

"I think we're ready," she said to our reflections.

It had taken almost a full school year, but we'd finally gotten invited to our first real high school party, a Memorial Day Weekend "day drink" that her latest crush, a sophomore soccer player named Aaron Reingold, was throwing while his parents were out of town. We'd spent the last two hours in Maren's room, blasting iTunes from her clunky white MacBook and getting ready.

I smoothed my jean skirt, which I'd paired with my favorite white tank top, while she swiped on a bubblegum-pink lip gloss, then handed it to me so I could follow suit. I remember thinking that I looked good—pretty, even—if a bit plain in comparison to Maren, with her sparkling blue eyes and cascade of naturally curly blond hair. Middle school hadn't been the kindest to either of us in the looks department (think: a near-unibrow for me and a conspicuous palate expander for Maren), but ninth grade had proven to be transformative. And while I wouldn't exactly consider us part of the popular crowd at Brantley Beach High, we fell somewhere in the middle. Respectable. That was more than enough for us—and apparently it was also enough to get us invited to the first legit party of the summer.

Maren and I chatted nervously with Mr. Murphy the whole drive to Aaron's. He was under the impression that this was a chaperoned barbecue, and our bodies practically vibrated with the knowledge of our fib. It was 12:30 in the afternoon when we pulled up (exactly thirty minutes after the start of the party—the absolute latest we could force ourselves to wait for our fashionably late arrival), agreeing to meet Mr. Murphy out front again at four to go back to Maren's. I'd brought my overnight things when I had come over earlier, and although I'd never admit it to Maren, I was already sort of looking forward to *after* the party, when we'd throw on comfy clothes and stay up late rehashing it.

"Thanks, Mr. Murphy!" I called as we leapt from the car. Maren grabbed my hand, and we speed-walked around to the front of the house, following the sounds of voices and music.

The house was gorgeous. It was clearly one of the newer constructions that had begun popping up around town, with a modular look and floor-to-ceiling windows with black trim that stood in sharp contrast to the quaint, old-fashioned beach houses on either side. The front of the property faced the water, with a firepit and Adirondack chairs on one side and a keg and two white folding tables lined with red Solo cups on the other (a temporary setup for this occasion, I assumed).

Aaron waved us over to one of the tables where at least a dozen other kids—some from our rising sophomore class and others I vaguely recognized from the hallways of BBH—were congregating. Aaron and his buddy from the soccer team, Chris Cappelli, began arranging the cups in the middle of the table. I watched as they cracked open a few cans of Natural Light, then doused each cup with a splash of the beer. Apart from the cup in the very center, which Chris filled to the brim. I made a concerted effort not to wrinkle my nose at the smell.

Maren and I had dabbled in alcohol here and there over the last year, but always in a controlled environment (her room, long after her parents had gone to sleep, *Gossip Girl* reruns playing on her MacBook to drown out the sounds of our nervous laughter). Our drinks of choice were red wine pilfered from a cabinet that was gathering dust in her parents' dining room and—once—a fifth of New Amsterdam her older cousin Leah had (reluctantly) procured for us while home from TCNJ for Thanksgiving break.

All this to say: Beer was new territory. As was drinking out in the open.

"Stack cup!" Aaron announced, with no additional explanation. Maren and I exchanged a worried look, but thankfully the game started at the opposite end of the table. We watched as Shelby Daniels and Melissa Cruz each grabbed a cup from the middle, downed the contents and then attempted to bounce ping-pong balls into their empty cups with the seriousness of competitive athletes. Shelby made her shot first and passed her cup to the right. Then Melissa made her shot and passed it to Shelby, and so on until Isaiah Thompson beat Mary Douglas and, with great enthusiasm, stacked his cup inside hers. The rest of the table broke out in cheers and whoops as Mary grabbed a new cup from the center, drank and started the whole process over again.

By the time my turn came the cups were stacked five high. My hand shook as I bounced the ball, which landed nowhere near the cup and instead rolled off the other side of the table. I reached underneath and grabbed it, popping back up just as the freshman boy to my left, Manny Nelson, was stacking his cup into mine. Everyone yelled, "Drink!" I followed orders and then (to my relief) successfully bounced the ball into a new cup and passed it on.

The game continued like this, and once Maren and I started getting the hang of it, we got just as competitive as everyone else, celebrating when we made shots in time, pouting when we missed and had to throw back bready gulps of beer.

Each drink didn't seem like much, but they added up, and soon the whole scene was becoming fuzzy at the corners. The game ended when Aaron failed to bounce his ball into the now-swaying tower of stacked cups before Chris. As punishment, he feigned reluctance, pulled the full cup of beer from the center and chugged to everyone's applause.

Aaron and a few other boys immediately got to work resetting the cups for another round when Sebastian walked in with Theo Louros and Andre Silva. He wore a white T-shirt, khaki shorts and his signature Vans, his skin already tanned from the mornings he spent surfing after school. They seemed to know everyone, hugging the girls hello and clapping the other guys on the back. Sebastian's eyes landed on me and I offered a little wave. He smiled in response, and I felt fire on my skin.

Aside from brief acknowledgments in the hallway, I'd barely interacted with Sebastian that school year. We didn't share any classes or even a lunch slot, and after school I spent most nights either at home with my family or working on the student newspaper, while Sebastian helped out at the restaurant and surfed with his buddies. We were summer friends, and it quickly became clear to me that that wasn't the same thing as real friends. Maren rolled her eyes whenever I said this, but it was the truth.

There was some more shuffling as the setup continued, which Maren took as an opportunity to hip-check me halfway down the table. I stumbled (conveniently) right next to Sebastian.

"Hey, Mariano," he said, his expression unreadable. "Wasn't expecting to see you here."

I crossed my arms. Was running into me at a party so shocking?

"Aaron invited us," I said, defensive. Before I could say more, the game started up again.

I realized I was now standing to Sebastian's left and shot Maren a hot glare. She shrugged innocently.

My turn came, and despite my shaking hand I made my shot on the third try—respectable—then passed my cup to Sebastian. But I made my next shot on the second, beating him. Confident from my beer buzz, I stacked my cup into his with a satisfying *thwack*.

The table erupted in cheers. Even Sebastian applauded me before taking his drink. My luck didn't last long, though. Theo was to my left, and on the next round, he beat me and I had to drink. Then Sebastian made his shot on the first try, which meant he could send his cup to anyone. He reached over me and passed it to Theo, who beat me again. They were teaming up to crush me, and the crowd was loving it.

I tried to catch up, but Sebastian made his shot first again. This time, though, he sent his cup across the table to Andre. A few people booed this decision. I felt conflicted. Part of me was relieved that he saved me, but part of me felt defensive. Did he think I wasn't mature or experienced enough to handle a game like this?

As the cups remaining in the middle dwindled, I willed the tower to stay far away from me. But of course it came, right as Theo grabbed the second-to-last cup from the center. A hush fell over the table, the only sounds coming from the clinking of ping-pong balls. We both missed shot after shot, but ultimately it was Theo's that went in. Everyone but Sebastian cheered as Theo grabbed the full final cup and handed it to me, beer sloshing over the rim in the process.

Just as I raised the cup to my lips, Sebastian leaned close to me—close enough for me to smell his sweat, feel his body heat—and whispered in my ear, "Just pretend to drink it until they look away. Then pass it to me."

I bristled at his offer, which was really more of a command. Sebastian took a nonchalant step back, keeping his eyes locked on me as I forced myself to take a couple of defiant sips. He was right: Within seconds everyone lost interest in my suffering, dispersing to refill their drinks and set up a different game.

I kept drinking, but the discomfort must have been written all over my face, because he stepped toward me again, until he was standing unnervingly close.

About halfway through I gave in, lowering the cup and discreetly passing it to Sebastian.

He downed it in three swift gulps, as if it were water.

"Thanks," I said, glancing down at my Havaianas flip-flops. "You didn't have to do that." I felt relieved and embarrassed and annoyed and grateful all at once.

He shrugged, as if to say *no big deal*. Then his expression turned serious for a moment. "Hey, is your mom picking you up later? You shouldn't be biking after drinking."

Heat crept into my cheeks. Again, I couldn't decide if I should feel flattered or embarrassed by all the attention Sebastian was paying me. Was he doing all these things—going easy on me in the game, finishing my beer, asking how I was getting home—because he cared about me? Or was it simply because he still saw me as a kid, too young to be at a party, too inexperienced to finish my own drinks and make responsible decisions about how to get myself home? If I got sick or hurt, Bubba would hear about it. Maybe he was just covering himself.

"I'm staying at Maren's. Her dad's picking us up," I said, meeting Sebastian's eyes and hoping I looked and sounded more confident than I felt. Then I added, "You really don't have to worry about me."

"Nikolaou!" Theo called from farther down the beach, where a few of the boys had gathered. He waved a football in the air, gesturing for Sebastian to join them.

"All right, Mariano," Sebastian said to me, his expression unreadable again. "Have fun." And then he jogged off to join the guys.

Maren and I spent the rest of the party sitting in a circle with a group of about ten kids, sipping boxed wine from our plastic cups and playing card games. Aaron sat next to Maren, and I could tell by the way he looked at her and acknowledged everything she said that, for the first time, one of our crushes was mutual. When she volunteered to bring out another round of drinks, he jumped up to help her, and I winked at her when she shot me a glance over her shoulder. They returned a few minutes later, Aaron with a little more swagger in his step and Maren blushing transparently. I knew immediately that my best friend had just had her first kiss.

Sebastian was still with the other guys when Maren's phone buzzed with a text from Mr. Murphy letting her know he was out front. As we said our goodbyes, a sophomore named Nia Reilly-Brown invited us to a bonfire at her house the following weekend. Maren and I didn't even bother downplaying our enthusiasm—we told her we'd be there. We were officially on the party circuit.

If Mr. Murphy could smell the evidence of the day's festivities when we got in the car or deduce anything from our nervous chatter, he didn't let on. We attempted small talk about the "barbecue," offering the briefest possible answers, afraid we sounded drunk, when in reality we were probably buzzing more from hormones than alcohol.

After we'd showered, changed and devoured a pizza with garlic knots—our sleepover special—Maren gave me the play-by-play of the moment with Aaron. When they got into the house, he'd pulled her into the hall next to the kitchen and said she looked really pretty. Then he'd kissed her.

"It was so quick!" She clutched a pillow to her chest, blue eyes wide. We were sitting across from each other on her bed. "It was over before I could even, like, figure out if it was good or not."

"At least you can say you've kissed someone." I sighed, grabbing the pillow from her and shifting so I could lay my head on it. It was only 8:00 p.m., but I felt liked we'd lived a thousand lives in a day. "And I'm sure you'll have an opportunity for a do-over soon. Aaron is super into you."

Maren blushed. I was genuinely happy for my best friend. Sure, I was also a little worried I'd lose her to Aaron at the next party. But mostly I was happy.

"Your time is coming soon too, Leens, I can just feel it." Maren squeezed my arm. "How was talking to Sebastian?"

I shrugged, still horizontal. "I just don't think he sees me as any more than this girl who works at his mom's restaurant in the summer. Like a little sister he's responsible for."

"Is that actually how he sees you, or is that how *you* see yourself?" Maren raised an eyebrow at me, clearly impressed by her own eloquence. "If you keep convincing yourself that you're someone he would never be interested in, that's exactly who you're going to become. You're not even giving yourself a fighting chance!"

I sighed. "What I want is to finally be over this crush. I want to stop reading into every little interaction I have with him, wondering if it means anything. I want to be free of Sebastian Nikolaou." I pressed my face into the pillow and let out a muffled little cry. Dramatic? Sure. But it felt good.

"Then that's what we'll do," Maren said, rubbing my back.

I opened one eye to look at her. "What are you talking about?"

"We'll swear off the Sebastian talk. No obsessing, no overanalyzing. We won't give him any airtime this summer."

"Mar. I start back at Bubba's when school's out in two weeks. And I'm in the main dining room this year, like him. I'm hardly going to be having a Sebastian-free summer."

She shook her head. "It's not about the time you're physically around him. It's about the space he takes up in your mind." She tapped a finger to her temple for emphasis. "You've gotta kick him out of there."

Later, after we'd shut off the lights and slipped under the covers, I contemplated what Maren had said. She was right, of course, but as much as I wanted to believe I could simply banish Sebastian from my thoughts and regard him with ambivalence that summer, I doubted it would be that simple. The pull I felt toward Sebastian was so strong, it felt physical. What if I wasn't strong enough to resist it?

Chapter 8
Now

"Sebastian. Fucking. Nikolaou. Back from the dead," says Maren.

It's Friday night, and we're about five minutes away from her parents' house. I'd sent her a vague WhatsApp message that morning, warning her that the Sebastian Situation had some new developments I wanted to discuss in person. After work I drove to Newark airport to pick her up, and less than a minute after getting in my car she'd cut the small talk and demanded an update. Thirty minutes later, I'm about to finish relaying the gruesome details.

Claire had been delighted to receive an email from me yesterday, letting her know I was interested in featuring her and Sebastian's wedding in my column. She'd replied that same day with an array of links and attachments, including a vendor list, an hour-by-hour wedding day itinerary, a Pinterest mood board and a band set list. I felt nothing as I reviewed the files, then downloaded each to a folder on my desktop. After six years, I've come to see these once alluringly romantic details for what they really are: pillars of the wedding industrial complex. Once you've written about enough weddings—and seen "Here Comes the Sun" by the Beatles listed as the recessional song at least two dozen times—you realize how impersonal and interchangeable it all actually is.

Only the final attachment—the invitation proof—momentarily tripped me up.

Together with their parents,
Sebastian Alexander Nikolaou
&
Claire Elizabeth Cunningham
request the honor of your presence at their marriage ceremony
Saturday, the Thirty-First of August,
Two Thousand Twenty-Four
Five o'clock in the evening

I hovered my cursor over the ampersand. How many times had I pictured Sebastian's name on a wedding invitation, but with mine below?

I pushed *that* thought away as quickly as it arrived and got back to business.

Claire and I emailed back and forth about wedding details a few more times that day. I'd asked if she and Sebastian would be available for a three-way call or Zoom soon—my best stories were ones that really captured the couple, not just the event, and I knew next to nothing about their relationship. She let me know that her busy schedule as the marketing lead for a celeb-backed beauty brand made it difficult to find time.

"So then she sends me this," I say, handing Maren my phone. "Open Outlook."

I smile when Maren successfully taps in my password on the first try. It's the date I got my first AIM screenname, a combination of numbers I've been using for every digital footprint since then.

Maren perches her designer sunglasses atop her sleek blond blowout—she got in the habit of taming those wild curls into submission sometime after college, but I have a feeling they'll be back after a day or two at home—and clears her throat dramatically. "'Lina—fast follow,'" she reads in her best corporate voice. "'Thoughts on joining Sebastian for a few appointments next week? I'll keep playing calendar Tetris but don't want to hold up the story in the meantime. I've cc'd him here—will let you two take it from here!' Oh my God, it's like she's his *manager*."

"Cringe, right?"

"Completely cringe."

I pull into the Murphys' pebble driveway, finding comfort in the familiar sound of tiny rocks crunching beneath tires.

"So what happens now?" she asks as I put the car in park.

"We drink wine with your parents and pretend you're staying forever?"

"Duh. And then what happens with the Sebastian Situation?" She looks a little wary.

I wave to a beaming Mr. and Mrs. Murphy, who are coming outside to help with their daughter's luggage. I feel like I've gone back in time.

But then again, I've been feeling like that a lot lately.

"Let's worry about that tomorrow," I say, popping the trunk.

Chapter 9

Then
Fourteen Years Ago

I biked to my first shift thinking about Maren's advice. As I pedaled, her words played on a loop in my mind, like the lyrics of a pop song I couldn't get out of my head.

We won't give him any airtime this summer.

A flash of Sebastian at the party, whispering in my ear.

It's about the space he takes up in your mind.

His lips pressing against the rim of the plastic cup, where mine had just been.

You've gotta kick him out of there.

I eased to a stop, dropped my kickstand.

His eyes like sea glass, curls blowing in the breeze.

His voice this time: *All right, Mariano.*

All right!

I locked my bike and walked inside.

Chapter 10

Now

I sip the last of my coffee as I watch Sebastian parallel park his Jeep on the street outside my apartment, hating myself for thinking of the older, beat-up version of that same car that used to pull in my parents' driveway before a shift. I wonder if, after spending enough time together this week, I'll get to a point when every interaction doesn't dredge up a parallel memory from the past.

Maren and I had a jam-packed weekend. Dinner with her parents Friday night. Brunch with mine Saturday morning. Back-to-back beach days. Rum buckets on the pier with David and his fiancé, Henry, who first met Maren last summer (and who I'm now convinced like her even more than they like me). It was fun and restorative and perfect.

But now it's Monday morning. Back to work—and on this particular Monday work involves running wedding errands with Sebastian Nikolaou.

"Morning," he says as I climb into the passenger seat. He's dressed casually again, in a local brewery tee, shorts and Vans. Most of his hair is hidden beneath a backward baseball cap, but

I notice a few unruly curls peeking out from under the band. I definitely don't think about running my fingers through them.

The car smells like coffee. I smile when I trace it to the Yeti tumbler in his cup holder. *Adult Sebastian drinks coffee.* A big step up from ninety-nine-cent iced tea cans.

"Dentist said I had to kick the Arnold Palmer habit," he quips, reading my mind.

He switches the gear into drive, and I switch the subject back to the present. "What's first on the agenda?"

"I need to drop off the florist deposit. That will just take a minute, but he said he's happy to show you sketches of the bouquets and centerpieces if it's helpful for your article."

"That's great. Thanks."

"We'll pick up the invitations after that. Then around lunch my mom and Omar should be ready for us."

"To run through the menu?"

He laughs. "If by 'run through' you mean serve us a full-blown tasting."

Now, *that* I'm looking forward to. My stomach practically growls in anticipation.

"And the last thing is my tux fitting."

I suck in a deep breath as quietly as I can. Maybe I can fabricate a reason for him to drop me off before that last one.

According to the GPS we've got a ten-minute drive, so I pull out my notebook.

"So how did you and Claire first meet?"

"We met my junior year of college, in a business class," he says. He drives the same way he did back in high school. Seat pushed back to accommodate his long legs. One arm stretched straight toward the wheel, hand at twelve o'clock. The other resting along the window.

"And then?" I ask when he doesn't elaborate.

He checks his mirrors, then changes lanes. "She asked me to a sorority formal. I asked her to be my girlfriend a couple weeks later." He shrugs. "Pretty typical college story."

I close my notebook. Clearly I don't need it for this conversation.

"Sorry," he says. A muscle in his jaw flexes, which accomplishes the unfortunate task of reminding me how compelling his jawline is. Jesus, I've got to just keep my eyes on the road. "I know I'm probably not being very helpful. Claire's better at telling these stories." He glances sidelong at me. "What about you? Seeing anyone?"

I can practically feel my face redden. I bet Sebastian is smirking at my discomfort, but I don't allow myself to check.

"I go on dates here and there," I reply. "Nothing too serious at the moment." This, I'll admit, is somewhat of an exaggeration. I've been on exactly two dates in the last year. One was a college acquaintance who slid into my DMs and asked me out to dinner, then proceeded to spend most of said dinner pitching his podcast idea to me. The other was with a guy I matched with on Hinge who ordered a glass of milk at the bar.

Definitely nothing serious.

"I'm focused on my job right now anyway," I add. I wiggle my notebook, hoping he'll take the hint and change the subject back to my article.

"I don't blame you. It's awesome," he says. For a second I actually wonder if he's making fun of me. After all, I learned the hard way that beneath that kind, charming exterior lies an ability to be heartbreakingly cruel. But when I glance over, his expression seems sincere.

"It's not exactly groundbreaking journalism, but it's a solid job," I say. "I like it, for the most part."

"Seems like a great job to me. You're a writer, just like you said you would be. And I'm not surprised at all, by the way."

I try to resist the swell of gratitude forming in my chest, but it crashes through me anyway. Back when I'd told Sebastian about my career dreams, I'd been envisioning myself writing sweeping travel features or long-form human interest stories—the stuff of magazine covers and awards. But Sebastian's words don't carry a hint of judgment. He sounds genuinely impressed. Proud, even.

"What about you?" I ask. "Do you like your job?"

"I'm not sure it's what I'm meant to do forever, but I like it for now. The company I work for helps restaurant owners improve their supply chain strategy. We review everything about their situation and then advise on inefficiencies that are wasting them time or money. Usually both. Unreliable vendors, outdated inventory tracking software, that kind of thing."

"Sounds like the sort of advice we could have used at Bubba's back in the day," I say, thinking of one particularly memorable shift when the snack bar ran out of ketchup packets, Snapple *and* plastic spoons before noon. I'd never hated working the register more than I did the moment I had to hand someone a cup of ice cream with a fork.

"Oh, definitely," Sebastian says, looking thoughtful. "But you know how stubborn my mom is. I think if I ran a model showing she'd save a million dollars a year by switching hamburger bun vendors she'd still insist on using Tony Suppa's guy."

"Tony Suppa's guy!" I cry. "Do you think he ever found out about the detailed mob history we invented for him?"

Sebastian shakes his head, chuckling. "We had way too much time on our hands."

"Or maybe it was the perfect amount, and we've just gotten used to not having anywhere near enough."

I say it nostalgically, my thoughts momentarily lost to the past. But when I glance back at Sebastian I find him looking a bit sullen.

"Anyway. The job." He grips the top of the steering wheel with one hand and scrubs the back of his neck with the other. "It's pretty flexible, which is the main thing I appreciate about it. Very 'human-oriented.' I'm grateful they let me take some time off to be out here."

I clock his tone shift to ponder later and nod, thinking about how *in*flexible my job is—or at least, that's how I've treated it. I haven't taken more than two vacation days in a row since . . . ever. Maren and I have been casually planning my London visit for years, but every time she sends me a flight suggestion or a concert date, I picture Mandy reviewing my PTO request, brow furrowed in concern. I always tell Maren I'll get back to her. I never do.

"Sounds so California," I say, detecting a smile in my periphery as he turns into a small parking lot.

Inside the florist's office, as I flip through sketches of roses and ranunculus, votives and hurricane vases, I think that maybe this day won't be so difficult to navigate after all. Flowers are flowers. Weddings are weddings.

My confidence briefly wavers at the stationery shop, where a staffer assumes I'm the bride.

"Oh, we're not—" Alarmed, I look to Sebastian, who's stifling a laugh, whether at the assumption or my reaction, I'm not sure. "I'm not the bride." I think of the paperwork shamefully stuffed in my workbag that suggests otherwise. I really need to find an opportunity to tell him. The longer I wait, the bigger a deal it's going to become.

Sebastian doesn't bother explaining further, so I nervously rattle off questions about fonts and paper stock, ignoring the names that the letters form. I am a professional who can separate the details of the event from my complicated feelings toward the groom.

"I'm starving," I say once we're back in the Jeep.

Sebastian smiles. "You're heading to the right place, then."

We drive in silence apart from the Spotify playlist he's playing via Bluetooth, and it takes every ounce of willpower in me to keep my eyes on the road and not on the subtle cord of muscles that snake along his right arm as he steers. I find myself noticing that every song lyric these days seems to be about love:

finding it, losing it, longing for it. Or maybe that's how music has always been—but right now it feels personal.

Sebastian makes the familiar turn into the employee lot at Bubba's and parks the Jeep. Then he leads me through the back entrance to the kitchen, which smells incredible. We find Omar at his usual station, tossing something in a giant basket of sizzling oil and nodding along to whatever Bubba is saying to him. Three cooks whom I don't recognize—two men who look to be around my age and a woman who is probably in her fifties—are heads down, engrossed in various prep tasks.

Omar looks up at us, his broad, familiar smile forming. Flecks of gray speckle his once jet-black hair and the lines around his eyes have deepened a bit, but otherwise he looks the same. "Lina Mariano," he says. "Took you long enough to stop by."

His words send a pang of guilt through my chest. All these years living around the corner . . . I *should* have stopped by. Instead, I'd let certain memories of this place haunt me into staying away from people who had cared so much for me.

"It's so good to see you," I say as he gathers me into a hug. I turn to Bubba, who's been watching us with a serene smile. "Both of you."

"Normally I'm skeptical of food critics, but I told Sebastian I'd make an exception for my favorite server," Bubba says, folding her arms around me. "Good to have you back, honey."

Omar nods toward the dining room. "Grab a seat. We'll have the first round out soon."

The dining room looks mostly the same. It's shaped like a semicircle, the diameter of which runs parallel to the kitchen and snack bar, while floor-to-ceiling windows and dark wooden booths with navy-cushioned benches line the arc. The ocean view is as spectacular as ever. A mix of two- and four-top tables fill the rest of the room, with the exception of the table Sebastian leads me toward now, which is a small high-top draped in cream and baby blue linens.

"A sample of what we're renting," he says as we approach.

"Modern coastal," I say, standing across from him. We each have a cream stoneware plate with a gilded, scalloped rim. The votives between us appear to be encased in sea glass. I've covered enough local weddings to know that a coastal theme can quickly veer into beachy kitsch, but this is tastefully subtle.

"When in Rome," he says, gesturing to the view, and I roll my eyes at his intentional cheesiness. "We're going for elevated, but . . . familiar. And fun," he adds. A crooked smile tugs at one corner of his mouth. "I'll let you be the judge."

But it only takes the first round, delivered by Bubba herself, to convince me.

"Let me know what you think," she says with a wink, presenting us each a silver basket filled with balls of fried dough. I bite into one and the flavors pop in my mouth. I immediately groan in approval.

"It's like a breakfast sandwich and hash browns all in one," I say, reaching for another.

"Tater tot breakfast bites," says Bubba. "Half are pork roll, egg and cheese. Half have bacon."

"Ma," Sebastian says, "they're incredible. Tell Omar I'm glad he listened to you."

Bubba squeezes Sebastian's shoulder, then disappears into the kitchen.

"So the food critic approves?" Sebastian asks when it's just us again.

"I've covered some restaurants in the area—openings, new seasonal menus. Whatever I can get my editor to approve, really. But I'm not critiquing anything. Except tacky wedding trends."

He cocks his head, piercing green eyes locked on me. "I take it you're ready to move on from the wedding beat."

"Weddings are a serious industry, just like any other. I've gotten really good at covering them, and for a long time I enjoyed it. But it can get"—I glance at the view to our left, trying to ignore the heat his gaze seems to reflect—"repetitive." I shrug. "I feel a bit stuck, to be honest. Ready for something new."

"I can definitely understand that," he says.

Of course he can. Hadn't that been the whole reason he left this restaurant—this whole town—behind in the first place? It hadn't taken him long at all to realize he wanted more out of life than what Brantley Beach had to offer. He's probably thinking *I told you so.*

One of the younger cooks appears with the next round: paper cones filled with fried calamari and shrimp.

"Handheld fritto misto," I say, popping a crunchy ringlet in my mouth, "is most definitely elevated fun."

Sebastian squeezes a lemon wedge over his cone and follows my lead.

"Seriously," I say around another bite. "This food is so creative! It should be on the menu. You should invite the Diamond Group people to your wedding and have them take notes."

Now Sebastian is the one avoiding eye contact. Was it cavalier for me to bring up Diamond Group so flippantly? So Sebastian never wanted to take over the family business—that doesn't mean he's indifferent to the fact that it's about to be absorbed by a bougie restaurant group from the city. The restaurant means everything to his mom, and for that reason alone it's probably a tender subject.

"Sorry," I say. "That was probably a little insensitive."

He rakes a hand through his hair. "It's really okay. It's going to be a big change for sure, but I need to get used to talking about it."

A question pops into my head. I hesitate, then think, *Fuck it.* He won't answer it if he doesn't want to. Wouldn't be the first time a source has done that.

"What made her want to sell? If you don't mind my asking."

I follow his gaze toward the kitchen. When he sees no one's coming he continues.

"She doesn't want to," he says, spinning the votive between his fingers. "She needs to." Sebastian looks up at me, and the pain in his eyes crushes me. "My mom's sick."

Oh.

"She's had health issues since I can remember," he continues. "Lymphoma is the main thing. But she's always managed it well. Responded to medication. Until recently."

I try to reconcile this information with the vivacious, energetic woman I've always known. I'd always assumed Bubba was perfectly healthy. Invincible, even.

"Shit. Sebastian, I'm so sorry. That's terrible."

"Yeah. It is. Honestly, when I found out, my first thought was to call the whole wedding off. The last thing she needs to be doing is working even more hours turning this place into a venue. But she wouldn't hear any of that. You saw how excited she is." He smiles softly, shaking his head.

"I'm sure it's nice to have a distraction," I offer gently.

"Yeah. Exactly. And I know she's relieved to see me settling down. I'm lucky I at least got her to agree to let me take leave from work so I can stay out here for a while. Omar and I will handle as much as possible. The wedding logistics. Getting ready for the restaurant's last season. Finalizing the negotiations with Diamond Group. She can work as much or as little as she wants, depending on how she's feeling. Focus on her treatments."

"It's probably a huge relief to have you here to help. Even if she's too stubborn to admit it." He lets out a soft laugh. I almost reach across the table to touch his wrist but I think better of it. A little distance is good. Safe. "Will Claire stay in Santa Barbara while you're out here?"

He nods, but before he can elaborate Omar appears with the entrées, smiling in a way that tells me he totally crushed this round and our tastebuds are about to take a journey. We sample each of the three choices: a deconstructed lobster roll, a slider trio and mushroom gyros ("a vegetarian option compelling enough to tempt meat eaters," I jot in my notebook). The food is so good that Sebastian and I don't speak until we've polished our plates clean.

"That was in-cred-i-ble," I tell him. "Jersey wedding food is already top tier, but this is on a whole other level." I flip to a fresh page in my notebook and switch into interview mode. "Which reminds me. I always like to ask couples for their Big Three."

Sebastian arches one thick, beautiful eyebrow at me.

"The vendors or elements that are most important to them," I say, elaborating. "Would you say food was one of your Big Three?"

"For me, definitely. I'd say food, location and music."

"Are you doing a band?" I love a good wedding band. I hope he says yes, which is nonsensical considering I won't be at this wedding. (In fact, I'd like to be on another planet during it.)

He nods. "The Geeks."

I squeal. "No way you got the Geeks!" The Geeks play all the local beach bars. They have a bit of a cult following, mostly in our parents' age bracket.

"We had an in," Sebastian says, grinning. "The drummer was Mom's prom date."

"Shut up. Of course he was."

He clears his throat. "So, yeah. Those are my Big Three. But Claire would probably have a totally different answer. Flowers for sure. Her dress, maybe. The photographer."

I nod but keep my mouth shut. For J.Lo in *The Wedding Planner*, choosing "I Honestly Love You" as your wedding song is matrimonial suicide. For this wedding writer, it's not being on the same page about the Big Three.

"Well, from what I've seen today, it seems like you guys have all the bases covered. It's going to be a beautiful wedding." I arrange my mouth into a smile. "And your guests will be dreaming of this food for days. *I'm* going to be dreaming of this food for days."

He tips his head toward the kitchen. "I'm just glad my mom and Omar have had so much fun with it."

"Omar deserves an award!" I cry. "Bubba's been wasting his talents on burgers and hot dogs."

Sebastian cocks his head thoughtfully.

"What?" I ask, suddenly self-conscious. He looks like he's about to tell me I have aioli on my face.

"Omar worked in the city for, like, ten years before he started here. You knew that, right?"

I shake my head slowly. I never really knew anything about Omar's life before the restaurant, I realize, or even just outside of it. I think of one time my mom and I ran into one of her students at the mall. He greeted her with a deer-in-the-headlights look, like he assumed she slept under her desk in the classroom.

Youth is wasted on the self-absorbed.

"What kind of restaurants?" I ask.

"Fine dining, mostly. And a gastro pub that was doing some really creative stuff." He drops his voice slightly. "He'd married his high school sweetheart right after culinary school. Cynthia was her name. When she got sick, they decided to move out here to be closer to her family. Slow down a bit. He responded to an ad for a line cook that my mom had put in the paper. Her parents still technically owned Bubba's at the time, but she was running the day-to-day. So of course she takes one look at his résumé and puts him in charge of the whole kitchen. The head cook had been considering retiring anyway." Our eyes meet across the small table. A pit forms in my stomach as I anticipate what he's about to say next. "Cynthia passed about a year later."

I swallow. "Jesus. I had no idea."

Sebastian's gaze drifts out the window, toward the rolling waves. "He's always telling my mom that this place saved him. I think it means as much to him as it does to her."

"Could he stay? If he wanted to."

"I doubt it," he says, the wistfulness gone from his voice. He runs a hand through his hair again. "Diamond Group made it crystal clear that they plan to turn this into a whole new concept. Bring in their own people. And to be honest? I don't think Omar would want to do this without my mom. He's planning to finish out the season, help us with the transition. Then he'll move down to Philly to be closer to his brother."

"That will be hard for her," I say, more of a statement than a question.

Sebastian nods, spinning one of the votives between his fingers. "You know what drives me nuts? People would always say how impressed they were that my mom kept running the restaurant by herself after my dad left. As if he had anything to do with it even when he was in the picture."

I'm surprised by Sebastian's candor. He seemed to idolize his dad when we were growing up, but it's clear from his tone and the pained look on his face that a lot has changed. I'd heard at some point after college that his parents were no longer together, but I never caught any details about exactly when or why they split. For all Bubba knew about the residents of Brantley Beach and their personal lives, she remained remarkably immune to gossip herself.

One thing I do know, though, is that Mr. Nikolaou had never really been involved in the restaurant. That was all Bubba.

"That must have pissed her off," I say. "Those kinds of comments."

He snickers. "Yeah. But you know Mom—never one to say a bad word to anyone. She'd just wave them off. Say she wasn't doing it alone, because she'd always have Omar."

Right on cue, Omar appears holding two dessert plates. Despite the heavy conversation topic, I can't help but smile at the slice of wedding cake he sets in front of me.

Well . . . not typical wedding cake.

"An ice cream wedding cake," I say, my voice ridiculously giddy. There's a chocolate top layer and a vanilla bottom layer, separated by a strip of cake crunch suspended in fudge.

Just when I think this meal couldn't possibly get better, I take a bite and realize that the top layer actually isn't chocolate. I look from Omar to Sebastian and back, incredulous, and ask with more than a hint of awe: "Honey fudge?"

Omar winks. "Can't take all the credit for this one. Twisters doesn't normally do cakes, but I convinced them to make an exception."

I shovel another bite into my mouth as Omar turns to Sebastian and says, "Your mom was feeling tired, so I sent her home."

Sebastian smiles weakly. "And she listened?"

"Not without a fight." Omar claps a broad hand on Sebastian's shoulder, chuckling to himself.

Now that I've scraped my plate clean I clear my throat. "Omar, the food was incredible. Thanks for letting me join."

He waves a hand. "It was great to have you back." He glances at Sebastian. "Both of you."

We carry our plates to the kitchen and thank the staff. I hug Omar, hoping he feels the apology in it. And the gratitude. The smile he offers when I pull away tells me that he does.

Back at the Jeep, Sebastian opens the passenger door. I climb in and click my seatbelt into place, then lace my hands over my stomach, groaning. "Holy crap. I feel like I just ate Thanksgiving dinner."

Sebastian switches the gear into reverse and says, "Same. Might have to let my tux out a little."

Right. Sebastian's fitting is our last appointment of the day. I conjure an image of him that would make James Bond cower—then quickly shove it out of my mind.

"Actually," I say, sitting up, "would you have time to drop me off? I was too busy eating to take notes. I should type something up while everything's fresh in my mind." I tap the side of my head for emphasis, because I'm an embarrassing person.

"Oh, yeah. Of course," he says, switching blinkers and taking a left out of the parking lot. "Shit. I do have to make one other stop first if it's okay. Before the place closes."

I nod, and we drive in silence for a minute. Then Sebastian glances over at me. "You know, I'd been kind of dreading all of these appointments, Mariano. But today wasn't so bad."

I look to my left and find his eyes back on the road, a hint of a smirk on his mouth.

I almost say something self-deprecating. "I'm good company," I say instead.

"You did always have a way of making the most tedious tasks ever so slightly more enjoyable."

An image flashes in my mind: Sebastian and me in the kitchen of the restaurant, rolling silverware into napkins while singing along to Bubba's *Rumours* CD. When the "Dreams" chorus comes on we take turns singing into a roll-up microphone.

I keep my eyes trained on the road, ignoring the magnetic tug of his presence on my peripheral. "And here I thought you always picked me because I was efficient."

Sebastian sputter-laughs, like I've just told a joke. Bubba loved me because I worked hard and was good with the customers, and because I cleaned the bathrooms without complaining. But all of that was mostly to make up for the fact that I was clumsy. I volunteered to unclog toilets as penance for breaking plates and spilling coffee.

I *was* joking, but I give him a playful shove anyway.

Then I look up, and horror sets in as I realize where we are. Parked at the city clerk's office.

"Just need another copy of our application for the officiant," Sebastian explains. He reaches into his glove compartment and pulls out a familiar envelope.

"Wait!" I grab Sebastian's arm. He shoots me a curious look but sits back down. Waits, as he's told.

Here we go.

"I've been meaning to tell you something." I blow out a breath. "That day we ran into each other here, when I was your witness? There was a mix-up with the paperwork."

"A mix-up, huh?"

I nod to the envelope. He slides the papers out, and I watch as he scans them, waiting to see his eyes widen or maybe even for an audible gasp of shock to escape from his mouth. But his expression doesn't change. He shuffles the papers back into the envelope and locks eyes with me again.

And then he *laughs*.

I can practically feel my cheeks redden. I knew it. He thinks the mistake ridiculous—laughable, even—and he probably thinks I did it on purpose. One big, sick joke.

I cross my arms. I'm not embarrassed anymore; I'm fuming.

"Sorry," he says when he realizes I'm glaring at him. "I'm only laughing because I already knew. I honestly just didn't think you'd ever find out about it."

He knew?

"I had a copy, too," I remind him.

He shrugs. "I figured you'd never look at it again." His mouth contorts into an infuriatingly smug smile. "Or maybe you'd shove it in a filing cabinet and come across it years later while doing a deep clean."

I scoff. No wonder he was smirking when I found him at the restaurant and laughing at the stationery store.

"Come on, Mariano. I'm just messing around. You have to admit it's kind of funny."

"A mistake that could have ruined your wedding. How hilarious."

He shakes his head. Sighs. "Claire and I fixed it the next morning. No harm, no foul. I do have one question, though."

I drag a hand down my face. "Go on."

"If you thought we didn't know, when were you going to tell one of us? Or were you just going to let us figure it out at the altar?" The smirk has returned, I notice with annoyance.

I wave him off. "I obviously would have told you eventually. I just didn't want to make it a big thing."

"Right," he says, opening his door. "It was an honest mistake. And luckily annulments are easy to get these days."

I roll my eyes but I can't help it: For the first time, I let myself actually laugh about the situation.

"Thanks for letting me tag along today," I say when we pull up to my apartment building. "Tell Claire I'll call her this week with any follow-up questions."

"I should be thanking you," he says. I'm standing outside the car now, the passenger door still open, and he ducks a little so I can see him through it. "Especially for indulging my mom and Omar. They loved seeing you."

"Well," I say, "I felt the same way."

And maybe it's because I'll probably never see him again—I've already decided I won't be at the wedding. I'll file my story based on my emails with Claire and notes from today. My first few years at Shore Life I attended every wedding I covered. More than a dozen per year. But now I usually only go if the venue is brand new so that I can write a few bounces on it, or if a vendor has planned some sort of bespoke installation that Mandy thinks I should experience in person. Otherwise, when you've seen as many weddings as I have, you really have seen them all. There are only so many times one person can hear an aunt who can barely see over the church podium read 1 Corinthians 13:4–8, or raise a glass to a teary father of the bride, or squat on the dance floor while whisper-singing "a little bit softer now" before they all start to blur together.

Or maybe it's because something about today, something

about driving around our hometown together and being back at the restaurant with Omar and Bubba and laughing until my stomach hurt, has made me feel nostalgic in a way that I haven't allowed myself to feel in a long time, that I shut the door, saying, "And Nikolaou? It wasn't so bad spending the day with you, either."

Sebastian's mouth curves into a lopsided smile as he switches the car into drive. Then, just before he turns those green eyes back to the road, he says, "See you around, Mariano."

Chapter 11

Then
Fourteen Years Ago

When I opened my eyes, my first thought was that my room smelled weird, almost like a hospital. I blinked a few times to clear my vision, revealing rows of white ceiling tiles. *Strange*, I thought. My bedroom didn't have ceiling tiles.

I propped myself up on my elbows. As my surroundings came into focus, I realized this wasn't my room at all. Instead of my bed, I was on a cot, facing an open door to a hallway. A woman in scrubs hurried past the doorway.

I *was* in a hospital. An emergency room, to be more specific.

Then I felt the pain.

I reached for my left leg where the jolt of fire had come from, then immediately clasped both hands over my mouth at the sight of the stitches that started halfway up the side of my thigh and disappeared into the bottom of my hospital gown.

Was I in an accident? Had I gashed myself on a piece of equipment at work? I shifted to my right, expecting to find my mom or dad so I could ask one of them.

Instead, I found Sebastian. He was slumped in the lone visitor's chair, asleep.

What. The. Heck?

I'd spent all of June following Maren's advice to the letter. The first two weeks were my training period for the main dining room, which involved shadowing a more experienced server. I let out a sigh of relief when Bubba assigned me to shadow Tina; Sebastian would be training a rising senior from the city named Ravi whose parents had a Shore house for the summer.

I signed up for as many shifts as possible that didn't overlap with Sebastian's, and when we did work together, I kept a safe distance. He continued to joke around with all of the staff, but whereas last summer I acknowledged everything he said within earshot in hopes of extending our interactions, I now offered no more than a tight smile in response.

We developed an unspoken rhythm, navigating around the restaurant and each other while exchanging no more than a brief word or gesture. Last summer, working at Bubba's had been the heartbeat of my social life, but this year Maren and I were attending parties multiple nights a week. Work, as far as I was concerned, was just for the paycheck.

Maren and I eliminated the *S* word from all conversations, instead shifting our focus to Aaron (who had officially asked Maren to be his girlfriend a week after their first kiss) and various prospects for me. I'd wound up having my first kiss in mid-June during a game of spin the bottle, which Maren insisted didn't really count. It had been with a boy named Josh from the all-boys private school a couple of towns over. It was brief, but I remember thinking his lips were soft, his breath minty fresh, like he'd just popped a Tic Tac. I decided that I agreed with Maren—it didn't count—but at the very least, maybe it would take some of the pressure off of my real first kiss. I was familiar with the motions now.

It wasn't a Sebastian-free summer—but it was pretty damn close.

Which begged the question: Why was he the one here with me now?

I took in his sleeping form, searching for any details that

might clue me in to how we ended up here. His curls were windswept and flecked with sand. His face was deeply tanned, his nose peeling a little, probably from a previous sunburn. He wore a BRANTLEY BEACH CLASS OF 2011 T-shirt with the sleeves cut off, exposing equally tan shoulders and long, ropey muscles. Faded red board shorts. Dirty white Vans.

He was sitting close enough for me to reach over and touch his forearm. So I did.

"Sebastian."

He stirred, squinting open those green eyes. At the sight of me he jolted upright.

I wasn't sure what question to ask first, but for some reason I landed on, "Did I pass out?"

Sebastian nodded. "When you first saw the blood." The concerned expression on his face shifted to one of mild amusement. "And then again on the way to the emergency room. And one more time while you were getting stitches. But just now you were sleeping—I asked the nurse, like, three times to be sure. Apparently fainting is exhausting."

I cringed with embarrassment, and then I remembered that I was wearing a flimsy hospital gown after getting stitches from my thigh to my ass, possibly while Sebastian Nikolaou watched. My proclivity for fainting was the least of my worries. In fact, I wouldn't have minded passing out right then.

At the same time, I felt a bit of relief. If Sebastian was calm enough to make jokes, then I figured I was going to be okay.

"Do you remember what happened?" he asked.

I shook my head slowly.

"Does the word *jetty* ring any bells?" he asked, leaning forward and resting his elbows on his knees. He was close enough for me to smell the salt on his skin, either from the ocean or sweat or some combination of both, and I thought it was this, more than anything, that jogged my memory.

Maren and I had both had the day off and decided to spend

it at the beach. She was into designing her own handbags that summer and had a vision for one studded with seashells and sea glass. We'd spent hours walking up and down the shore, stopping every few feet so she could examine ones that caught her eye. My parents were in Boston for the weekend visiting my aunt and uncle, so I truly had no schedule, nowhere to be but the beach.

At one point when we reached the surfing beach, Maren hopped up onto one of the huge black rocks that formed the jetty.

"C'mon." She gestured for me to follow, a hint of mischief in her expression. "We'll find some good stuff up here." I rolled my eyes, because I knew she wasn't really talking about shells anymore; she was hoping for a glimpse of the surfers. Not that I really minded that idea.

I climbed up on the first rock and stood, following her. She was already a few rocks ahead of me when she called over her shoulder, "Careful, Leens. There's algae—"

The next thing I felt wasn't pain—it was the cold, slick surface of the rock against my hands. I saw a flash of blood, and a wave of nausea pulled me under. Then, darkness.

So I'd slipped on the jetty, cut my leg and . . . hit my head? Or maybe I had passed out at the sight of the blood alone, like Sebastian said. That seemed more likely; I'd always had a weak stomach for anything medical.

Another memory flashed—a combination of feelings and sounds without images. Maren calling for help. Strong arms cradling me. Half my face pressed against warm, salty skin, the taste transferring to my lips with each step.

A bumpy car ride, my head cradled in Maren's lap, her hands shakily stroking my hair while shouting directions for the shortest route to the hospital to whoever was driving.

Sebastian.

He'd carried me off the beach. Driven me here.

Stayed.

"I should call my parents," I said, searching the cot for my phone. Sebastian reached over the rail and handed it to me.

"Already did," he said. "They're driving back from Boston now. Should be pretty close, actually. And Maren's in the waiting room. We've been taking turns," he said, answering my next question.

"I'm surprised they let you guys back here with me."

"The nurse is my mom's friend," he said, shrugging. "She says rest and don't worry about your shifts this week, by the way—my mom."

I smiled weakly, thinking of the gnarly scar I'd likely have for the rest of my life thanks to a moment of carelessness.

"Thank you," I said, turning to him. "Not just for getting me here. For staying."

I forced my eyes to meet his, so clear and green they put the sea glass Maren and I had found to shame.

"I had to make sure you were okay," he said, his tone soft but serious. He looked at me for a beat longer and then straightened up, clearing his throat. "My mom would kill me if I didn't," he added.

With that amendment, all my temporarily forgotten doubts resurfaced. Did he stay because it was me, or because it was what his mom would want him to do?

A nurse appeared in the doorway, clipboard in hand.

"Angelina Mariano?"

I nodded.

"Your parents are checking in now," she said, smiling gently. "They just have to sign some paperwork and then we can discharge you."

The nurse handed me a stapled packet of papers with my discharge instructions. Just in case I wasn't feeling embarrassed enough, Sebastian listened while she summarized the steps—which included thorough instructions on how I should shower to avoid getting my stitches wet.

My cheeks turned redder than my wound.

"We'll see you again to remove the stitches in ten days. No biking for at least a week after that," the nurse added helpfully.

Crap. I hadn't thought about that. Mom had taken a curriculum-writing job that summer, so neither of my parents would be able to give me a ride to work once I was ready to go back.

After I thanked the nurse and she left, Sebastian put a hand on the rail.

"I'll drive you to work when you're ready to come back," he said.

"You don't have to do that," I said, my eyes on the hallway straight ahead. "We aren't even on the same schedule."

"Why is that, by the way?"

I turned to look at him and found something surprising in his eyes: a hint of genuine hurt.

I racked my brain for an explanation other than the truth but was saved by a knock on the doorframe.

"Oh, honey," my dad said.

And then my parents were flanking me on either side, a flurry of hugs and questions and fuss. I noticed Maren in the doorway behind them, still in her beach cover-up. She offered me an apologetic wave.

I filled my parents in on what happened (Sebastian's rescue mission becoming decidedly less *Baywatch* in my retelling—though I could tell by the look on Maren's face that it definitely was extremely *Baywatch*) and my care instructions. By the time they were satisfied with the level of information I'd provided, I looked over and found Sebastian's chair empty.

"Thank God Maren was with you," my mom said, turning to squeeze her hand.

"And Sebastian," my dad added. "That's a great kid right there." Coming from my soft-spoken father, it was the highest of compliments.

"Yeah," I said. "I'm pretty lucky."

Chapter 12
Now

At the office two and a half weeks later, I create a new email, type Mandy's address in the recipient field and attach a file named RW59. It's the outline for my "Real Weddings" column on the Nikolaou-Cunningham wedding. I shake my head at the screen.

It's certainly not my best work, but it will have to do.

The day after I'd gone to all the appointments with Sebastian, I'd sent him a carefully crafted and—I thought, at least—thoughtful text message, thanking him for everything from the previous day, including opening up to me about what he was going through with this mom. I know from past experiences that asking someone dealing with a family illness to let you know if there's anything you can do can feel more like a burden than support, so I also sent him a list of specific ways I could help, from dropping off groceries to picking up Bubba from a treatment. I haven't heard back.

Then Claire and I were supposed to talk on the phone, but she ghosted me. And neither she nor Sebastian has answered any of my follow-up emails since. I'm sure she's busy with work, and he's preoccupied with the restaurant and helping his mom. But still, the radio silence is a little odd. I debated just calling Sebastian but ultimately talked myself out of it. After the tasting I'd briefly wondered if we'd taken a step toward something resembling a friendship, but I realize now that was never the case. Just because we'd seen each other three times in the span of a few days and shared a difficult conversation didn't mean we were suddenly friends again.

The one person I did manage to get ahold of shortly after the tasting was Omar. I asked him a few clarifying questions about his inspiration for the menu and where he sourced the local ingredients, and we wound up staying on the phone for another twenty minutes catching up. When he asked about my old friend Maren Murphy, I told him that she had a fabulous London job and actually happened to be in town visiting for the summer. He invited us both to come to the restaurant this coming Saturday. It's Bubba's sixty-fifth birthday, and he's planning a little surprise party. I thanked him and said I'd get back to him soon. I'm still on the fence about whether or not we should go.

"Ready to get the hell out of here?" David asks, slamming his laptop shut decisively.

"You have no idea," I say, hitting SEND.

"We're obviously going," Maren says an hour later. We're at a bar on the pier overlooking Brantley Marina with David and Henry, eating coconut shrimp and drinking from rum buckets.

"Wouldn't you rather spend the day at the beach?" I ask, even though I know trying to change her mind is futile. "Or go to the city?"

"What I want," she says, "is to eat some greasy American food with my best friend."

"And maybe watch said best friend try to pretend her high school crush doesn't still have her heart in an absolute chokehold?" David asks, helpfully.

Henry laughs nervously.

"He does not! This can be strictly professional," Maren says, draining the last of her bucket and then gesturing to our waiter for another round. "Look: I know you, and I know you're overthinking the whole situation. It's actually really simple. You've been having trouble getting ahold of Sebastian and Claire for your article. This is the perfect way to get your questions answered. And you said yourself that you wish it hadn't taken you all these years to go by the restaurant. That place, the people—it all means a lot to you, and now you have a chance to reconnect. I don't think there's anything wrong with that."

Her wise words are undercut by the burbling sound her straw makes as she tries for one last slurp, pushing a curtain of unruly curls off her face. The chic Londoner is gone, the wild teenager back in her rightful place across from me.

"I completely agree," David says, shocking no one. "At this point it's more suspicious if you *don't* go." He points at me with a shrimp tail. "Makes it seem like you've been intentionally hiding all these years."

"I *have* been intentionally hiding all these years," I point out.

"They don't have to know that," David counters.

The waiter returns with four fresh buckets. We're silent for a full minute while we suck down the way-too-sweet concoctions.

"Are we too old for these?" Henry asks.

"Never!" Maren cries.

More silent sipping. Somehow we've already been here for two hours. The sky has turned pinky-orange, like sherbet, boats bobbing hypnotically below, and a solo guitarist has started strumming next to the bar. It's one of those quintessential summer nights that reminds me Brantley Beach has its perks.

"We'll go to the party," I say finally. David whoops, but I shoot him a look and he quickly reins it in. Then I turn to Maren. "Just promise me you'll act normal."

"Of course," she says innocently. "When have I ever steered you wrong?"

Chapter 13

Then
Fourteen Years Ago

Returning to work on the Fourth of July wasn't one of my brightest ideas.

I didn't realize this until about an hour into my shift, which started at noon. Because the first hour, I was too busy replaying the four-minute drive here to fully register the chaos around me.

I'd gotten my stitches out the day before, right on schedule, and after ten days cooped up at home I couldn't wait to get back to my normal routine. I'd been under strict orders to avoid swimming, sand and direct sunlight, and the antibiotics I was on to prevent infection had meant no sneaky sips of alcohol, either. Maren dutifully hung out with me for a few hours almost every day, distracting me with rom-com marathons or ambitious baking projects—activities we otherwise reserved for rainy days. Aaron had unceremoniously dumped her over text, so she hardly minded the excuse to disappear from our social circuit for a little while.

Maren had wanted to spend my first day of freedom at the beach, but after missing almost an entire paycheck I couldn't turn down time-and-a-half holiday pay. The beach could wait until tomorrow.

The sound of tires hitting the driveway sent a shiver down my spine. I opened the front door and waved to Sebastian, who waved back, then reached across the passenger seat of his Jeep to push open the door for me. As I got in, it hit me that this was my first time in a boy's car, or any friend's car, for that matter. (Well, if you didn't count the time I was in and out of consciousness.) Sebastian was old for his grade and had gotten his license in June when he turned seventeen. Maren and I would be taking Driver's Ed that fall in preparation for our learner's permits.

"Nice car," I said, because it felt like a thing you're supposed to say. I instantly regretted it.

"Thanks," he said. "It's old but it does the job."

He had a CD playing. The familiar beats of a Third Eye Blind song came through the speakers.

"How're you feeling?" His hand braced the back of my seat as he looked over his shoulder and reversed out of the driveway, his other palm spinning the wheel.

"Great!" I chirpcd, but reflcxively I covered my scar with my left hand. I'd have worn pants if it weren't eighty degrees today. (I almost did anyway.)

"That was a pretty nasty fall, Mariano," he said, glancing over at me.

My eyes darted to the road ahead, face neutral, but inside I was reeling. I'd hoped Sebastian had only caught the aftermath of the . . . *incident.* But apparently he'd witnessed the main event.

"Not my finest moment," I said, shifting in my seat. "But it could have been a lot worse. I haven't officially thanked you for what you did. So, yeah. Thanks."

"Of course," he said, raking a hand through his luscious curls. "Glad I was there at the right time."

That certainly was one way of looking at it.

Two minutes later, he parked his Jeep in the employee lot, and we entered the lunch rush.

Along with Memorial Day and Labor Day, the Fourth of July was one of the three biggest weekends down the Shore, which meant all hands on deck at Bubba's. We all worked extended shifts to accommodate the influx of crowds during the day (for the beach) and at night (for the fireworks show over the ocean). Tina was the morning shift leader, Sebastian the afternoon, and during our midday overlap they kept spirits high with the promise of a reward after the restaurant closed at 9:00 p.m.: a staff party at Tina's house while her parents were out of town.

I barely saw Sebastian all day, not that I really had time to notice. Our staff was thrown a new curveball almost every hour. At 1:30, the ice machine broke, so Sebastian and a busboy named Sean Wilkinson wheeled empty coolers to the 7-Eleven, filled them up and lugged them back. Just before three I lost a coin toss with Ravi and had to unclog a toilet, and sometime around four we ran out of ketchup. By eight, my feet were throbbing in my Payless shoes, my skin caked with a layer of sweat and grime.

I powered through the final hour knowing the restaurant would be dead as soon as the fireworks started at dusk. I exhaled a literal sigh of relief when I heard the crack from the first test go off and the remaining customers began scrambling to finish their meals and snag a spot on the beach.

After my last table signed their bill, I reached into the utility closet to grab the mop and start my closing duties, but someone touched my arm to stop me. I turned and found myself inches from Sebastian.

"The floors can wait, Mariano," he said, taking the mop from me and resting it back against the wall of the closet. "Come watch the show with us."

I peered around him to the dining room, which had been bustling just a couple of minutes ago. Now it was nearly empty; the rest of the staffers must have already gone outside. I spotted

Bubba near the hostess stand and felt my skin flush, worried she'd caught us all slacking off. I never wanted to disappoint Bubba. But she winked at me and mouthed, *Go*.

Sebastian led me out the back door, past the dumpsters and around the corner of the building to a small stretch of boardwalk with a ramp that led to the parking lot behind the restaurant. Someone had moved the Bubba's delivery truck that was usually parked there to make space for the staffers to sit on the ground with a perfect, unobstructed view of the fireworks above the ocean. Normally I'd sit next to Tina, who had clocked out hours before and come back for the fireworks, but she was sitting cross-legged between Ravi and a middle-aged waitress named Kelly. Sebastian dropped to a spot on the ground and I decided that it would be more conspicuous if I *didn't* just sit next to him, so I gave in and took a seat, crossing my legs.

We were silent for a few minutes as pinwheels and weeping willows exploded above us. I sucked in deep breaths of the fresh, salty air, thankful to be outside.

Then, eyes still trained on the fireworks, Sebastian asked, "So how have you been, Mariano? I feel like you've been avoiding me this summer."

My face felt hot. I shrugged. I wasn't exactly a smooth liar, but I could handle some strategic downplaying.

"I've just been trying to focus on training," I said, my eyes locked on a constellation of red and blue sparks that spelled U-S-A. Tina glanced over at us, eyebrow raised. I hoped the sound of the fireworks prevented her from actually overhearing our conversation.

Sebastian leaned back onto his elbows, one long leg stretched out in front of him and the other bent at the knee. "Worried I'll distract you?"

I turned to him just as he was doing the same, a smirk dancing across his mouth. I sensed the flirtation in his tone, but instead of exciting me like it would have last summer, it put me on guard. Sebastian acted this way with everyone, I reminded myself. I wasn't special; I just happened to be the one sitting here.

I rolled my eyes and said, "I just don't want your mom to relegate me to the snack bar again."

"She never would," he said, his tone serious now. "You're one of her favorites these days. Always on time, willing to cover shifts at the last minute. The customers like you . . ." His voice trailed off, then the smirk reemerged. "It's like that whole ice cream machine saga never even happened."

At this I rotated my whole body to face him, my voice low. "Does she seriously remember that?"

Sebastian laughed. "Relax, Mariano. I'm kidding. That thing is ancient and she probably didn't even notice."

I turned back to the fireworks, a little embarrassed. But mostly I was glad to hear how much Bubba liked me.

We watched the show for a few more minutes, any awkwardness in the silence between us masked by Bruce Springsteen via a nearby speaker, singing "Jersey Girl."

Sebastian stood up quietly.

"Where are you going?" I hissed.

"Everyone's beat," he said, gesturing to the rest of the staff, who were in various lounging positions to relieve what I imagined were feet that throbbed as much as mine did. "I'm going to start closing."

"I'll help."

Inside, Bubba and Omar were already making good progress on closing up the kitchen, so we started on the dining room. Sebastian cranked up the volume on the speaker system, which broadcast the same Pandora beach vibes station all summer long—a mellow-meets-punk mix of Jack Johnson, Sugar Ray, Red Hot Chili Peppers and Third Eye Blind.

We didn't talk as we worked, but we fell into a companionable rhythm. First we disinfected all the tables, then he stacked the chairs and swept, and I followed each finished section with the mop. It was an efficient system—we finished closing the dining room with two people faster than we would have been able to with the full staff and all their shenanigans.

"Do you want a ride to the party?" Sebastian asked me as I tossed my apron in the laundry basket with the dirty kitchen towels.

My feet ached in response. "Honestly? I'm exhausted. I think I'm gonna bail."

Sebastian surprised me by saying, "I was thinking the exact same thing. I'll drop you at your place on my way home."

"Okay," I said. "Thanks."

He turned to the long expo counter that connected the dining room and the kitchen. Through the hatch, I could see Bubba and Omar hunched over the sink, speaking in hushed tones. Bubba looked upset.

"Mom?" Sebastian called.

Bubba snapped up. Omar pivoted to one of the prep stations.

"Hey, honey," she said, attempting to arrange her face into its usual sunny expression. But her weariness was clear.

I glanced at Sebastian. I knew he must have clocked the tense moment, too, but if it concerned him he didn't let on.

"All closed up out here," he said. "I won't be late tonight. Just dropping Lina off and then I'll see you at home."

Bubba smiled gratefully at her son. Then she looked back and forth between us, eyes narrowing in a way that seemed playfully suspicious. "You're both angels, thank you. I won't be far behind you."

We drove for a few minutes without talking. Normally I would have agonized over something to say to avoid coming across as awkward or uninteresting, but I was too tired for my usual mental gymnastics. I couldn't wait to get home and fall into my bed.

"How do you feel about a pit stop?" Sebastian asked about halfway to my house. I meant to respond with something along the lines of *No thanks, I'm ready to sleep for a year*, but instead the words that came out of my mouth were: "What kind of pit stop?"

Instead of answering, he offered me a crooked smile and flicked on his turn signal just in time to pull into the parking lot of Twisters, my favorite ice cream shop in town.

"Don't they close at ten?" I asked, glancing at the dashboard clock. It was 9:52.

"Eight minutes is plenty of time to scoop two honey-fudge cones. And I trust you aren't going to argue with me and say that isn't the superior flavor."

I kept my mouth shut and opened the passenger door, because he was right: I wasn't going to argue.

A bell above the shop door tinkled as we opened it, and I recognized Isaiah Thompson from school behind the counter. A look of annoyance flashed across his face at the sound of such late arrivals, but a smile quickly replaced it once he saw Sebastian. *Everyone* loved Sebastian.

"Hey, man," he said. "Honey fudge on waffle?"

"And whatever she wants," he said tipping his head toward me.

"Same, please," I piped up.

Sebastian pulled a ten-dollar bill out of his pocket before I could object, and I felt too awkward to offer to pay him after the fact so I just accepted my cone and thanked him. My first car ride with a boy and now my first time being treated for anything. Maren's voice thrummed in my ears: *Are you on a date with he who shall not be mentioned? So much for a Sebastian-free summer.*

I followed Sebastian to a bench outside. The sugar worked its magic quickly, and I found myself no longer thinking about my aching feet.

"You gotta go way faster than that in this heat," Sebastian

said, stifling a laugh as chocolate dripped down the side of my hand. His scoop was already more of a mound. I shot him a glare, racing to catch up.

"Tina will be bummed we're missing the party," I said once we'd both gotten to our cones and the drip-risk had subsided. "Do you regret skipping it?"

"Nah," Sebastian said. "There will be plenty more parties this summer, I'm sure. They're all the same, really."

His blasé attitude surprised me. Most of the rising seniors I knew jumped at every invitation, because they knew there were only so many left.

"And I try not to stay out late when my dad's traveling," he added. He still sounded casual, but his gaze drifted across the parking lot. I could tell he had something on his mind. I wondered if it had to do with whatever Bubba and Omar were discussing in the kitchen.

"Is he somewhere cool, at least?" I asked, trying to lighten the mood. Mr. Nikolaou was a bit of a mystery to me. He traveled a lot for his fancy New York City job and didn't come by the restaurant often, but whenever he did Sebastian beamed with pride. I could tell how much he looked up to him.

Sebastian laughed derisively. "Philly." He glanced sidelong at me, which I took as permission to laugh, too. No shade on Philly; it just wasn't the far-off city I'd been expecting.

"He was supposed to come home tonight," Sebastian continued, "but now he won't be back until tomorrow."

I nodded slowly, feeling like I was starting to understand. Philly was less than an hour and a half from Brantley Beach—certainly close enough for Mr. Nikolaou to drive home for the night, even after a long workday. Maybe that was what had upset Bubba.

We were quiet for a moment, and then I surprised myself by asking, "Is it weird to think about graduating next year?"

He paused before answering, as if seriously considering the

question. "Yeah," he said, "I'd say weird is the right word. It's weird to think that this time next year, I'll be getting ready to move, and I don't even know where. There are so many unknowns."

"Sounds scary," I observed.

He shrugged. "It's a little scary, yeah. But at the same time I feel kind of ready to move on. When I was a freshman I never would have thought I would feel that way, but it's the truth. I just feel like every year that I'm here is the same: school, working at the restaurant, surfing, parties."

"Do you think you'll go far away, then?" I asked, willing my tone to register somewhere between completely apathetic and vaguely curious.

"Yes," he answered without hesitation. "Only because I know myself, and I know my mom, and if I stay close she'll never fully accept that I'm not going to stay here and help her run the restaurant forever. My mom was born here and never lived anywhere else. She's only been to a few states, never outside the country. The restaurant is her whole life. I need her to understand that it isn't going to be mine."

I thought about how, no matter how early I clocked in, Bubba was already there, poring over piles of paperwork in her office. How she stayed even after everyone else clocked out, tinkering with leaky pipes and loose floorboards. Whenever anyone on staff (lovingly) joked that she practically lived at the restaurant, she waved them off. But there was clearly some truth to it. And Sebastian didn't think that was a good thing.

"You don't want to feel stuck," I summarized.

"Yeah. Exactly."

"What does your dad think? About college," I clarified.

He shrugged. "I don't think he really cares how far away I go, as long as the school has a good business program."

I nodded, though this made me a little sad for Sebastian. My parents and I were already starting to talk about colleges, mostly in the tristate area and a few farther up the East Coast. My mom and I loved mapping out the visits we wanted to take during my junior year, and my dad spent at least a few hours every month researching local and national scholarships I might be eligible for. Although I knew finances would play a big factor in my decision, I also knew that my parents very much cared about where I ended up. And—above all—they wanted me to be happy.

"What about you?" Sebastian nudged my shoulder playfully. The unexpected contact made my spine go rigid.

"I'll definitely stay on the East Coast for college," I said. "After that? I don't see myself moving too far away from Jersey, but I'd love to work in the city. I want to be a writer. Maybe work for a magazine or a website."

"That's so cool," he said. "What do you want to write about?" It was the first time someone took my interest in writing seriously enough to warrant a follow-up question. I forced myself to look up at his mossy eyes. They dazzled with the reflection of the shop lights.

"I'm not sure, exactly. Definitely something happy." I felt vaguely self-conscious about the fact that this was the longest I'd spent talking about myself with Sebastian, but he seemed genuinely curious, so I continued. "My mom always has these depressing news shows on, and my dad's forehead is always, like, scrunched in concern when reads the paper. Maybe I could write for one of those fluffy travel publications, or do feature profiles."

"You could always write about ice cream," Sebastian said, raising his cone. "I can't really think of anything happier."

I laughed. He was joking, of course, but I imagined capturing a honey-fudge cone in words to someone who had never tasted one. It struck me as a fun challenge.

"You will be," he said, his tone matter-of-fact.

"I will be what?"

"A writer. I bet you'll be a great one."

The bell above the door tinkled to our left as Isaiah exited, waving to us on his way to his bike.

"This," I said, turning to Sebastian and holding up the bottom inch of my cone, which was packed with the last bit of honey-fudge goodness, "is the best part."

"You are correct." He tapped what was left of his cone against mine in a cheers. "To not getting stuck."

"To not getting stuck," I repeated.

A swell rose in my chest. I didn't fight to tamp it down. Sebastian had shone his light on me, and I let myself melt from the warmth.

Chapter 14
Now

"Maren Murphy," says Andre Silva in his signature flirtatious tone. "Aren't you a sight for sore eyes."

At this, Maren rolls *her* eyes, but accepts the two glasses of champagne he offers her, passing one to me. We've just arrived at Bubba's for the surprise party. Bubba herself isn't due to arrive for another thirty minutes.

"Nice to see you, too, Andre," Maren says, tucking her curls behind one ear. She sounds bored, but I can tell by the quick up-down she gives him that she sees what I see: The years have been kind to him. "Playing greeter for the evening?"

"Anything for the Nikolaous," he replies, flashing a dazzling smile. He'd been a star soccer player in high school and one of the most attractive guys in the grade two above ours—maybe even hotter than Sebastian, depending on who you asked and how much they valued muscle mass, which Andre had no shortage of. He'd also definitely had a thing for Maren the summer before our junior year, but she'd always dismissed him. The jock thing, she'd insisted, "just didn't do it" for her. I know from Instagram that he'd gone to Villanova on a soccer scholarship and wound up staying for law school, and that now he splits time between his firm's Philly and Jersey offices. No girlfriend, to my knowledge. And, as if to emphasize just how far behind him his jock days are, he's shown up to the party dressed the part, in a sharp navy suit with a crisp white button-down.

In other words: Maren is doomed.

Andre finally says hi to me, then makes a sweeping gesture toward the door, as if he's welcoming us into a much fancier establishment. *Right this way.*

The dining room looks like it's been dipped in sunshine. A tribute to Bubba's favorite color, no doubt. A pale yellow balloon arch shoots up from either side of the hostess stand, which has been turned into a makeshift bar, complete with a metal ice bucket of Coronas and Surfsides. Half the tables have been removed, and the half that remain are topped with vases of dahlias, tulips and marigolds. Close to forty people are here already, greeting one another and mingling.

Maren tugs me toward a table with familiar white baskets of food and picks up one that holds a hot dog and onion rings. She closes her eyes and takes a bite.

"Ohmygod. Home."

I laugh, then snag a cheeseburger and French fry combo for myself. We find an open table and arrange ourselves so we have a discreet yet unobstructed view of the entrance. Maren and I are both people watchers to our core.

"So what's our game plan?" Maren says around an onion ring, eyes on Andre as he bends down to hug a white-haired woman who's just arrived.

"You tell me, Coach," I say, dunking a fry in Omar's scratch-made honey mustard sauce. "I'm not even sure we should be playing this game in the first place."

It's the truth: An uneasiness had come over me while I was getting ready for the party that I haven't been able to shake. Why did I keep throwing myself back into Sebastian's orbit like this? He and Claire had ignored my texts, emails and calls. Showing up in person feels like a statement—and not the good kind. Then again, I'd thought as I'd swiped on my mascara—the only makeup besides lip gloss I wore in the summer, if I wore any at all—*throw* felt like too active of a word. I felt more like I was being pulled, and doing little to stop it.

I wipe the grease off my hands and smooth the front of my pale green sundress. I'd picked it because it was simple yet flattering, with a flowy cotton skirt and spaghetti straps that tied at my shoulders. I'd initially paired it with white espadrille wedges but ultimately dressed it down with my go-to tan flip-flops. I wore my hair natural, in loose layered waves, the longest of which fell just above my elbows. I'd sent Maren a mirror selfie, as is our tradition any time we go out in public together, so that we could match each other's vibes. She'd gone with a dark green tank top with a similar neckline, white jeans and a pair of raffia mules, curls fully embraced. I picked Maren up thinking we'd dressed appropriately for the occasion, but now that we're here all I can think about is how well we match the shades of Sebastian's eyes, and I feel extremely creepy.

Maren nudges me. "Hm?" I mumble, realizing I've missed something she said.

"You know I can't resist a suit," she groans. "And it's even tailored properly."

She's still looking at Andre, who's left his post at the door and is now headed for the "bar" with Theo Louros. Sebastian had once told me that Theo was his oldest friend—they'd met as kids in Greek school. By the time I met Sebastian, he, Andre and Theo had become an infamous trio in the halls of BBH. Andre, the charming jock. Theo, the mysterious introvert. And Sebastian, the cool, laid-back surfer with a heart of gold. They were the kind of ridiculously handsome guys you assumed were total jerks but had the audacity to actually be on track to becoming good people. Or at least that's how it seemed. They were cool without being exclusive. Fun without being reckless. Confident without being smug. They respected the teachers. Spoke highly of their moms.

It was hard not to fall in love with at least one of them.

"Let's get a drink," Maren says suddenly. She clasps my fry-free hand and tugs me toward the bar, stifling laughter while I roll my eyes like we're fifteen again.

We walk up as Andre is helping Theo fill a cooler with the craft beers he brought. I recognize the cans immediately: They're from Kane, a popular local brewery based one town over in Ocean. A good choice.

"Strange to see you two drinking anything other than Natty Light or Franzia," Maren says.

The guys look up. Andre smirks. Theo looks from me to Maren and back with a raised brow, curious.

"Hey, Maren," Theo says, rising. He smiles at me. "Lina." I flash to another time he was smiling, but at my expense. All three of them were. This smile is much kinder.

"Drinks?" Andre asks.

Maren and I accept two Surfsides and crack them open while the guys finish filling the cooler. Then the four of us migrate to a nearby table.

"You're living in Europe these days, right?" Theo asks Maren. "How is that?"

"London, yes. It's lovely. But I'm stateside for a bit." She glances at Andre. Internally I roll my eyes at her suddenly prim vocabulary—and her intentionally vague timeline.

"And Lina, you're still in Brantley Beach."

I don't love the lack of question in his tone—or his inclusion of the word *still*—but I nod.

"Yep. I worked in the city for about a year, but when that

job didn't pan out I started at a local outlet." Maren shoots me a warning look like she always does when she's worried I'm about to go into self-deprecation mode, so I leave it at that. And anyway, I have nothing to be ashamed of around this group: They're still here, too, and they don't seem to mind.

We spend the next few minutes catching up on our jobs and parents and even our relationship statuses, which come up when Theo tells us he'd married his college sweetheart, Hana, a couple of years back and that she'll be arriving later with their two-year-old daughter, post-nap time. They're both teachers. Andre had dated someone seriously in college, too, but they'd broken up a few months into their respective grad programs. For the time being, he says, he's focusing on his career and enjoying the single life.

We, of course, have already gleaned most of this information from Instagram, but part of being a member of our particular age group is never revealing who you keep tabs on.

Maren's update is characteristically brief and cryptic: She dates here and there, nothing serious. I think of the string of suitors she's had since college—plenty of attractive men (usually older and wealthy) had pursued her, but she always cut them loose within a couple of months. I wonder if she'll ever find someone who can make a compelling enough case for her to settle down, but I hope someone rises to the challenge one day.

Andre produces another round of drinks and passes them around.

"What about you, Lina?" Theo asks.

My love life isn't much to talk about, but this question comes up more frequently than I'd like, so I've perfected a canned response. "I had a boyfriend senior year of college. Nice enough guy, smart. But it never felt like a forever thing. He wound up going abroad for a Fulbright, and we both agreed it was best to just end things. I've dated a bit since then, but I don't know,"

I say, deviating from my script. "It's hard to meet new people here."

"And she knows too much about the old people," Maren chimes in.

A clanging sound draws our attention toward the middle of the room, where Omar stands, holding a pot lid in each hand like two cymbals.

"She's one block away," he announces. "Quiet on the set!"

A hush falls over the dining room. It's filled up since we've been talking, but no sign of Sebastian.

A minute later, Bubba appears in the doorway. I glimpse a broad shoulder behind her just as everyone yells, "Surprise!" It's clear by the look on her face that she's genuinely shocked. She shoots Omar a playfully angry look. Then she turns and reaches up to hug her son to the tune of about fifty *awwws*. When Sebastian guides her inside, she's swiping away tears.

She hugs Omar next, and Sebastian begins greeting some of the other guests. He looks ridiculously handsome, in a white linen polo, navy chinos and Vans. I can tell by the way that the middle-aged lady he's greeting smiles at him that I'm not alone in this opinion.

He sees me as he's shaking hands with a man wearing a GREETINGS FROM ASBURY PARK, N.J. T-shirt. I wave . . . and get a curt head nod in reply. He doesn't smile, and the look in his eyes tells me: A) he wasn't expecting to see me here; and B) he's not necessarily thrilled by the surprise.

In the shuffle of greetings and another round of drinks we lose track of Theo and Andre, and Maren and I somehow wind up in a conversation about British versus American humor with our high school PE teacher and his wife. I keep an eye on Bubba and Sebastian in my periphery, watching for an opportunity to say hello, but they never quite make it to our region of the dining room. I vacillate between thinking this is intentional and thinking that I've really lost it.

Bubba finally spots us a little while later, at the dessert table. She pulls me into a hug, and I breathe in her familiar scent: rose perfume and coconut shampoo.

"Happy birthday, Bubba," I say as I pull away. "You might remember my friend Maren Murphy?"

"Of course. Your other half!" She hugs Maren, too. "Your parents still come in for dinner. They told me all about your fancy London job. They're so proud of you."

"This has always been their favorite place in town," Maren says. "They're going to miss it terribly."

I feel a pang in my chest. At the end of this summer, Bubba's will be gone, a Diamond Group restaurant in its place. The food will probably be more impressive—or at least more complicated—and the prices will almost certainly go up. But the biggest change, I realize as I look around this room, will be the absence of Bubba herself. She not only remembers her regular customers' orders, but also their stories. When I worked in the dining room I remember her frequently making rounds, catching up on everyone's news. She always remembered whose son or daughter was about to get married or have a baby, and who was one month closer to retirement or finally planning a bucket-list trip. Without her at the restaurant, who will keep tabs on what becomes of us? Who will track our milestones and report on our accomplishments big and small?

I mean to ask Bubba if she knows where Sebastian went, but by the time I quiet my thoughts she's being whisked away again.

"He's avoiding us," Maren says, offering me a spoonful of her gelato. I accept and follow her gaze to the open kitchen door, through which I see Sebastian, hunched over a prep table while scrolling on his phone.

"Glad I'm not imagining it," I say. "What I can't really understand is, why?"

Maren takes the spoon back and taps it against her lips,

thinking. "Maybe this is all just a lot for him. His mom being sick. Selling the restaurant. It's a lot of change. I'm sure a night like this makes it hard to ignore all that. And he definitely can't ignore it while talking to you." She points the spoon at me. "You *know* him."

"I used to know him," I correct. "He's different now."

"I don't know, Leens. People change, but not as much as you think."

Theo and Andre wave us over when Theo's wife and daughter arrive a few minutes later, and we spend the next hour taking turns chasing little Esther around and asking way too many questions about what life with a toddler is like. Maren and I are well into appropriate child-rearing age, yet neither of us can imagine taking care of anyone but ourselves. Hana jokes that she'll happily let us watch Esther for an hour or five for research purposes.

At one point Sebastian's eyes catch mine again, and he immediately diverts his gaze, as if even his vision doesn't want to risk touching me with a ten-foot pole.

I must look as disappointed as I feel, because Maren steps closer to me, lowering her voice. "Hey. He's being a total jerk, but don't let that make you regret coming here tonight. It isn't a waste."

She nods toward the bustling dining room. I know she's right. Even if I don't get the answers for my column—even if I never see Sebastian Nikolaou again—I know that this night won't have been for nothing. I've missed this place, these people. Not just Bubba and Omar, but all the regulars who still know me by name. When Hana and I exchanged numbers, she said she couldn't believe someone Theo had grown up with was living nearby all these years and they'd never run into me. Brantley Beach is a relatively small town, but I've been so busy working and avoiding the past that, clearly, I've missed out on a lot.

When Theo and Hana announce they're leaving, I assume Maren and I will be close behind. Across the room I see the windows have darkened, and guests have started saying their goodbyes. The night is coming to an end. That Sebastian still didn't materialize even when Maren and I spent half the night with his closest friends confirms that I was right: He has no interest in being friends with me—or even civil acquaintances. He and Claire got what they needed from me and that was that.

I leave Maren to what I hope will be a brief final conversation with Andre about the state of menswear and take myself to the restroom.

The door to the snack bar swings open right as I'm passing it, and I crash into a hard body.

Thankfully I don't hit the floor this time, but the stack of papers Sebastian was holding does, the pages fanning out at our feet.

"Dumb door," I mutter.

"You all right?" Sebastian asks, bracing my shoulders to make sure. The feeling of his hands on my skin is more jarring than the collision.

"Fine." We both bend down to pick up the papers, and I force myself to look him in those obnoxiously beautiful eyes.

They look . . . tired. My anger briefly shifts to worry, but I shift it right back.

He's not mine to worry about.

We rise, and I hand him the stack I collected.

"What are these?" I ask. There's some sort of drawing on the top page.

He's silent for a moment, as if he's debating whether he wants to tell me or not. But he ultimately nods toward the snack bar entrance. "Come on. I'll show you."

The snack bar looks exactly the same as it always has—cramped, chrome and outdated—so I'm not sure what I'm supposed to be looking at. Sebastian leans back against one of the steel counters, then pulls himself up onto it in one effortless motion.

"Take a look," he says, offering me the papers.

Upon closer inspection I realize the drawing is a detailed pencil sketch with a layout that roughly resembles that of the room we're standing in, though everything else about it is different. The ancient ice cream maker and other unsightly equipment have been replaced with sleek, updated appliances: an espresso machine with dozens of knobs and attachments, a juicer, a built-in dishwasher (luxury!). The customer window has been reimagined as a café counter with taps for drinks on draft and a row of barstools on the other side. The pastry case, previously hidden in the back corner, has been moved to the front near the register, the basic bagels typically inside replaced by glazed scones and cinnamon rolls.

I shuffle to the next page, which turns out to be a menu for "Bubba's Café." I smile as I read through. There are all of the usual modern café drinks—single-origin coffees, cold brew (hence the taps), lattes and cappuccinos and flat whites with various flavor options—and below that some quirky breakfast and lunch items. Better Than Your Packed Sandwich is a mix of almond and apple butters with sliced bananas and local honey on a cinnamon raisin loaf. The Snack Bar Sampler is a shareable option consisting of sliders, housemade pigs in a blanket, truffle fries and onion rings with a side of spicy ketchup.

I look up at Sebastian, who I realize has been staring at me.

"This is amazing," I say. "You came up with all of this?"

He nods once. For maybe the first time in his entire beautiful existence, Sebastian Nikolaou looks shy.

"When?" I ask.

"It's something I've always worked on in my downtime. I think I first got the idea in high school."

"You never told me."

"I never told anyone." He gestures to the sketch. "At first

it was just about upgrading what's always been here—a layout that's easier to navigate, more modern equipment. But then in college my work study was at the campus coffee shop, which was honestly a pretty legit place. I loved learning how to make all the drinks, what the differences were between lattes and flat whites and cappuccinos and cortados. That's when I started playing around with menu ideas. And my current job is all about vendor logistics and efficiencies, so I have a pretty good sense of that part of the business, too."

"It's a good idea," I say, and I mean it. "Smart. With all the tourists coming in from the city, the boardwalk could use an elevated option. And to be honest, I think locals are craving something like this, too, especially the younger ones. All we really have in town are the chains."

"Or the bagel shops," Sebastian says. "Where the coffee is very much an afterthought."

I drop my jaw. I'm very defensive of our bagel scene. "Sure—but there *is* something about a pork roll, egg and cheese with a vaguely burnt drip coffee on the side. And if it comes in a paper cup with a peel-back lid . . ." I press my pinched fingers to my lips: *chef's kiss.*

"To each their own," he says, sounding amused. "The thing is, there's plenty of good coffee and espresso up and down the Shore. Offshore in Long Branch—"

"Booskerdoo in Asbury," I jump in. "Coffee Corral in Red Bank."

"Rook," he supplies.

"Obviously—there's one in almost every town now."

"Right. But not ours. The idea would be to partner with a local roaster that's ready for another location. Arrange a deal where they're our exclusive supplier and we buy the beans wholesale. Keep costs low while giving them another revenue stream."

"The margins on coffee are so high," I say. "It'd be great for business."

"And the snack bar was always seasonal," Sebastian adds, "but the café could stay open for takeaway year-round."

"Definitely." Pause. Then I ask the obvious: "Have you showed your mom any of this?"

Sebastian looks at the sketch and shakes his head slowly. "What would be the point? It's all just stuff I messed around with when I was bored." He rakes a hand through his curls. "It's not real."

"Why couldn't it be, though?"

Sebastian blinks a few times. (His lashes are offensively thick.) "Money, for one thing," he says. "A big part of preparing to sell the restaurant has been helping my mom get the books in order, and the story they tell isn't pretty. Honestly, I don't know how she's been able to keep things running this long. Not to mention the fact that the money we get from Diamond Group could go toward her treatments, which are expensive as hell."

Hard to argue with that. I find a familiar groove on the counter that's been there for more than a decade and run my fingers over it, racking my brain for something useful to say.

I settle on: "I'm sorry, Sebastian. The whole situation is beyond shitty."

"I'm sorry, too," he says, rubbing the back of his neck. "Sorry I didn't come over and say hi. And for not returning your messages."

"I know you're dealing with a lot right now." I can hear the coldness seep back into my tone but struggle to warm it. "I totally get it."

"The way you offered to help out with my mom—it meant a lot. Even with everything going on I should have gotten back to you. Thanked you."

"It's seriously okay, Sebastian," I say, softening. "I offered because I wanted to. You don't owe me anything." I tilt my head and manage a slight smile. "Although an email would have been a nice gesture, just so I can wrap up my column and not miss my deadline."

His eyes narrow, then shift back and forth ever so subtly, searching my face. And in that moment I begin to suspect what's actually going on, even before he confirms it.

"Claire never called you." He says it like a realization rather than a question.

I shake my head slowly. "I haven't heard from her in a while."

"Me either." He smiles weakly. "We called the wedding off."

"Shit," I say—out loud, apparently.

"She said she'd take care of 'alerting all of the vendors.' Sent me a list of names including yours, but I guess she never got around to it. I should have just called you myself, but honestly I've been kind of off the grid since everything happened. If this puts you in a shitty spot with your editor . . ." He shakes his head. "I really am sorry."

I now see the tiredness in his eyes for what it really is: physical and emotional exhaustion. "Dealing with a lot" was an understatement.

"The last thing you need to do is apologize for that," I say. "Can I ask what happened?"

He blows out a breath, and I wait to see if he'll elaborate. "Claire is a force," he says finally. "She has her whole life figured out, and she needs a partner who can fit into it. For a long time that worked perfectly for me. Drew me to her, even. I had no idea what to do with my life, and I thought that if I could just stick with someone like her, I'd keep moving in the right direction. But then everything with my mom . . ." He drags a hand down his face. "I realized I was definitely going in *a* direction, but not necessarily the right one—or even the one that would make me happiest.

"Long story short, I told her I needed to spend the summer out here, and that I wanted to reevaluate our situation after that. Discuss all of our options. Moving to the opposite coast would have been a major change, but her company has a New York City office, and mine is remote-friendly—to me, it definitely seemed in the realm of possibility. We stayed up all night talking, and she absolutely understood where I was coming from, but I could tell she just wasn't going to consider it. Her whole family—her entire life, really—is in California." He shrugged. "I honestly couldn't blame her."

"When was that conversation?" I ask when he pauses for a beat.

He gives me a sheepish smile. "The night before you showed up at the restaurant and asked if you could write about us for your column."

I wince, but internally I'm trying to get a handle on the timeline.

"So you didn't call off the wedding right away."

He shakes his head. "Her solution was long distance. After the wedding I'd stay out here as long as I needed to, and she'd stay in California. Try to visit each other once a month. I told her I wanted to take a few more days to think about it, talk it through. But to be honest I think we both knew where things were headed. I kept going through the motions that week—going to those appointments with you. Doing the tasting. Working on the seating chart with Mom. Helping plan this wedding has made her so damn happy. I almost could have gone through with it for that reason alone." At the worried look I'm no doubt emitting, he adds, "She knows now, though."

"I'm sure she understood," I say gently. "Right? A wedding is wonderful, but if you truly weren't happy, she wouldn't want you to go through with it just for her sake."

"She did understand, yeah. I mean, at first she accused me of throwing my life away so I could babysit her, but once we talked more she got it. Claire loved our life together, but in the end I'm not sure that love had much to do with me specifically. Not exactly the strongest foundation for a marriage."

"Damn. That's . . ."

"A lot?"

"Yeah." It *is* a lot. "I'm tempted to say at least you found out now instead of ten years down the line, but I'm sure everyone is telling you that and it isn't actually comforting."

"It was kind of comforting the first two or three times, I guess." He laughs half-heartedly. "You know what's funny about the whole witness thing?"

I shake my head once, fighting the urge to groan with embarrassment. I'd be thrilled to never discuss "the witness thing" again.

"She signed first," he says. When I narrow my eyes, he elaborates. "She signed the application before you did. She's the one who made the mistake. Signed the witness's line instead of the bride's. I'm not saying she did it on purpose, but I don't think it's out of the question that something subconscious could have been going on there."

She signed first. Of course she did. I'd been so quick to blame myself that I'd forgotten the facts. Silently, I absolve myself of the embarrassment I've been carrying around for weeks. If anyone was subconsciously sabotaging this wedding, it was Claire, not me.

We're silent for a minute or so. I brace for the awkwardness, but it doesn't come.

"So," I say eventually, "what happens now?"

"Always with the big questions, Mariano."

I swallow, cheeks heating, but I hold his eye contact. I want to know the answer.

"I think what happens now is just . . . this." He gestures toward the dining room. "Helping out at the restaurant for one last season. Taking care of my mom. Making her smile as much as possible. Being around people who care about her as much as I do. That's as far as I've gotten." He shrugs again. "For once, I'm trying not to think beyond the summer."

"Sounds like a perfect plan to me," I say. And it does.

"What about you?" I cock my head, and he clarifies. "Will you find another wedding to cover in August?"

I wave a hand. "Maybe. I'll see if my editor wants to take a couple off the backup list." He gives me a quizzical look. "Weddings get called off more often than you'd think."

"And here I thought my plight was unique," he says. "What about after that? I know you said you've been wanting to try something new. If you could write about anything, what would it be?"

I barely remember telling him this at the tasting, so I'm shocked *he* remembers clearly enough to follow up about it.

"Divorce?" I joke. He laughs, but waits for a real answer. "I love writing about food, actually. Interviewing catering leads and pastry chefs has always been my favorite part of my job. The restaurant scene here is so interesting—so many long-standing institutions like Bubba's alongside openings from talented newcomers, and everything in between. The Italian, Greek and Jewish influences run deep, but it's becoming more and more diverse—some of the best new restaurants are Japanese, or Oaxacan, or focused on soul food. You can understand so much about a place and its people—and how it's changing—through the food."

My words hang in the air a moment as he considers me. "You should do it, then."

"Do what?"

He shrugs, not in an apathetic way, but as if the answer is obvious. "Tell your editor you want to shift your focus."

"I have," I say. "What I want to do doesn't seem to carry much weight."

His brow furrows. "Then find somewhere else to work where it does."

"You make it sound simple," I say. "But publishing jobs aren't exactly easy to come by. I started out in New York City and was laid off after a year. As much as I'm over my job, I'm also grateful to have one."

"Maybe you're looking in the wrong places," he offers. "You're right, I don't know anything about your industry, so maybe I'm totally wrong here. But I do know that you're crazy talented, and I think you should work with people who value you enough to give you a say."

"I do want that, at some point," I admit. "But you know what? I'm into this whole not-thinking-beyond-the-summer thing. Maybe I can try that out with you."

He doesn't push it. "I'd like that," he says. "We can check in on each other. Give progress updates."

"Like we're in a twelve-step program for overthinkers," I add.

He laughs again, and it's a beautiful sound. I can't help but think of the last time we were alone in the snack bar like this. The sensory reminders—the coolness of the metal counter under my palm, the smell of fryer oil, the low hum of the air-conditioning unit—are almost too much to bear. I feel like we're fifteen and seventeen again, on the brink of a moment that will change everything.

The urge to reach out and touch him hits me like a wave. I want to comfort him, and words don't feel like enough. I imagine covering his palm with mine, or reaching up to hug him. But the days when we could casually touch each other are long gone. I settle for the companionable silence and hope he takes comfort in my energy. The way he's looking at me tells me that he does.

He's still looking at me this way when the door swings open and Andre steps through, wielding a half-eaten sheet cake with pink frosting. He looks from Sebastian to me and back again, a smirk forming.

"Are the candles in here?" he asks. "Your mom said we can sing to her now that 'only the real ones are left.'"

I laugh, glad some things haven't changed. To Sebastian's embarrassment, Bubba has always loved adopting what she calls "young people lingo."

"I'll grab them from the kitchen," says Sebastian, lowering himself off the counter. "Come on, Mariano."

I follow him out of the snack bar and send my past self a mental thank-you for having the foresight to tell Maren to pack an overnight bag so she could crash at my place tonight.

We're going to need all the debrief time we can get.

Chapter 15

Then
Fourteen Years Ago

"Leens. It's getting out of control," Maren announced during a sleepover the week before Boardwalk Night. We sat facing each other on her plush pink comforter, a dwindling container of her mom's chocolate chunk cookies between us. "What are you going to do?"

"Hard to say," I said around a bite of cookie. "But I'm leaning toward nothing?"

Maren's white-blond eyebrows shot up two inches.

"You're the one who said I shouldn't read too much into it. That he's nice to everyone."

"Yeah, I did think that. At first. But I changed my mind! There's no way he's *this* nice to everyone."

She had a point.

Everything had changed after that night at Twisters.

The most obvious example? Sebastian drove me to and from every shift we shared for the rest of the summer. Even after my leg healed, his Jeep kept showing up in my driveway. Sometimes we'd stop at Wawa or QuickChek on the way so he could get gas and an Arnold Palmer, and I'd pick up a pack of Twizzlers if the stash in my work locker was running low. The rides were short, but the minutes we spent singing along to CDs he'd made at Sam Goody—they were usually heavy on Boys Like Girls, Yellowcard, Blink-182, Third Eye Blind and Sugar Ray, a combination I'll forever think of as beachy pop punk—and talking about everything from work gossip to celebrities added up. We got to know each other.

If we worked a morning shift, we'd bring bathing suits to change into, then join whoever else was off for the day and a bunch of kids from our high school on the beach, dispersing to hang out with our respective classes. Usually I'd meet up with Maren and either my parents or one of the Murphys would pick us up, but he always checked in with me, made sure I had a way to get home.

But it wasn't just the rides—his whole demeanor around me shifted, too. Sebastian had always been friendly to me in a we're-all-part-of-a-group way, but now he treated me as an individual and sought out my company. He picked me for two-person tasks like silverware rolling or sweeping and mopping. At lunch he snuck me extra waffle fries from the kitchen (everyone knew they were my favorite). On more than one occasion I even caught him clearing one of my tables for me when I wasn't looking.

And then there was the touching. A lot of it. A chummy arm slung across my shoulder while Tina divvied up our closing tasks. Surprise bear hugs from behind to startle me while I counted out change at the register. On nights when we closed alone and he finished stacking all the chairs before I'd wiped down the last window, he'd throw me over his shoulder and do it himself while I kicked my legs in mock distress the whole time. Once, during a painfully boring all-staff training for the new computer system, he absently played with my hair for seven agonizing minutes.

I wasn't an idiot: I knew that there was a strong possibility all that touching was his particular brand of teenage flirting. But I also constantly reminded myself that he never quite crossed that invisible line. If friendship were a room and other possibilities lurked just outside, we lived at the threshold.

I let out a sigh of frustration and collapsed backward onto the bed. "Why can't he just be a jerk like a normal guy? That would be much easier to deal with."

Maren smiled at this. "Crazy idea here, but have you ever considered just telling him how you feel?" We'd officially abandoned our pledge of a Sebastian-free summer. Time to devise a new game plan.

"Do I imagine myself doing that? Sure. But then I imagine him rejecting me and decide I'd rather have some of his attention than none of it, even if I'm making half of it up in my mind."

"That sounds healthy," Maren said.

"He could be with any girl at school," I went on. "Actually, he could probably be with any girl at any school in the tristate area. I just find it hard to believe I'm even on his radar. Romantically speaking."

A pillow connected with my face. It was remarkably soft (the Murphys had the best pillows) but still startling.

"What gives?" I asked, shooting up.

"Don't talk about my best friend like that."

I crossed my arms.

"I'm serious! You've always been smart and thoughtful and talented and cute—and then you grew *those*." She gestured to my chest and I crossed my arms tighter. I'd recently had to buy my first D-cup bra. "You're totally hot."

I snorted. The truth was I did sometimes catch glimpses of myself at certain angles—in the car's side mirror while driving somewhere with my parents, or while taking ridiculous selfies on Maren's Photo Booth app—and think: *Pretty. Attractive, even.* But for every good glimpse there were at least four bad ones. Angles that exposed my nose as too long, my jawline too masculine, my skin too oily. The notion that someone like Sebastian might find me attractive wasn't inconceivable, but it did feel unsustainable. Sooner or later, he'd see something he didn't like.

"You said it yourself just now: It would be easier for you to move on if he gave you a reason to. Even if you don't get the answer you want, I think it's worth asking the question. And Leens? You're running out of time. He graduates this year!"

"He does, doesn't he? Thank God you reminded me."

"What's with the sass? I'm trying to help!"

I huffed. "Fine. So what's your grand plan? You want me to confess my love to Sebastian by the end of the summer? Invite him on the Ferris wheel and deliver a speech out of a romcom?"

"I was picturing the Zipper, actually," she deadpanned. "Something with a little more danger."

"Hot," I said, grabbing the last cookie. "I'll bring a barf bag."

We stayed up late watching *Gossip Girl*, but I found my mind drifting from Blair and Chuck's latest tiff to my own dilemma. Maren was right: My time with Sebastian was running out. If what he told me that night at Twisters was true, he'd be far from Brantley Beach starting next fall. What did I really have to lose, if I knew I'd lose him either way?

Chapter 16

Now

"High Noon or beer?" I ask Maren, pulling one of each out of a small soft cooler nestled in the sand. Technically there's no drinking allowed on the beach, but only the bennys ever seem to get caught. We, on the other hand, know how to be discreet.

"Noon. Black cherry," Maren replies, leaning back and arranging her body under the shade of the umbrella she borrowed from her parents' house. Growing up, I'd always envied how quickly her skin would develop a deep tan within the first days of summer, contrasting with her white-blond hair, but now she looks pale in comparison to me. The world of designers and models she inhabits has given her a newfound preoccupation with all things skin care and antiaging.

I crack open one of the vodka seltzer cans, decant it into a tumbler and hand it to Maren, then do the same with a Corona for myself. "Three years in London and you've become a vampire," I say.

"I'm sorry we can't all live at the beach," she says, doing that thing only she can seem to do: make my life seem a lot cooler than it is. I spread out a towel between her Tommy Bahama beach chair and David's gear, which he dropped in a heap before immediately heading for the water. I lie on my stomach, propping myself up on my elbows so I can look out at the waves rolling in.

It's been two weeks since Bubba's party—and two weeks since Maren and I split a bottle of rosé on my balcony, her jaw hung open in disbelief as I recounted the story of Sebastian and Claire's demise. Sebastian texted me the next morning. His message said, **Overthinkers' Support Group** with a little "TM" next to it, the trademark emoji. I responded: **Not to immediately overthink, but we need a better name.** I haven't seen him in person, but we've been texting somewhat regularly ever since, mostly about work or his mom's treatments.

Maren has expressed reservations about this new line of communication, which is pretty rich, considering I'm only in this situation because she practically forced me to go to the party. David, on the other hand, is quickly becoming Team Sebastian's number one representative. I've assured them both I'm not getting my hopes up.

I'm not thinking beyond the summer at all.

"God, we were so lucky to grow up here," Maren says now, "and we didn't even realize it."

I follow Maren's gaze toward the water, trying to see Brantley Beach through her eyes—the eyes of someone who left. I think guiltily of the twinge of shame I've always felt about ending up back here while so many other people have moved on. Would I see it differently if I'd known anywhere else for longer than a year? Or if Maren had stayed, too?

"Would you ever come back?" I ask. I realize I'm not sure what her answer will be.

She considers the question for a moment, pursing her lips as she thinks. "I don't think so," she says finally. "I'm a *city person* now."

"Careful. Beach patrol might be listening," I joke. "But I

don't blame you. Who needs Jersey when you can bop over to the French Riviera for a beach getaway?"

Maren snorts, but I know I'm not far off. Maren can downplay the glamour of her life on our FaceTimes and in our messages all she wants. I know she goes on frequent holidays with work friends, and that she has no shortage of suitors abroad who are skilled in the arts of wooing and whisking.

"It's not the same," she says, turning to me. "Here has you."

My heart swells with affection for my best friend. I reach for her hand and squeeze it.

"All right all right, enough of that," Maren says. "I promise not to get sentimental again until my last day."

David returns, his skin glistening with salt water, and the three of us lie out for a few blissful hours, alternating between chatting and reading (a paperback thriller for me, a media mogul tell-all for David and the latest issue of *Vogue* for Maren).

We're all dozing off when I hear a loud *thud*. A soccer ball lands in a spray of sand at Maren's feet.

I stand and whip around, already annoyed at the half-hearted apology I'm about to get from some high schooler or college kid, but instead I find myself face-to-face with Sebastian.

A conspicuously shirtless Sebastian.

In theory, this particular detail shouldn't affect me. After all, Sebastian was frequently shirtless during the summers of 2009 and 2010. His mom would often scold him for peeling off his shirt the second his shift ended and he was ready to hit the waves, or for stopping by to distract her and the staff on his days off, sandy, sunburnt and barefoot, wearing only his faded red board shorts.

But seeing adult Sebastian shirtless is a different thing entirely. His arms are corded with lean muscle, his long torso smattered with the subtle outline of his abs. He has the effortlessly athletic body of a guy who doesn't spend hours a week in a gym but instead has an active lifestyle. Maybe he surfs a few mornings a week and goes for a couple of easy jogs over the weekend. Whatever he's doing, it's working for him.

"Sorry. He thinks he's still on the team." Sebastian gestures over his shoulder to Andre, who's a few yards back, stifling a laugh.

I toss the ball to him, feeling basically naked in my bandeau bikini. Why couldn't I have been wearing my coverup?

"We'll let it slide, Sebastian, but next time you can just say hi," Maren perches her sunglasses on her head, one blond eyebrow arched in suspicion. "No need to endanger us to get Lina's attention."

Sebastian's eyes widen a little. I shoot daggers at Maren over my shoulder, catching David's giddy expression in the process.

"You're right. I'll try again," Sebastian says, playing along. "Hi, Lina. Enjoying the weather?"

"Ha-ha," I say, crossing my arms over my chest.

I half expect Sebastian to turn back to his game but he tosses the ball between his hands, eyes on me. "We were actually about to grab a bite at the restaurant. You guys want to join?"

Maren and I both start to shake our heads, but before we can answer David chimes in. "We're *starved*. I'm David, by the way. Lina's work husband. Although not her first, I hear."

Maren swats him with her magazine.

"A bite sounds great," I say, masking my mortification with a tight smile.

"Meet you up there in ten?" Sebastian asks with a little smirk.

I nod, and then he jogs back over to Andre.

"What are you *doing*?" I hiss at David once Sebastian's out of earshot. "I thought we were going out to dinner tonight." He's already standing, shaking the sand from his towel. Maren is still in her chair, uncharacteristically quiet.

"I'm forcing you to actually figure out what's going on with him," David hisses back.

"There's nothing going on!" I'm full-on whining.

"You're right, there isn't anything right now, and maybe there never will be. But you can't let this drag on like last time—it's crazy! Don't you want to find out for sure, one way or the other?"

Maren stands with a sigh and slings the strap of her folded chair over one shoulder.

"Wow. You both think I'm still hung up on him, don't you?" I ask.

My friends exchange a knowing look that makes my skin heat, and then Maren says gently, "I don't know if it's him, or if it's the idea of him, or maybe even if it's *you*—the person you were back when you had this crazy crush. But there's something you're holding on to."

"And I think the fact that he's back in town—and, conveniently, single—is the perfect reason to figure out what that something is," David adds.

"*Convenient* is a bit of a stretch," I argue. "Are you forgetting that he literally just broke off his engagement? I'm sure he's nowhere near ready to even think about someone new."

David perches two steadying hands on my shoulders. "You're not someone new, though. And I'm not saying you have to rush into anything, okay? You can take things slow. Get to know each other again—as adults this time—and see where it goes."

I look to Maren. It's clear to me that these two have been scheming behind my back. I'm sure I'll be sorting through my feelings about that later. "And you agree with this?"

She shakes her head wearily. "I don't know, Leens. It worries me, to be honest." She doesn't have to say why for me to understand: *Because I know what happened last time.* "But I do think it's something you have to figure out."

There's not much I can say to that, so I take a deep, grounding breath and let it out. I flip my sunglasses down from their perch atop my head. Then Maren and David each wrap an arm around my back and steer me toward the boardwalk.

Chapter 17

Then
Fourteen Years Ago

The third week in August was the rainiest any of us could remember. I was working the closing shift—my fourth painfully slow one in a row—with Sebastian, Tina and Ravi. We were bored out of our minds, killing time in the dining room while Tina regaled us with gossip, the sound of incessant rain hitting the roof in the background.

"So they're still kissing when she feels something wet on her foot," Tina said, eyes gleaming. She was sitting on one of the four-tops at this point, legs crossed, not even pretending to work. Next to her, Ravi was sanitizing menus, looking bored. (I knew better: Ravi loved our small-town gossip.)

"Do I even want to know where this story is going?" I asked, laying my head on the table where Sebastian and I were rolling silverware. He met my eyes, amused.

Tina waved me off. "Just wait. So she pushes him away and looks down. Turns out it was the cockapoo! Little bugger peed all over her to mark its territory."

"That is maybe the worst first-kiss story I've ever heard," Sebastian groaned.

"I told you! My first kiss, on the other hand—now that was perfect," Tina said, kicking her feet, a wistful expression on her pretty face. "Eighth grade. Bobby Garcia. On the Ferris wheel. I had the biggest crush on him. I swear we would have gotten married if he hadn't moved to Bergen County."

"That sounds romantic," I said, earnestly.

"Mine was lame," Ravi chimed in. "I kissed Izzy Lane at homecoming freshman year. She said 'thanks,' then told me she just wanted to be friends because she really needed to focus on soccer."

We all burst out laughing, Ravi included.

"What about you, Nikolaou?" Tina asked, eyebrows dancing.

I stiffened but didn't look up, pretending to be intensely focused on my millionth napkin roll. In my periphery, Sebastian fidgeted with a packet of Sweet'N Low.

"He probably can't remember," said Ravi, his tone the vocal equivalent of an eye roll. "Too much action to keep track of."

I looked up as Sebastian whipped the napkin he was holding at Ravi, who held his hands up in surrender.

"I remember, obviously." Sebastian glanced at me, then turned to Tina: "Julia Simmons."

I knew of Julia Simmons. Everyone did. She was Tina's age, a year older than Sebastian. National Honor Society president. Field hockey captain. Just as much a shoo-in for "most likely to succeed" as she was for "best smile." Headed to Princeton in the fall. The kind of girl you couldn't even hate for being so perfect because she was actually a nice person. In other words: exactly the kind of girl I'd expect Sebastian Nikolaou to be kissing.

Tina motioned with her hands for him to go on.

"There's no story, really," Sebastian continued with a shrug. "A bunch of us were at this beach bonfire. She lives a block from me so we walked home together. It was cold. I gave her my sweatshirt. When she handed it back to me she kissed me."

Ravi whistled, impressed. Tina cooed. I gripped the fork I was holding so tightly that I nearly impaled myself with the tines.

"Then what?" Tina was leaning forward, elbows propped on her knees. "Did you guys hang out again after that?"

"Sure," he said casually, fiddling with the hot sauce now. "We hung out a few times at her place. Nothing serious."

"Mmm. I bet." Tina grinned mischievously.

My stomach flipped. I could certainly imagine the sort of unserious things Sebastian and Julia Simmons were doing at her house.

"Your turn, Mariano." Ravi said.

The dining room's soft lighting suddenly felt as harsh as a spotlight.

"Oh." I cleared my throat. "Mine isn't really a good story, either."

Silence. I busied myself reaching for more silverware and realized—too late—that we'd run out of napkins. Crap.

When I looked up, I found three pairs of eyes blinking back at me. Clearly that response wasn't going to cut it.

"It was with a kid from St. Christopher's," I offered, thinking of Josh and his Tic Tac breath.

"I love a man in uniform," Tina said wistfully. "Details!"

"It was at a party." And then, because I apparently have the moral code of Abraham Lincoln, I clarified: "During a game."

"That's cute," Ravi said, at the very same time Tina said, "Spin the bottle doesn't count."

She nudged me playfully. "Tell us about your *actual* first kiss."

I shot her a pleading look, and I could tell by the way her eyes widened that she clocked her mistake—and immediately felt awful about it. Everyone went quiet.

"Enough story time for tonight," Sebastian said, chair screeching as he stood. "Let's divide and conquer so we can all get out of here."

"I'll close down the snack bar," I said, pushing through the swinging door before anyone could argue.

Alone in the snack bar, I worked my way through the closing checklist, sanitizing the counters and breaking down cardboard boxes and restocking the condiment station. All the while Tina's words rattled around in my head: *Spin the bottle doesn't count.* They were the exact words Maren had said to me, and while I knew that neither she nor Tina had meant to be unkind, the sentiment stung. I was beginning to sense that there was a divide between girls like me and girls like Tina—and, now, Maren. Girls who didn't just talk about boys but who actually had "real" experiences with them.

Girls who didn't spend all their free time daydreaming about silly crushes.

"Need a hand?"

I jumped, activating the soda fountain nozzle I'd been cleaning and earning a spray of seltzer to the face. I looked up to find Sebastian in the doorway, one hand in his pocket, the other tugging at his mess of hair.

He grabbed a clean towel and handed it to me. As I dried my face, I considered the likely possibility that he was only here because they'd all been whispering about me, and he'd been the one to feel bad enough to come check in. But then I searched his face for any trace of pity. I couldn't find one.

"I'm almost finished with this, if you want to close out." I nodded toward the cash register.

He obeyed. I turned back to the soda machine and took my frustration out on a particularly stubborn ring of congealed Mountain Dew while Sebastian counted the cash in the drawer.

After a few minutes, he broke the silence. "They were just messing around, you know." He sounded tentative. "You shouldn't feel, like, embarrassed or anything."

I felt my cheeks get hot. As if I didn't feel childish enough right now. The last thing I wanted was to be told how I should or shouldn't feel.

"Shouldn't you be concentrating?" I said instead, and I took his silence as a concession.

Just as I was drying the clean drip tray, I heard the cash register click closed. I tossed the rag I'd been using in the sink.

And then I was in the air.

"Put me *down*!"

"Only if you promise to stop sulking," said Sebastian, who had swept me off my feet and over his shoulder in one effortless motion. "What did Big Soda ever do to you?"

I kicked my feet a few times to no avail.

"I'm not in the mood, Sebastian," I whined to the grimy tile floors. I realized, with a huff, that they still needed to be cleaned. I was never getting out of this place.

I felt the rise and fall of his shoulders as he sighed. Then, gently, he deposited me into a sitting position on the counter. We were eye level for once, his torso pressed against my knees, hands lingering on my hips. I assumed he was just making sure I was steady, but he didn't pull away. At some point during the acrobatics my shirt had ridden up a little, which meant Sebastian's right thumb was now grazing the bare skin just above my right hip bone.

I frowned at him, but he just kept on looking at me in that playful, unserious way he always did when he was messing around at work, trying to make me smile no matter how tedious the task or aggravating the customers. To Sebastian, I knew, this was just another silly game between coworkers—*ha-ha-ha*.

Only I wasn't laughing anymore.

He leaned a little closer, one corner of his mouth curled up in a half smile, and said, "Enough scowling."

"I'm not—"

But before I could finish the sentence, his free hand—the one that wasn't bracing my hip—swept up to brush his thumb over my lower lip.

"Scowling," I said softly. His touch felt like an electric current against my trembling lips.

Sebastian's smile faltered, green eyes flashing as they scanned my face. Then, before I could process what was happening, Sebastian shifted his hand to my jaw, tugged me closer and kissed me.

"There," he said softly, his mouth hovering an inch from mine. "That definitely counts."

Chapter 18

Now

Inside the restaurant, Maren, David and I find Bubba at the hostess stand, flipping through paperwork. I know from my texts with Sebastian that she's been skipping some days altogether, but that on good days she loves nothing more than working. My annoyance at my friends' meddling dissipates: I'm glad it's a good day.

When Bubba looks up and sees us, she beams at Maren and me. "You two look like a million bucks!" She hands me a stack of menus. "Sebastian's out on the patio."

"Thanks, Bubba," I say, clocking that she didn't mention Andre.

My hackles are already up on our way to the patio when David gasps dramatically, his phone held up to his face.

"What now?" I ask, stopping short.

"I double-booked myself today and just realized: trivia night. The one Henry's cousin hosts."

I glower at him. David has complained to me on numerous occasions about Henry's insufferable cousin. He wouldn't be caught dead at that trivia night.

I turn to Maren, who's chewing her lower lip. "Let me guess. You can't stay either?"

"Please don't kill me," she says, shooting David a glare. "I have a *real* reason. My parents texted me earlier to see if I can do dinner with them tonight. Mom's getting sappy about my trip ending. She wants me to come home and help her make all my favorites."

I glance at the patio. Through the windows I spot Sebastian, alone at a four-top. He's donned a white T-shirt (probably at his mother's behest). Without his shirtlessness to distract me, I notice that his hair has grown longer since that day I saw him at the clerk's office, his curls back in full force. He looks more like he did back in high school—wild and natural.

"Go ahead," I say, turning back to my friends. "I got this." (Whatever "this" is.)

David pulls me into a side hug. Maren kisses me on both cheeks, European style.

"I love you." She whispers it like an apology. "Call me after?"

I nod, and then they're gone.

"We need to find less flaky friends," I say as I sit down across from Sebastian. I immediately avert my eyes to the menu. Sebastian against an ocean backdrop is too ridiculous a view for me right now.

"Funny, I was going to say less intrusive," he says. I look up and find him smirking.

What the hell does *that* mean?

"I don't really mind, though," he continues. "I wanted to get your opinion."

That's when I notice two takeout coffee cups on the table, one with a hot drink and one with some sort of iced coffee drink. He slides both toward me. I sip the hot one first. It's a latte—or no, maybe a flat white. Rich, bold espresso cut by just the right amount of frothy milk. Even on a hot summer day, it tastes perfect. I switch to the other drink, which is an equally delicious iced latte, and refreshing.

"These are excellent," I say, then take another sip. "Where are they from?" Bubba's only serves basic drip coffee: hot and acidic, or iced and slightly watery.

"I've been to dozens of cafés and coffee shops up and down the Shore the last couple of weeks—all places that source and roast their own beans. This place in Manasquan is my favorite. Family owned. The sister was a chemical engineer and the brother was a hedge-fund guy in the city. She figured out the small-batch roasting process, and he got an investor. I've been talking to them about what a partnership might look like, if we kept the restaurant and they became our sole bean supplier. I still want to talk with a few more places, but they seem like a great fit, and the numbers weren't as much of a stretch as I was expecting."

"Sebastian, that's incredible. I knew Bubba would love the café idea. You showed her the sketches?"

He surprises me by pulling the flat white back toward him and taking a sip. The casual intimacy of this gesture—with him, here—hits me with a wave of déjà vu. I feel like we're teenagers again, splitting a fountain drink during a shift. I half expect Ravi or Tina to round the corner.

"Not yet," he says. "But I'm going to. I just want to get the details right first. And I have a little time. We aren't supposed to finalize the contract with Diamond Group until later this summer. As long as I can secure a vendor and prove the numbers make sense, I think I can convince her not to sell."

"You will," I say, meaning it. "Besides Bubba, no one knows this restaurant better than you. She'll see that."

He smiles softly. "Thanks, Leens."

"So what does this mean for you?" I ask tentatively. "You have a whole life in California."

He nods slowly, looking toward the ocean. "I do. And if

you'd asked me a few weeks ago, I'd have insisted it was a life worth getting back to as soon as possible. But now?" His eyes land on me, and my skin heats. "Now I'm not so sure. I just know I have to see this through."

I know he's talking about the restaurant—of course he is. But I feel a flutter of something anyway. Something exciting and dangerous and familiar all at once.

Hope.

We sip our coffees in surprisingly comfortable silence for a moment. Then he asks, "How are you? Does your editor hate you because of me?"

"Ha. She's disappointed we won't be getting all those impressions from Claire's Instagram followers, but she'll survive." I twirl the plastic cup between my palms. "Sometimes I think if I have to write about one more wedding I may wind up murdering the bride and groom."

"Dark. Who's the next potential victim?"

"A couple from Philly. They're getting married this weekend at that new hotel on LBI." Long Beach Island is one of my favorite areas of the Jersey Shore, about an hour south of Brantley Beach. Eighteen miles of white-sand beaches, gorgeous homes and a local population of 15,000 that grows to 200,000 from June to August.

"Love LBI. Sounds beautiful."

"It does. And since it's a new venue I'll get to go see it for myself. I'll write my usual column about the wedding and another article all about the hotel."

"Do you get a plus-one on this assignment?" Sebastian leans lazily back in his chair, almost like he's trying to look as casual as possible while asking the question.

I nod, holding that incessant eye contact. After a beat I add, "I'm taking someone." I don't specify that the someone is David because, frankly, he's on my shit list right now.

Sebastian raises an eyebrow in curiosity and says, "I'm jealous."

I nearly choke on my latte.

Sebastian definitely notices, because the corner of his mouth curls up into a smirk. "I've been meaning to get down to LBI to check out the coffee scene," he explains, and my esophagus muscles begin working properly again.

I'm about to offer to do some recon for him when a clap of thunder breaks out overhead. Rain follows, fast and heavy. And by the look of the gray storm clouds rolling in, this won't just be a passing summer shower.

Sebastian and I duck inside the restaurant, where there isn't an open table in sight. Everyone else who has been sitting on the patio with us had the same idea, along with all the sopping wet beachgoers who are now pouring in to take cover.

"Shit," I say, leaning against the wall. "I picked the wrong day to bike here."

"I'll drive you home," Sebastian says, running a hand through his already wet hair.

Outside, we walk around the perimeter of the restaurant, under cover of the awning, to grab my beach chair and towel, then my bike from the rack. But there's no choice but to weather the rain as we dash across the parking lot to his Jeep. I hop in and slam the door shut while Sebastian wrestles my gear into the trunk. Once he's behind the wheel we both break out in a fit of laughter at how ridiculous we look. My soaked cover-up sticks to my body. His T-shirt and shorts sop onto the seat.

When he asks, "Want to DJ?" and offers me the lightening cable that connects to CarPlay, I feel a wave of déjà vu for the second time today. It's the 2024 version of letting me choose a CD from his six-disc player. I accept the cable, plug it into my phone and press SHUFFLE on my favorite summer driving playlist. I hear the first chords of "Invisible String" by Taylor Swift and immediately skip it, then skip five more songs to cover it up. Shaboozey feels much safer.

Over the course of the short drive to my apartment my senses go into overdrive. Sebastian's profile tugs at my periphery. I feel the warmth from his body, smell his sweat mixed with the rain. I shiver.

It's the longest six minutes I've experienced in a while.

We pull up outside my apartment and Sebastian puts the Jeep in park.

"Thanks for the ride," I say, reaching for the door handle, "and the coffee."

I'm about to push the door open, bracing myself to reenter the rain, when his hand catches my forearm. His touch sends a ripple of goose bumps along my wet skin.

He says, "Wait."

I do as I'm told. I turn to face him, but instead of contextualizing the request, he just stares at me.

I stare back.

I don't have the best track record when it comes to reading signals from guys. Junior year of high school I was convinced Isaiah Thompson was going to ask me to prom. Turned out he really did just want my help editing his Common App essay. On the flip side, when Justin Taylor from my freshman intro to journalism course kept bringing an extra coffee and a chocolate pretzel to study group for me, I thought he was just being friendly. I was shocked when he asked me to a fraternity mixer the next semester, and we wound up dating on and off throughout college.

But I don't think the way Sebastian is looking at me right now leaves much room for misinterpretation. And even if I'm wrong, I know that what Maren said to me on the beach earlier is true.

I need to figure out what's going on with Sebastian Nikolaou.

"Do you want to come inside?" I ask, finally. "We could dry off. Order a pizza. We never did get to eat lunch."

It's an absurd question, considering the state we're in. Surely he wants to get home as fast as possible, away from the rain and into a dry change of clothes. But as his green eyes continue to hold mine I think maybe it isn't so absurd at all.

He kills the engine and says, "I have some gym clothes in the trunk. I'll grab them."

We dart through the rain to get to the entrance of my building, then run up the two flights of stairs to my unit, my flip-flops squeaking the whole way. The key is slippery in my hands but I manage to get us inside on the second try. I close the front door behind us, then lean against it and slide to the floor, doubled over in another fit of laughter, the shock of the rain momentarily quelling the fire that had been burning between us in the Jeep.

"Holy shit," Sebastian says, kicking off his Vans. His shirt drips water onto the floor. And then he's sliding down next to me, laughing just as hard.

When we both start to catch our breath, he turns to me. "I wanted to kiss you in the snack bar the other day," he says.

The admission is a ripple in my universe. How many hours have I dedicated to decoding Sebastian Nikolaou—attempting to decipher the meaning in his words and actions? I'd spent years wishing we were on the same page, and now that we finally were it was disorienting.

"I did, too," I say, shakily. "Yesterday, and a lot of other times."

He closes the distance between us in one quick, graceful motion, and then his lips are on mine. His palm is cool from the rain as it cups my cheek, but his mouth is impossibly warm. I've thought about our brief, hesitant kiss all those years ago a thousand times, but this—this is something entirely different: slow and hungry and *sure*.

His tongue brushes my lips—a question—and I part them in reply, letting his heat fill my mouth. His hands find my hips and guide them until I'm straddling him, running my hands through his curls. Each kiss is harder and more urgent than the last.

My hands wander from his hair to his arms to the hem of his shirt. I slip one hand beneath it, press my palm against his stomach. The faintest groan escapes his lips, which I take as permission to add my other hand. He winds up pulling the shirt over his head, doing away with it altogether. Even better.

I'm suddenly desperate to get out of my wet clothes, too. Reading my mind, he places a hand on each of my hips, slowly pushing up the hem of my cover-up, exposing my thighs. I raise my arms over my head so he can pull it off the rest of the way, leaving me in the white bikini I'd felt so self-conscious in when I'd run into him at the beach just a few hours ago.

Only now, I want him to see me.

He presses his lips to mine again and I let my hands rove over his chest, his arms. He pulls back, locking eyes with mine as he reaches his hands around my back and touches the bow that holds my bathing suit top in place. I'm about to suggest we relocate to my room when I feel him slow down our pace, then stop altogether.

He presses his forehead to mine and says, "We should dry off."

I try not to let this sting. He reaches into the drawstring bag he grabbed from the trunk and produces a dry T-shirt with the sleeves cut off. Tugs it on. The moment has passed.

And then another thought occurs to me: Maybe he thinks he's made a mistake. Crossed a line. It's so soon after Claire. He's probably on the rebound, and realizing the potential complications of rebounding with me.

Suddenly feeling exposed, I pull the wet cover-up back on and brace myself for his exit. I'll send him a text tomorrow. Apologize for getting carried away. Assure him I didn't get the wrong idea. Downplay the whole thing.

I'm already drafting the message in my head when he pulls

out his phone and begins scrolling. Maybe he'll pretend his mom needs him. *Sorry to run, but something came up at the restaurant!* Fine. I'll play along.

He turns the phone to me. On the screen is a contact page for Gio's—a pizza place a few blocks away.

"Why don't you go change?" he asks, with an encouraging smile. "I'll call it in."

Chapter 19

Now

It takes David exactly one glance at me as I'm walking into the office Monday to realize something is up.

"Spill," he says, before I even sit down.

"We'll talk at lunch," I reply, hooking my laptop up to the monitor.

"Nuh-uh." He grabs me by the elbow and leads me toward the break room. "This can't wait until lunch. This is coffee talk."

We wedge ourselves between the coffee station and the water dispenser and I spill the details. The conversation about Sebastian's café idea. The stormy drive home. The steamy make-out. And the tame but pleasant three hours that followed.

As Sebastian had suggested, I changed while he called in a large special pizza for delivery. We spent the rest of the evening on opposite ends of my couch, talking and eating with Bravo on in the background. When the rain let up around eight o'clock he said he should probably get going. His mom was going to bed earlier these days, and he wanted to catch her before she fell asleep. I walked him downstairs, wondering the whole way if he'd kiss me goodbye. Preparing for it just in case. Instead he'd hugged me quickly and wished me good night. That was Saturday night, and I haven't heard from him since.

I finally stop talking and brace myself for David's reaction.

When he doesn't immediately offer one, I ask, "So what do you think?"

"He's into you," David says, his tone matter-of-fact. "Obviously. How do you feel about what happened?"

I've been asking myself this same question. "I felt happy at first. But now . . . confused. A little scared. I mean, he *just* broke off his engagement. I doubt he's thinking clearly. He's hurt, and I'm here. It's convenient. Classic rebound situation."

"I don't know, Leens. If it were about convenience, I can think of way less complicated options than someone he has as much history with as he does with you. Maybe it's not a rebound at all. Maybe it's . . ." David strokes his chin, searching for the right word. Then he snaps his fingers. "A realization."

"Damn," I say, booting up the espresso machine. I need caffeine for the rest of this conversation and the day of mental gymnastics I have ahead of me. "That's deep."

"I'm serious. Let me ask you this: What did you guys talk about for three hours?"

I shrug. "Our jobs. His mom. How Brantley Beach has changed over the years. The breakup with Claire, a bit. The ideas he has for the restaurant, if he can convince his mom to keep it."

"Sounds intimate. Anything else?"

"He feels like he let his mom down by being away for so long. We talked about that for a while. Regrets. How much he wants to make up for lost time. Get his priorities straight."

"Okayyyy. Why am I right about everything? He's opening up to you, Leens. That's not a conversation a guy has if all he cares about is convenience." I chew my lip, and David lowers his voice. "I know you're just trying to protect yourself, Leens.

And that's okay. But I think you're reading this one all wrong. Not to mention lying to yourself about your own feelings."

I know he means well, but something about David's tone sets me off.

"What do you want me to say?" I ask, not bothering to mask my frustration (though I do keep my voice down—Debbie's always listening). "That after losing literal years of my life to obsessing over this guy and finally getting over him, he came crashing back into town and sucked me right back in? That I think about him constantly? That I can't focus at work because I'm too busy dissecting our conversations just like I did back in high school? You're right, I *am* protecting myself. Because trust me when I say I know what happens when I don't, and it isn't pretty." I cross my arms and push back my shoulders, but instead of intimidating I probably look ridiculous. David has about a foot and a half of height on me.

"Leens," he says, his voice gentler this time. "I know that, historically, this guy has wielded way too much power over your heart. I've been there, so I get it. Trust. But also, this isn't high school anymore! You're different people. Don't let what happened back then determine what happens now."

I know, on some level, that he has a point. But I also know that the situation isn't as simple as he makes it sound. With Sebastian, *nothing* is simple.

I feel my work phone vibrate in my hand. It's a calendar reminder: I have a call with the planner for the LBI wedding this weekend.

"I've gotta jump on this call," I tell David. "But I hear you. And sorry for getting snippy. We'll talk more at lunch?"

"Duh," he says, handing me my forgotten latte. "Let's do dim sum."

Chapter 20

Now

"I can't believe you're leaving Sunday," I say to Maren. "This summer has flown."

We're seated at the Murphys' expansive kitchen island on a Thursday night, drinking too-strong margaritas and flipping through both of our old yearbooks. We always get nostalgic during Maren's last week home.

"If we stop talking about it, maybe it won't have to be true," Maren says. "Look at this one!" She points to one of the collages, which includes a tiny picture of us during Battle of the Classes. The freshmen wore red that year, and Maren had made us matching outfits: She'd added fringe to our class T-shirts and complemented them with Soffe shorts and tie-dyed soccer socks. We'd even box-dyed the tips of our hair, much to my mother's dismay. To this day my bathroom sink at my parents' house still has a faint pink tinge.

I laugh. "We look . . ."

"Happy," Maren supplies.

"I was going to say like we're about to get our asses kicked in dodgeball."

"Well. That too."

I flip to the back of the book—it's one of the ones I brought over—where all the signatures are, and run my fingers over the ink-rippled pages.

Maren's *LYLAS!!!* takes up half a page. *HAGS! See you at the beach!* wrote Tara Rizzo from Algebra I. Billy Wortman (a kid who had a standing table in detention) wanted me to HAKAS, which is an acronym I can't say I remember. I Google it now: Have a Kick-Ass Summer. How edgy. Then I spot Sebastian's loopy signature in the bottom corner.

I remember working up the courage to ask him to sign my yearbook during lunch. He smiled and asked if I had a pen. I proudly handed him a Sharpie. He finished quickly, then closed the book and handed it back to me. I made myself wait until I was sitting in World History the following period to read it, only to find that there was no message (however short) for me to decode. He'd only written his name. The friendly two-sentence message I'd drafted in a notebook and memorized before writing in his suddenly felt like an embarrassing love letter.

My phone buzzes on the counter, and the screen illuminates with a new message. I press the lock button and the screen fades to black before Maren notices.

I'd mentally prepared myself for Sebastian to pull back after what happened at my apartment. He's the one who stopped whatever might have happened next, after all. But he wound up texting me a niche New Jersey meme a couple of days later, which sparked a good-natured debate about whether jughandles actually help traffic or worsen it. We've been texting pretty regularly ever since, mostly humorous observations about our days or more discussions about how Brantley Beach has changed since Sebastian last spent a significant amount of time here. I know we're dancing around the elephant in the room, but I can't bring myself to be the one to bring it up.

To say that it's been difficult to concentrate at work this week is an understatement. I find myself glancing at my phone between every task, hoping to catch Sebastian's name on my screen. In the evenings, I force myself to keep my phone buried in my bag so I can focus on whatever story Maren is telling me over dinner, or the movie we're seeing. Then the moment I get back to my apartment I pull my phone back out with relief, and text with Sebastian until I can't keep my eyes open.

"Are you seeing him again soon?" Maren asks, eyes still on a cringe-worthy picture of us at the winter ball. I should know by now that nothing gets past her.

I'm sure Maren hasn't been blind to my distracted state, but it's the first time she's probed since I gave her the rundown of what happened at my apartment. She'd been decidedly less encouraging than David. To Maren, what happened indicated that Sebastian is just as unpredictable and indecisive as ever. It's not like me to hide things from Maren, but the situation feels new and fragile, so I'm protective of it, worried that if we talk about it too much I'll start overthinking and morph it into something else entirely. Plus, I only have a few days left on the same continent as my best friend. I need to keep my priorities straight.

"Eventually, maybe?" I say, like I don't care either way. (We both know that I do.) He'd asked what I was doing this weekend, and I reminded him I'd be at the wedding Friday and was throwing Maren a small going away party Saturday night. I considered inviting him, but thought better of it. This weekend I need to focus on work and Maren, and that requires keeping Sebastian at a safe distance. The texting is distracting enough.

Maren narrows her eyes at me but doesn't push for more, which I appreciate. She knows me well enough to understand that when I'm ready to fill her in, I will.

"Another?" I ask, twirling her empty glass.

"After I pee."

When I hear the bathroom door shut I swipe open Sebastian's message. It's the Google Maps listing for a coffee shop on LBI called How You Brewin'? I save it to my "Want to Go" list for this weekend, then get to work on the margaritas.

Chapter 21

Then
Fourteen Years Ago

"So does this mean you guys are, like, together?" Maren asked the day after Sebastian kissed me in the snack bar. We were sitting cross-legged on our favorite bench outside Bubba's, putting every second of my thirty-minute lunch break to good use.

I grabbed the basket of fries we were supposedly sharing from her lap. Her yellow bikini was coated in crumbs.

"I have no idea *what* it means," I admitted.

The kiss had stunned me. It was over in an instant, but the sensations lingered. The warmth radiating off Sebastian's body. The softness of his lips pressed against mine. The roughness of his skin as his hands braced my hip and fumbled for my jaw. It was an instant, I knew, that would set up roots in my memory bank, forever accessible for me to replay.

I was excited, and more than a little anxious, to talk to him about it. We hadn't gotten a chance to last night.

Right after he pulled away, Ravi had swung open the snack bar door to let Sebastian know his phone was ringing in his locker. I practically jumped off the counter as Sebastian ducked out to answer it. He poked his head back in a couple of minutes later, looking apologetic and maybe even a little shy. He asked if I would mind getting a ride home with Tina. His dad had gotten home a day early from a work trip and wanted to pick him up.

"Of course," I'd said, looking up from the spot I'd been pretending to mop. As much as I wanted to pick up where we left off, I couldn't help but smile at the excitement on his face. He was clearly looking forward to spending time with his dad. "We'll talk tomorrow?"

He'd smiled and said, "Yeah. I'd really like that."

"Well, at least you'll find out tonight," Maren said now.

I nodded. Sebastian wasn't scheduled to work that day, but I'd see him later, for the staff's annual Boardwalk Night.

"What's your game plan?" Maren asked, her excitement growing. "What are you wearing?"

"I probably won't have time to change," I said, ignoring her first question. I had no game plan to speak of. "I'll just go straight from here."

"You're going to let Sebastian Nikolaou ask you to be his girlfriend wearing *that*?" She pointed at my greasy polo, aghast.

The insult barely registered. My heart was too busy absolutely soaring at the word *girlfriend*.

"The uniform didn't seem to be a turnoff for him last night," I pointed out.

"*Angelina!*" Maren squealed.

I rolled my eyes, but I felt myself blushing. "What do *you* think my game plan should be?"

She tapped a fry against her lips thoughtfully. "I think you should just be yourself," she said finally.

"That's your grand advice? *Be myself?* I want my fry money back."

Maren laughed, but then her expression turned serious. "I just mean, maybe this is one of those no-game-plan situations.

You and Sebastian have become close this summer. He clearly likes you for who you are. Be confident in that."

I chewed my lip. Maren had always been the confident one, not me. But a lot was changing; maybe that could, too.

Later, after I'd raced home to shower, I shimmied into the thrifted mini eyelet sundress Maren had lent me. Then I pulled out my trusty Urban Decay Naked palette, skipping over the muted shades I usually favored and swiping until my eyelids shimmered. Confidence armor.

"Want me to drive you, honey?" My mom leaned against my doorframe, smiling softly. I'd been fussing with my hair in front of the full-length mirror next to my closet. "You look beautiful, by the way."

My cheeks burned. Mom always saw the good angles. "If you don't mind. Which shoes?" I turned toward her. I had a high-top Converse on one foot and a gladiator sandal on the other (they were all the rage, I swear).

She thought for a moment, then pointed to the sneaker. "Less expected. I like that."

I thought about what Maren had said on the bench, about Sebastian liking me for who I am.

I smiled and said, "Me too."

Chapter 22

Now

I'm standing in my closet, steaming my dress for tonight, when David calls.

"Hi," I say, putting him on speaker so I can keep working on the fabric, which the website described as a chic powder blue linen but arrived as a rumpled square that had been stuffed into a packing envelope, then shoved into my mail slot.

He fake-coughs twice. "I'm sick."

"Are you bailing on me or quoting *Mean Girls*?"

"Two things can be true at once?" I don't acknowledge this with a response. Instead, I try smoothing a particularly stubborn wrinkle by switching to "turbo mode" and steaming the lining from the inside. The dress falls off the hanger in the process. Oh well. I'll give it another go at the hotel.

"I'm sooo sorry," David says, the pace of his words picking up. "But would you totally hate me if I didn't go? Basically Henry's aunt and uncle—the rich ones who have the house in Spring Lake and breed labradoodles? They have floor seats for Bruce at MSG tonight. Which, I know. Ridiculous. Only they can't go anymore, because one of the labradoodles might be going into labor. And apparently they were going to just eat the price of the tickets, because what's three grand when you've got doodle money? But they told Henry we could take the tickets for free! So, yeah. I obviously hate to bail on you but I think I have to?"

I wrangle the dress back onto the hanger. The steamer is at a rolling boil now and spurting water. I shut it off and pick up the phone.

"David? It's really okay. No further explanation needed! Let me go, though, so I can see if my mom or dad can come. Mandy let us pay for two heads out of the budget and she'll be pissed at both of us if she finds out I went alone."

"What about Maren?"

"She's on the goodbye circuit. Tonight's dinner with her grandparents in Montclair."

There's a pause, and then David says, "Surfer Boy?"

I drag a hand down my face, because I had a feeling this was where this was going as soon as I answered the phone. My stomach does a little flutter at the suggestion, but I don't tell David that. Let him feel guilty a little longer for ditching me.

"Goodbye, David," I say. "Tell the Boss I say hello."

"Let me know what Sebastian says!"

I end the call and slide down to the floor, my back resting against a shelving unit. I tap into my message thread with Sebastian. Our last exchange was around midnight last night, about a new Apple TV series he's watching with his mom that he thinks is absurdly bad. I start typing.

Are you still free tonight . . . and do you have a suit with you? I hit SEND before I can convince myself otherwise.

The dots that indicate he's typing appear almost instantly, and then his reply comes through.

Yes. And I can get my hands on one.

Chapter 23

Now

The hotel's check-in starts at four o'clock, and it's an hour drive south, which leaves me just two hours to freak out between the time I invite Sebastian to the wedding and when he's due to pick me up. (I'd been planning to drive, but he insisted.) It's not nearly long enough.

I distract myself with my pre-wedding guest-slash-reporter primping routine. (The routine has nothing to do with Sebastian, I remind myself.) I start by taking what Gen Z calls "an everything shower," during which all of my products get some love: shampoo, conditioner, body scrub, body wash, razor. Back in the day—before TikTok decided you should only wash your hair once a week and maybe not shave at all—this was just called a shower, but I digress. Once out, I twist my hair up into a microfiber towel and apply more makeup than I normally would. I even incorporate a long-forgotten eyeliner. (Which, okay, may have something to do with Sebastian.) Then I blow-dry my hair, curl it and brush the curls into loose waves. A spritz of the perfume Maren sent me from London last Christmas is the final step.

I put on my comfiest gray shorts and a quarter zip. The ceremony isn't until five, so I'll have time to change once we get there. This seemed like a great plan when I thought I'd be traveling with David, but now I'm imagining changing in the same hotel room as Sebastian and I'm starting to sweat.

The truth is, I'm spiraling. This will be the first time I've seen him in person since the night we kissed at my apartment. We still text daily, but neither of us has acknowledged what happened, and the more days that pass the more unbearably awkward it feels like it would be to do so. In fact, I've begun to wonder if I imagined the whole intimate encounter, like it was some sort of pent-up fever dream. I'm perceptive enough to acknowledge that Sebastian clearly doesn't mind spending time with me—after all, he agreed to be my work-slash-wedding date with just hours' notice—but I also don't want to wrongly assume that his motivations are romantic. Sebastian is going through a lot right now, and something about me must comfort him.

Which is why I've decided to keep my guard up this weekend. If Sebastian wants to initiate another steamy make-out, I won't necessarily protest. But I also won't let myself think of it as something deeper than it is. No assumptions. No getting carried away.

My phone buzzes next to the bathroom sink. It's Sebastian, letting me know he's outside.

He's leaning against the passenger door of his Jeep when I come out. I've spent the last two hours mentally preparing myself for Sebastian in a suit, but apparently I should have been preparing for Sebastian in road-trip casual athleisure. Because, damn. He's wearing a thick navy T-shirt, gray waffle shorts, white crew socks and Vans. His curls have been gelled into submission, and he's got a pair of brown Wayfarers on that make my stomach do a somersault. I suddenly wish I were the one driving so I'd be forced to keep my eyes on the road.

"Hi," he says.

"Hi!" I chirp. He pushes off the car and takes the paisley Vera Bradley duffel bag I've been using since fifth grade from my shoulder and the dress out of my hand. "Oh—thanks!" I can't seem to stop chirping. I get settled in the passenger seat while he hangs my dress next to his suit in the back seat, then puts my bag in the trunk.

I smile when I notice the two coffee cups in the console. He'd texted me for my Rook order a few minutes ago. I grab my New Orleans–style cold brew, thankful to have something to do with my hands for a while.

"Thanks for this." I indicate my cup as he slides into his seat. "And for coming with me."

"That's not all." He reaches into the pocket of his door and produces a movie theater–size box of peanut M&Ms and a package of Twizzlers.

"Wow. I feel like a passenger princess." Either he has great taste in candy or he remembers Twizzlers are my favorite. The second possibility makes my skin heat up. I grip my cold brew a little tighter.

"You're taking me to a swanky beach wedding. And you have to work while I get to enjoy the open bar. The least I could do is fuel you with caffeine and sugar." He hands me the aux cord and starts driving.

"How's your mom?" I ask. "Good day?"

"Seems like one. She was getting ready to go to the restaurant when I left."

"I'm so glad." I queue up a few songs, then settle back into the seat. It's a gorgeous day for a drive—and an outdoor wedding ceremony. The brides, Bonnie and Amelia, must be breathing sighs of relief. We had a phone call this week during which Bonnie went over the forecast and various weather-related contingency plans in painstaking detail. She sounded like an amateur meteorologist.

I only last about two songs before I'm breaking into the Twizzlers. Sebastian gestures to the M&Ms. I open the box and pour him a handful.

He pops a few in his mouth, then asks, "Want to play a game?"

"Like 'I Spy'?" I don't say this with enthusiasm.

"Don't hate on 'I Spy.' But no, different one. You think of a number from one to ten. I'll come up with a category, and you have to pick something in that category that you think reflects your number. After five categories, I try to guess what number it is."

"So the number is a rating, essentially? And I'm picking things that go with that rating."

"Right. So let's say your number is ten, and I choose ice cream flavor as the first category."

"I'd obviously say honey fudge."

He smiles. "Exactly. You get it."

"All right," I say. "I've got my number."

"Okay, let me think of some good categories." He runs a finger over his lips while he does so. It's alarming how distracting this is. I grab another Twizzler. "We'll start simple. Sports."

"Like, to watch or to play?"

He shrugs. "Open to interpretation."

"Volleyball?"

"I'm sensing uncertainty. So probably not a particularly high number or low number."

I keep my poker face. "Just give me the next category."

"Tasks at the restaurant."

I smirk. "Snack bar register."

"Okaaaay," he says, stroking his jaw now. The light stubble he's had the last few times I've seen him is gone. He must have shaved for the wedding. "Not gross like bathrooms or mopping," he muses. "But on the other hand you're in front of customers the whole time, so 'no goofing around.'" He says this in the voice he's always used to imitate his mother. "I'm thinking we're in the four to six range. Bagel order?"

I purse my lips. This is harder than I thought. "Egg and cheese on a plain bagel."

"What kind of cheese?" he wants to know.

"American."

"Is it toasted?"

"Sure."

He nods, like he expected this. "That helps. But no bacon, no pork roll. Not even some avocado. This is very *mid*. I think we're at a five. It's a five, isn't it?"

"I get two more categories!"

"I'm locking in early, because I'm that confident. New rule."

I throw my hands up in mock frustration. "Fine! It's a five."

"I knew it!" He smacks the steering wheel, victorious.

"Yeah, yeah." I'm getting competitive now. "Think of your number."

"Okay, got it."

"Days of the week?"

"Good one. Tuesday."

"Holidays?" I ask, twirling a Twizzler.

He thinks for a moment, then says, "New Year's Eve."

"This is a low number," I say. His poker face isn't as good as mine, so I know I'm right. "Pizza topping?"

"Pineapple," he says, without hesitation.

"One. I'm locking in early."

"Damn, you're good. I thought I threw you off by not picking Monday."

"Nah, I get your thinking there. Mondays are rough but at least there's the motivation of starting a fresh week. Tuesdays are just . . . sort of irredeemable."

"Someone was on the right track with Taco Tuesdays. But still."

I nod in agreement. We play a few more rounds, and we both

do pretty well, even with just three guesses. I feel a rush of validation when I pick Twizzlers for candy, cheeseburger for sandwich ("I respect that," he said) and New York for U.S. city and he correctly guesses a ten. It feels good to know that, even after all these years, we still know each other pretty well.

"Do you think you'll ever work there again?"

It takes me a moment to register that he means New York. "I think about it sometimes, but I don't know. Probably not in the cards."

"You loved it, though." I look over just as he's repositioning his hand to the very top of the steering wheel, at twelve o'clock, the tendons in his forearm flexing in the process. I force my gaze back to the road. "I mean, it's your ten. That's a big deal."

I let out a breath. It's been a while since I've talked about my time in New York. "I did love it. I dreamed of saving up enough to move there, even if it meant having three roommates to be able to afford it." I laugh humorlessly. "I had a taste of this life I'd always imagined, and I wanted more."

"But. . . ?"

We glance at each other at the same time, then both turn our eyes back to the road. And something about that brief look makes me feel comfortable enough to be honest. "But then I had it completely ripped out from under me. I got laid off. Spent a couple of months searching for a new job when no one was hiring. Got rejected over and over. Felt like a failure. Like everyone and everything around me was moving forward and I was getting left behind. It was a pretty dark time for me, mentally. Then I started at Shore Life, and that was that. New York was finished with me. Sometimes I feel like I imagined the year I worked there. It feels like another life."

Sebastian nods, processing this. "That's definitely shitty," he muses. "But you've gained a lot of experience since then. You have more to offer. I bet if you applied for jobs in the city now, you'd get completely different results."

My skin warms in response to this, but as is my nature, I

can't simply accept his compliments. Shoulder-Maren appears, wagging a finger, so I forgo pure denial in favor of some light self-deprecation. "Sebastian Nikolaou moves back to Brantley Beach and immediately launches a campaign to send me away. I'm flattered."

He tuts. "You're right, I don't want you around. That's why I agreed to be your rent-a-date tonight."

I shrug. "That could totally be a front. You said yourself you needed an excuse to get on the island for research." He glances at me, eyebrow raised. "Don't act like you didn't notice that the hotel's in-house café has quite an impressive single-origin coffee program."

He dips his head toward me, conceding this point. "Can't I look forward to hanging out with you *and* sampling a Nicaraguan pour-over?"

I roll my eyes, but neither of us says anything more. His words echo in the silence, and I wonder if that's exactly what he wanted to happen. I turn up the music to quiet them just as we hit Exit 63. He flips on his blinker and veers right, taking us off the Garden State Parkway.

Long Beach Island is one of my favorite places on the Shore, and maybe on earth. It's a barrier island split into six cute little towns with names like Surf City and Ship Bottom. The hotel we're headed to is toward the southern end of the island, in Beach Haven. For the first time throughout the drive I have no problem keeping my eyes on what's outside the car. We pass the familiar businesses—a breakfast haunt called The Chicken or the Egg, a townie bar called Nardi's with a bright pink bus outside that drives patrons back to their beach homes or rentals each night, a mini golf course attached to a soft-serve shop. There are also rows and rows of quaint beach homes, with more of the newer, not-so-quaint mansions mixed in than I remember seeing when I was here on a weekend trip with my mom last summer.

I could tell from the photos I'd seen online while researching for my column that The Island Inn was a beautiful establishment, but as we pull up to it now I realize that it's even more stunning in person. It's impressive in size, but unlike some of the modern resorts that have popped up along the Shore in recent years, it has a traditional, grand-hotel vibe. A teenage valet in khakis and a polo rushes over to Sebastian's door, and two bellhops in matching uniforms are close behind, offering to take our bags. Sebastian helps them hang his suit bag and my dress and duffel on a cart, then hands them each a few bills as he thanks them.

Sebastian and I follow the bellhops between two white columns and into the lobby, which is somehow both grand and quaint, with robin's-egg blue banquettes, white coral-inspired chandeliers, marble floors and historic photos of New Jersey landmarks lining the walls. I check us in at the front desk while Sebastian says he's going to peruse the café menu. I turn around with our key (yes, an old-fashioned key rather than a card) just as he's returning with two take-out cups.

"Research?" I ask as he extends one to me. I'm heavily caffeinated from the Rook I drank in the car, but I'll rarely turn down any form of coffee.

"One is Nicaraguan and one is Costa Rican. I think I like the Costa Rican better, but I want a second opinion."

I take a sip as we walk toward the elevators, then swap with him. "They're both nice, but I think I agree with you."

He hands me back the Costa Rican, which may be the most selfless thing a man has done for me in a while. (I realize this isn't necessarily something to be proud of.)

I lead us to room 47 and insert the key. I see the corner of one bed, then let out a breath I didn't even realize I was holding when a second comes into view. I'd of course requested a room with two double beds when I'd originally made the reservation for David and me, but you never know.

The room is adorable. Light hardwood floors connect to

pale blue walls that match the accent pillows on the otherwise white beds. On the other side of the room is a kitchenette with a quartz waterfall island and two seagrass barstools, flanked by a den with an old-fashioned settee and coffee table. A sliding glass door leads to a small balcony with two white Adirondack chairs, overlooking the ocean view.

My gaze wanders to the open bathroom door, through which I can see a Jack and Jill sink and a frameless glass shower. I quickly blink away the image that appears in my mind of Sebastian's torso: shirtless, muscled and wet. I turn to face the beds again and am assaulted with more unwarranted images.

"Do you want me in the bedroom or the bathroom?" he asks. I freeze, gaping at him. But then he grabs his suit bag from where the bellhop must have hung it in the closet and I realize he's asking where he should change.

"I can take the bathroom!" I gather up my things and bolt there, shutting and locking the door behind me.

Once my breathing resumes a semi-normal pace, a quick phone check confirms we have about thirty minutes until we need to be seated outside for the ceremony. It's the perfect amount of time: I've already done my hair and makeup so I won't feel rushed, but I also won't have too much extra time to spend in this adorable room with Sebastian, banishing forbidden images from my brain.

I unzip the garment bag that's holding my dress. It's still got a few wrinkles, but I realize I forgot to pack my steamer, and there's no way I'm going to check the closet for an iron and risk a glimpse of a half-dressed Sebastian. It looks good enough.

After running a comb through my hair and touching up my makeup, I shimmy into a pair of shape-wear shorts, swap my comfy bralette for a strapless bra, and step into the dress. I get the zipper about halfway up before it catches just below my bra band. *Of course.*

Holding the top of my dress in place with one hand, I exhale, roll my shoulders back, and assess myself in the mirror. I am going to ask Sebastian Nikolaou for help, and it's not going to be awkward or embarrassing or flirtatious.

I begin turning the doorknob, then think again of stumbling upon Sebastian while he's still changing and stop myself. I text him instead: **Let me know when I'm good to come out! May need a hand with my dress.**

He replies by knocking on the bathroom door, which makes me jump. I crack the door and peer up at him through the opening.

"Need me to zip you?" he asks, and I wonder if he, too, finds this sentence unexpectedly sexual or if I've just really lost it. I nod, pushing the door open further.

I turn to face the mirror, and he steps forward until he's standing right behind me. "It's a little tight around the . . ." I say. Our eyes meet in the mirror, and I see the corner of his mouth curl ever so slightly. "But it definitely fits."

"I've got you," he says, and then I feel his hands on the back of my dress. The dress zips without a hitch on his first try, and I let out a relieved breath.

"Thanks," I say.

"Of course." He's still looking at me in the mirror. "No problem."

I step into the kitchen area so that Sebastian can use the restroom. Seated at one of the barstools, I yank on my block heels and fasten the straps. When he comes back out a moment later, I get my first good look at Plus-One Sebastian, who proves to be just as devastating as Road Trip Sebastian. He's wearing a blue summer suit with a crisp white shirt and the brown leather loafers he wore the day I'd run into him at the clerk's office a lifetime ago. He's also applied a little more gel to his slightly slicked-back curls. I prefer them wild, but the look suits him.

"You clean up nice, even on short notice," I observe.

"You can thank Andre," he says. "I was going to run to the

mall. Then I remembered we've always been the same size and he'd probably have even more options. Also, you look beautiful." The earnestness with which he says this sends a jolt through my belly.

"Thank you. Ready to go down?" Perhaps I just need to accept that no sentence will sound innocent this weekend. But he just nods, and gestures for me to lead the way.

"Need me to hold anything?" he asks while we wait for the elevator. He's a good date, I think. Considerate. I imagine him slipping my phone into his pocket, my ID into his wallet. Modern markers of intimacy. But then I remember that he's probably learned to ask this from years of dating Claire. I thank him and shake my head.

In the lobby, a hotel staffer registers our cocktail attire and guides us down a hallway that leads to the courtyard, where rows of white wooden folding chairs lead up to an impressive floral arch. A strip of private beach serves as a stunning backdrop. I lead Sebastian to the far corner of the last row and we each take a seat. Only about a quarter of the guests have arrived so we could sit much closer, but I like to stay under the radar—and out of the photographer's view. When I attend weddings for work, I'm always acutely aware of being the least important person there. Well, maybe behind Mom's work colleague the couple has never met, or Dad's recently divorced golf buddy's new girlfriend.

Sebastian lets out a low whistle. "How much do you think a wedding at a place like this costs?"

"A hundred grand," I say, snapping some pictures on my phone to help me remember the details later. He raises both eyebrows in shock. "I have a copy of the itemized budget."

"Damn. I just don't know how you don't think about everything else you could do with that kind of money."

I nod. "Yeah. I used to think that all the time when I first started covering weddings."

"Not anymore? I guess you probably get used to it."

I shrug. "That's part of it. I mean, not every wedding I cover is this nice. But for the ones that are, I think it's also that I realize now that a hundred grand probably doesn't mean the same thing to that particular couple—or their families—as it means to us. If you've got that kind of money, why not spend it on a day like this, I guess? One life and all that."

He nods, considering this.

"Although," I go on, "I should caveat that I've also realized an expensive cost per head doesn't necessarily equate to a great wedding. I've covered no-frills weddings at chain hotels and in backyards that were incredibly romantic and fun, and much fancier weddings where the father of the bride forgot to mention the groom in his speech. Or the best man showed up to the ceremony drunk with no clue where the rings were. Or everyone did their parts respectably but the A/C broke and all anyone talked about was how sweaty they felt. When it comes to weddings money helps a lot, but it's not the be-all and end-all."

"Fascinating," he muses. We're both facing forward, people-watching as the chairs in front of us fill up with smiling guests dressed in their summer best. "What's your favorite wedding you've covered?"

I smile. That's easy. "Maggie and Rob. May 2022. They were originally supposed to get married in May of 2020, but obviously that didn't happen. They canceled and rescheduled five or six times. I went to lots of micro weddings and even some Zoom weddings during the pandemic, and those were special in their own way. But this was the first one that felt almost like a pre-2020 wedding. It poured all morning and then the sun came out just before the ceremony. It was a beautiful event from start to finish, and everyone just seemed so happy to be there, celebrating something together. Hugging and dancing without fear. It was the first time in years that I felt truly hopeful. Like things might finally be getting back to normal."

Sebastian turns to me just as I'm glancing over at him, and his mouth curls into a smile. "Well. When you put it like that, the big wedding does sound worth it."

Despite the smile, there's a sadness to his eyes that reminds me he was supposed to be getting married at the end of this summer. Suddenly all this wedding talk—and the entire evening—strikes me as pretty insensitive.

A string duo begins playing "Come Away with Me" by Norah Jones, quieting the chatter among the guests and rescuing me from that particular thought spiral for the time being. The procession begins: first the bridal party, all dressed in navy, followed by a beaming flower girl and a ring bearer who loses his shoe halfway down the aisle. Then Bonnie and both of her parents appear, and everyone rises. She's enviably chic in a sleek bun, glowy makeup and a satin column gown with an oversize bow at her low back. At the end of the aisle her parents kiss her and take their seats, then she turns to watch Amelia—who is equally stunning in a classic ballgown, lace gloves and a cathedral veil—walk with her dad. I feel the familiar prick of tears as I watch Bonnie watch Amelia walk down the aisle. No matter how many weddings I attend, that moment never seems to lose its impact.

I blink back tears and glance at Sebastian to see his reaction. His brow is furrowed, like he's lost in a concerning thought. Is he picturing Claire walking down the aisle with him at the end? Is he grieving that he won't have this same moment next month like he was supposed to—regretting it, even? I think back to the night in my apartment. The way he kissed me, but then acted like nothing had happened. It was reckless of me to let my guard down like that. To think he could have any sort of emotional clarity so soon after a breakup of that magnitude.

I do my best to shake off these thoughts and focus on the wedding that *is* happening. My favorite ceremonies have two things in common: personal vows written by the couple and an under thirty-minute run time. Bonnie and Amelia's ceremony checks both boxes, so—my own thought spirals aside—the evening is off to an excellent start. The brides and their party recess back down the aisle, and then I check the monogrammed program I'm holding, which tells me that it's time for cocktail hour on the terrace.

"I'm ready for a glass of prosecco and something wrapped in puff pastry," I say as we stand and follow the crowd.

"If there's a raw bar, you can find me there," Sebastian says.

"Oh, there will *definitely* be a raw bar."

In true Jersey fashion, the cocktail hour is ridiculously over the top. Stations manned by attendants in white chef coats dot the terrace. There is, in fact, a raw bar, complete with a heart-shaped ice sculpture in the middle outlined in crab legs. There's also a sushi station with freshly prepared rolls and sashimi, a boardwalk-themed counter with waffle fries and sliders and a carving station with a choice of lamb or ribeye. And all the while additional waitstaff weave among the guests, offering passed hors d'oeuvres: spanakopita egg rolls, ricotta crostini, crab puffs, ahi tuna cucumber bites. It's an absurd amount of food, especially when you consider the fact that in an hour there will still be a seated dinner. But hey—I'm not complaining.

I'm about to make a beeline for a guy serving penne vodka out of a giant cheese wheel when Sebastian grasps my forearm. I turn to him.

"We should divide and conquer." He hooks his thumb toward the bar, where a line is forming. "You grab drinks, I'll make us plates?"

"Can we do the reverse? I should check out all the food myself. For research, obviously."

He half smirks. "Obviously. Prosecco?"

"Please. Actually, just get me whatever the signature cocktail is."

He salutes me and then he's gone.

Once I've piled two plates high with food, chatting with each attendant along the way, I spot Sebastian at a high-top with two copper Moscow mule mugs and join him. For a few frenzied minutes the extent of our conversation is phrases like "Ohmygod, the bacon-wrapped scallops" and "Wait, did you try this? With the sauce?" I've lost track of my nerves from the hotel room, distracted by our shared joy over the food. Maybe I don't have to overthink this night. It can be casual and fun, just like it would have been with David.

"I know you want out of this job," Sebastian says, skewering a shrimp and then pointing it at me, "but so far I'm seeing a lot of perks."

"This is the fun part. Watch me write a thousand words on how to control sweat on your wedding day and you may feel differently."

"To be fair, that sounds useful."

"Oh, I'm full of useful information. Foolproof tips for freezing wedding cake. Which vendors you should tip and how much." I count off each example on my fingers. "The difference between American, French, royal and ballroom bustles. Gifting etiquette. Invitation etiquette. Seating etiquette. There's even etiquette for calling *off* a wedding." I practically clamp my mouth shut when I realized what I've just said. "Sorry."

"For what?"

Suddenly the inside of my Moscow mule is fascinating. I'm afraid to look up, or to respond.

"It's fine, Lina," he says. "I wasn't thinking about that. Really."

"Okay. But it would be normal if you were, you know."

"I was supposed to get married and it didn't work out." I look up, and he shrugs. The sadness has returned to his eyes, the brightness that had been there a few minutes ago gone. "I can't avoid weddings for the rest of my life."

"Sure. But you were supposed to get married *next month.*

I'm just saying if the timing of this night is a little rough, I get it. During the ceremony you looked . . . distracted."

Sebastian watches me for a moment. His green eyes have gone a bit stormy. He doesn't deny it, but before I can probe more a member of the jazz ensemble that has been playing for the last hour announces that the reception will begin shortly in the ballroom.

We follow the crowd into an elegant room with white and gold-flecked marble floors and high ceilings. A full-length, antique-style mirror near the entrance relays the seating chart in loopy calligraphy. I find "Angelina Mariano and Guest" assigned to table 11 and lead us that way.

We choose seats at the long table and greet the guests sitting near us, who are a mix of family friends and distant cousins. I'm a pretty sociable person, but I always feel a little awkward at weddings I attend for work—so much forced small talk. Sebastian more than pulls his weight in these conversations, though. He really is good at the whole plus-one thing. At one point he even offers to switch seats with me so I can have a better view of the dance floor.

An MC hops on the mic, and the next two hours follow the familiar rhythm of so many weddings I've attended. Entrances. First dances. Speeches (this time, the fathers and mothers all speak, along with a best man and two maids of honor). Periodically I steal glances at Sebastian, who smiles and chuckles and claps at all the appropriate times. But the worry lines on his brow remain, as if he has tasted something sour and can't fully shake it.

Dinner is family style and better than standard wedding food, the standout being a summery pasta in a bright pesto sauce. I snap a picture and text it to David so he knows what he's missing. And then the band takes the stage and it's time to dance. This, admittedly, is the point at which I typically draw a line in the sand between wedding guest Lina and wedding writer Lina. I could live without dancing the "Cupid Shuffle" or belting the words to "Valerie" with Bonnie and Amelia's nearest and dearest. But Sebastian surprises me by rising immediately and reaching for my hand.

"Come on, Mariano," he says. "We might as well get the full experience."

And so we dance. The band is fine—I've heard better vocalists over the years—but they play what the people want to hear, and with each transition we grow more enthusiastic, as if we've been following this perfectly fine wedding band since their early days and would never dream of missing a show. We belt out the lyrics to "Mr. Brightside" with the bridal party and jump so much during "You Belong with Me" that I give in and kick my heels off. By the time the lead guitarist starts strumming the first few notes of "Tennessee Whiskey," Sebastian and I are both breathless and a little sweaty.

I'm about to cop out and say I'm going to the bar, but he takes a step closer to me and holds out a hand, eyebrow raised in invitation. I accept, and then he's pulling me close until our bodies are pressed together in a way that makes my breath hitch.

The male vocalist croons (almost) just like Chris Stapleton, and we sway along. I'm stiff at first, but then he tugs me even closer and I rest my head on his chest. He holds one of my hands in his; his other hand has settled on my hip, gentle but firm. He smells different from usual, like a woodsy cologne, and the thought of him taking this extra step while getting ready for tonight makes me smile against him. But I quickly rearrange my expression back to neutral, even though he can't see it either way. The dancing has been fun, but I remind myself how guarded he has seemed all night. The signs that his mind is somewhere else—with someone else. *Don't get carried away.*

"Do you still think I seem distracted?" he asks, his voice a low rumble next to my ear.

"Not since dinner." I force a lighthearted tone. "Maybe you just really couldn't wait to dance."

He laughs once, and the shell of my ear warms with the heat of his breath. Then he asks, "Want to know the truth?"

Do I?

"Yes," I say, even though I'm not sure I do.

"The truth is you're right. I *have* been a little distracted. When you asked me to come, I didn't think it would be a big deal. But I've been in my head more than I expected."

My stomach sinks, but I don't dare break our rhythm. Whatever he's about to say, I need to hear it. That he's not over Claire. That he regrets what happened between us. That tonight was fun and all but he hopes he hasn't given me the wrong impression.

"Not because I'm being reminded that I was supposed to have a wedding and now I'm not. It's more like . . . realizing I came so close to doing all of this with the wrong person."

Oh.

"Seeing the way Bonnie and Amelia looked at each other during the ceremony," he continues, "and the way their families looked at them. Claire and I, we had a fine relationship, but we didn't have *that*. I didn't realize it at the time, but I was essentially on autopilot for years. I came really fucking close to doing something I for sure would have regretted. And that's a scary thing to be reminded of. So, yeah. I've been a little distracted tonight. But not for the reasons you probably thought."

I tip my head back to look up at Sebastian, and I can tell by the way he's looking down at me that he's being honest, and that it isn't an easy thing to admit. But even if the reason isn't quite what I thought, the fact is that he's still processing the end of his engagement, not to mention his mother's illness. The biggest of my fears and doubts remain, don't they? That he's just spending time with me because it's convenient. That he'll remember why he didn't want to end up stuck here. That he's still trying to figure out the life he wants, and I'll be collateral damage along the way.

We've stopped dancing, but his fingers are still interlaced with mine, his thumb tracing circles absently on the back of my hand.

"Now you're the one who's gone somewhere else," he observes. "What's going on in your head?"

"I'm sorry," I say finally.

"You really need to stop saying that."

"I am, though," I say, dropping his hand. "I shouldn't have asked you to come. It's a lot."

"Lina—no." His hands come up to brace my shoulders, and he leans in close again. "I'm really glad that you asked. I've had more fun tonight than I have in a long time. Please don't think otherwise."

The way he's touching me, the tenderness in his voice—I know these are tactics designed to comfort me, to gain my trust, but they have the opposite effect. My walls shoot up.

"I mean it's a lot *for me*," I say to my bare feet. It's almost a whisper. "And I think you know that."

In all the years I've had feelings for Sebastian, this is the closest I've come to admitting them. I'm terrified to look up, to see the reaction in his eyes. I doubt it will be one of cruelty or even surprise, but it may be one of pity—and that might be the worst reaction of all.

But when he cups my chin and gently tips my head back, the hunger in his eyes looks nothing like pity. His gaze drops to my mouth, then back to my eyes, shifting and searching for a moment before he says in a low, soothing voice, "I'm okay with a lot."

Before I can fully process his words, the song changes, reminding me that Sebastian Nikolaou and I are staring at each other in a crowd of strangers. I excuse myself to get that drink. On my way to the bar I finally catch Amelia and Bonnie, who thank me profusely for coming and graciously accept my gushing compliments on the whole evening before a coordinator whisks them away to cut the cake.

Sebastian is already sitting at the table when I return, double vodka soda in hand. I've started to come down from the adrenaline rush I experienced on the dance floor, though I'm still not sure what to say to him next. But when I sit, Sebastian's hand brushes my thigh under the table, sending my heart racing again, and the way he turns to look at me under hooded eyes tells me it wasn't an accident.

We leave as soon as the cake is served.

Neither of us speaks on our way up to the hotel room. I'm still holding my shoes when we get to the door, and, wordlessly, Sebastian takes them from me so that I can dig the key out of my purse and let us in.

Inside, the silence continues, emphasizing our every breath and movement. I drop my purse on the counter with a clang. Sebastian places my shoes on the floor, then drapes his jacket over one of the barstools. I turn so we're facing each other, my back pressed against the island, and he steps closer to me, so close that I have to tilt my head back so I can look up at him and he has to curl his upper body a bit to look down at me.

"You're so tall," I say softly, stupidly, because I need to cover up the sound of my racing heart, my shaky breath, and it's the only coherent sentence I can form.

Sebastian's hands wrap around my hips, and in one quick movement he lifts me onto the counter. "Better?"

We're almost eye level now. I nod, and then, before I can overthink it, my mouth is on his.

He crushes his lips against mine in response. We're both a little rough at first. Urgent and chaotic. I hook my legs around his waist, tugging him closer, while my hands make a mess of his curls. The tempo slows a bit when his hand brushes the zipper at the back of my dress, his eyes asking permission. I nod, and he guides me off the counter, then slides the zipper down my back. As my dress falls to the floor I reach for the hem of his shirt, untucking the fabric in fistfuls. I move for his shirt buttons next, grunting in frustration when it takes my shaky fingers longer than it should to undo the first few. Sebastian smiles against my mouth and helps me finish the task, then moves his hands to my waist.

Here's something women don't talk about enough: There is truly no sexy way to remove shape wear. Sebastian reaches for the waistband—which, thanks to my lack of height, is nearly touching my bra—but I bat his hands away and roll the spandex down to my hips, then shimmy out of the shorts the rest of the way. It's ungraceful but quick, which is the best I can do.

Any flashes of awkwardness from SpanxGate are swiftly assuaged by Sebastian's lips, which meet mine again and then break away so that he can kiss me in other places: the bend between my neck and shoulder, my collarbone, my chest, the curve of my waist. He stops when he gets to the scar on my thigh and runs a hand over it, then kisses me there, too. A heat blooms between my legs and intensifies as he trails kisses back up my body. And then we're kissing again, this time slow and gentle.

One of the perks of this adorable little room is that the beds (the fact that there are two suddenly seems rather wasteful) aren't far from the kitchenette, and we stumble toward the closest one now. I fumble for his belt just as he reaches into his back pocket and produces a square blue wrapper. I think again of the cologne and wonder if Sebastian was thinking of this possibility when he was getting ready for tonight, or if he's just the kind of guy who carries condoms around in his wallet at all times, just in case.

I reach for the wrapper so that I can open it but he sets it on the nightstand instead. "Not yet," he whispers, pushing me back onto the bed.

I used to think a lot about what it would be like to sleep with

Sebastian Nikolaou. But as he reaches behind me to unhook my bra, then dips his hand below the hem of underwear while pressing his mouth to the curve of my breast, I find that I'm more than happy to wait a little longer to find out.

He takes his time with me, but he's a quick learner, taking cues from my body's responses to his fingers and his mouth. Part of me wants to let him keep doing the things he is doing to me all night, but eventually I come up for air long enough to place a hand on his chest.

"I want you," I say, meeting his eyes.

He cups my cheek in his hand and presses our foreheads together. "Have me, then."

He covers my body with his and I pull his hips toward mine, a little impatient now. I don't want to wait another second not knowing what he feels like.

I've waited long enough.

After, he holds me against his chest, stroking my hair while we talk late into the night. He tells me more about his vision for the restaurant, his mom's treatment plan, even the end of his relationship with Claire. I go into more detail about the year I spent in New York City and its abrupt end, Maren's glamorous life in London, the stories I dream of writing one day when I'm finally brave enough to leave the safety net of Shore Life behind. Like always, we do not reminisce about the years we knew each other as teens. We expertly avoid any topics that might inadvertently trigger thoughts of what happened back then, the night after he kissed me in the snack bar. Why we fell out of touch for so long.

I wake up early the next morning with one cheek pressed against Sebastian Nikolaou's left bicep, our legs entwined like a tree's twisty roots. I peer at the clock on the nightstand: 6:00 a.m. Sebastian is still sound asleep, his chest rising and falling in an even rhythm. Half of me wants to nuzzle against him and close my eyes again, but the other half jitters with nervous energy. I realize I need a few minutes to clear my head and think about everything that happened last night—and I'm not going to be able to do that as long as my mouth is in the vicinity of his.

I peel myself out of his grip and tiptoe past the kitchenette and into the bathroom, pulling the door shut behind me, then assess myself in the mirror. I'm wearing a far too big waffle-knit shirt that Sebastian had offered me out of his duffel bag some time before we fell asleep. Last night's makeup is smudged around my eyes, and my hair is a mess.

Images from last night come back to me in a jumble—not just the things we did but the conversations we had, and the things left unsaid. The uneasiness I'd felt upon waking develops a voice, and it has a lot to say. *Careful*, it warns. *Remember what happened last time?*

Don't get carried away.

I'm craving coffee, but I don't want to wake Sebastian by brewing a pot in the room, and the café downstairs doesn't open for another thirty minutes. I decide washing my face is a good first step, so I grab a makeup remover towelette from my toiletry bag. But when I tuck my hair behind my ears to get it out of my face it sort of crunches in the process, and I decide that what I really need is a shower. I always think better in the shower.

I lean against the sink while I wait for the water to heat up—I like it almost too hot for my skin to bear. As the room fogs up I pull Sebastian's shirt over my head. I've just stepped out of my underwear when I hear footsteps padding down the hall.

Two gentle knocks on the door, and then his voice from the other side: "Everything all right, Lina?"

And then, before I can think better of it, I'm slipping through the shower door and saying, "Come in."

Through the frosted glass I see a smudged outline of him. He's standing very still.

"Come in . . . like, all the way?" I detect a note of self-consciousness in his voice that makes me smile. Could I, Lina Mariano, be making Sebastian Nikolaou nervous?

"I'm guessing you need one as much as I do," I say, as if I am the type of woman who invites men to shower with her all the time. "So you might as well get in."

There's some movement, and then the shower door opens. He slides in quickly, and I take a step back to make room. We're both still and silent for a moment. Even though we're naked—and even though his body is objectively something to behold—the moment doesn't feel sexually charged. As the water runs down my back I think about how strange it is that two people can feel comfortable enough to take their clothes off in front of one another, yet do anything to avoid an awkward conversation.

Maybe it doesn't have to be that way. Maybe I could tip my head back, look Sebastian in those beautiful eyes and finally ask him what the hell happened that night. Maybe he'd say I had it all wrong, offer an explanation I hadn't considered, some piece of information that made it all make sense. Or maybe he'd confirm my worst fear: That there was, in fact, nothing wrong at all with the way I remembered what happened back then.

Just something wrong with me.

Sebastian tips my chin up so I'm looking at him. I blink away the sting of tears, thankful to have the water from the shower as an alibi. His thick, dark eyelashes are flecked with droplets, too.

"What are you thinking, Lina?"

Instead of answering I pull him down to me by his neck. I kiss him as the water keeps falling, streaming off our bodies in rivulets.

Chapter 24

Now

The buzzer to my building rings around seven o'clock Saturday evening. I told everyone to come over any time after eight with the exception of Maren, who's arriving early to help me set up for her own mini going away (again) party.

"Damn," she says a minute later when I open my apartment door. "You look hot."

"Is it too much?" I ask, smoothing the front of my dress. It's a casual midi, but it hugs me in all the right places. Maren is wearing jean cutoffs and a halter top that confirms the '90s are, in fact, cool again. I motion for her to give me the two canvas bags she's carrying, one slung over each shoulder. "Jesus, why are these so heavy?"

"I like wine," she replies, following me inside. "Even though anything remotely good out here is ridiculously overpriced for what it is."

"We're uncultured Americans," I say, setting the bags on the island. "We don't know what we don't know."

Maren opens the cabinet next to the fridge, retrieving two glasses and a corkscrew. "And to answer your first question," she says, "it's definitely not too much. Sebastian is your—what's that saying? Your white elephant?"

"I think that's the Christmas gift swap we do at the office. White whale?"

"Yes, that!" She unloads six bottles from the bags, then gets to work on the cork of a Cab. "You gotta pull out all the stops. Show him what he's been missing out on all these years."

Maren's still wary about Sebastian, but I appreciate that she's trying to be supportive for my sake. I called her the second Sebastian dropped me off at my apartment this morning, which timed up perfectly with her drive home from her grandparents' house, and fully briefed her on last night's events.

I detailed how, after the shower (which took a rather steamy turn), Sebastian and I chatted over flat whites (mine iced, his hot) at the café. Then we checked out of the hotel and spent a couple of hours driving up and down the island, splitting various coffee and espresso drinks until I had a caffeine headache. I had to have him pull over so I could beg to pee at the Ron Jon Surf Shop just before we exited the island.

It was one of the best mornings I've had in a long time.

So much so that I didn't want it to end. Which is why, not long into the drive home, I wound up inviting him to come tonight.

"Count me in," he'd said, glancing over at me from the driver's seat. (There'd been a lot more glancing from both parties on the ride home.) "I'm grabbing dinner with Andre and Theo and Hana, but I'll come by after."

The moment he'd said this I immediately regretted extending the invitation. Not because I didn't want to see him again so soon (I definitely did), but because the thought of giving Maren and David a front-row seat to whatever is going on between us—with only Henry as a buffer—made me want to jump out of the moving car.

"Tell them they can come, too," I blurted out. "The more the merrier!"

It's honestly a good thing Maren brought so much wine.

"Maybe I needed those years to figure myself out first," I say now, spinning the stem of the glass she's just poured for me. "I was kind of a loser back then."

"Don't insult me," she says, pouting her bottom lip. "That loser was my best friend."

I laugh mid-sip, but Maren doesn't join in.

"I'm serious," she says, handing me a paper towel so I can wipe the wine from my chin. "You let his approval carry so much weight back then. But what he did was a *him* problem. I hate the thought of him showing up after all these years and making you feel all insecure again." She nudges my shoulder. "Especially when I'm not down the street to remind you how perfect you are."

"I know you're worried, Mar," I say, feeling a familiar pang in my chest. I miss my best friend already and am dreading tomorrow, when she'll get on a plane and our interactions will once again be limited to WhatsApp and FaceTime. Maren is the kind of friend best experienced in person. "All I can say is that things are different now. I joke about myself, but I'm not that insecure teenager anymore. I know my worth."

This seems to satisfy Maren for now. She arranges the contents of my Trader Joe's haul into an Instagram-worthy charcuterie board while I transfer the stuffed mushrooms and cocktail meatballs I'd prepped earlier from the fridge to the oven and set up a drink station. By the time the buzzer sounds again an hour later, we've killed the first bottle of wine and polished off half of the brie.

I open the door to David and Henry, who come bearing cookies and even more wine. (I really love my friends.) We all exchange greetings and hugs—Maren squealing with excitement—and then gather around the appetizers.

After turning my back for approximately four seconds to uncork the next bottle, I find the three of them with their heads together, whispering. I'd sent David a slightly briefer debrief over text after my call with Maren. He'd replied with a barrage of emojis and seven follow-up questions, to which I'd replied with a plea to act normal tonight and the praying hands emoji. I clear my throat.

"Sorry," David says. "We have no chill. But can you blame me for wanting just, like, three more details?"

I sigh and check the time on my phone. "We probably have a few more minutes until they get here. What do you want to know?"

David and Maren exchange a conspiratorial glance. Even Henry, who usually tolerates but doesn't share our gossipy nature, looks curious.

"Was it as hot as you thought it would be?" David asks with a mischievous smirk.

I feel a blush creep up my neck—I've always been a little prudish at heart—but I soldier on. "Way hotter."

Even this is an understatement. Sex with Sebastian was . . . different. Not polite and efficient like the sex I had with my college boyfriend, or sloppy and slightly awkward like hooking up with a guy from Hinge or a mutual friend setup. I'd long accepted that I was probably one of those women for whom sex is fine but not earth-shattering. Maybe I was more likely to be "turned on" by a good conversation than by anything physical, so what? No shame in that. I listened attentively to Maren's tales of serial orgasms across the continents with the bemused curiosity of someone who isn't even enlightened enough to be jealous.

But Sebastian debunked all of that in one evening. Many times over.

Tonight, I'll have to school myself from gawking at his elegant fingers, the bow of his lips, the rumble of his voice. From sweating with the knowledge of how swiftly any one of those things is capable of becoming my undoing.

"What about after—was it awkward at all?" Henry wants to know.

"Honestly? It wasn't," I say. "I kept waiting for the awkwardness to come, but we just talked for a long time after, and then we fell asleep. Everything felt really . . . comfortable, I guess."

"Did you cuddle?" Maren turns to David and Henry. "She's a huge cuddler. And a cover stealer. I know from years of sleepover experience."

I toss a cracker at her.

"There was cuddling," I concede. "It was very nice."

Maren smiles at that. Then the buzzer sounds.

"Sorry," I say, moving toward the door. "I'm not taking any further questions at this time."

Maren and David groan. Henry quiets them by topping off their wineglasses. At least they're easily distracted.

"Let's party!" Andre proclaims the second I open the door, hoisting a case of Michelob Ultra in the air. Hana and Theo follow, shooting me apologetic glances. I thank them for the olive oil and flowers they've brought and direct all three of them toward the kitchen.

And then there's just Sebastian in the doorway, wearing a white polo shirt that emphasizes his tan so much it's borderline ridiculous, along with a pair of navy shorts that make me wonder if knees are in fact a very sexy body part that I've been overlooking. He's holding a big paper bag and looking at me in a way that makes me want to pretend there's a gas leak and send everyone home.

"Hi," he says as he steps inside, towering over me. An image flashes of the last time he crossed this threshold, with rain-soaked clothes and hungry eyes. I need another glass of wine, stat.

"Hi." I look up at him. "Long time, no see."

I want to pull him down to me by the curls at the nape of his neck, but I'm not sure that's an appropriate greeting, especially in front of an audience. To give my hands something else to do I take the bag from him, then lead him into the kitchen.

I deposit the bag on an empty sliver of counter next to the fridge and peer inside. It's a box of pastries from the best bakery in Brantley Beach and an unmarked bag of coffee beans.

I feel a hand on the small of my back, strong but gentle. "For tomorrow morning," Sebastian says against my ear. A shiver runs down the length of my body, because I know he means the food but now I'm thinking of his hands.

I whirl to face him, pressing my back against the counter. "Assuming you'll stay over, huh?" I don't allow myself to flatten my palms along the planes of his chest. I deserve a trophy for my self-restraint. "That's quite presumptuous of you."

"I never said you had to share," he says, shifting his hand from my lower back to my hip. He leans closer, invading my space. "I do love those chocolate croissants, though. A guy can hope."

With no small amount of effort, I peel away from his gaze, expecting to catch at least a few gawkers. But everyone has moved to the living room. Someone has set a beer can in the middle of the coffee table, and Andre and Maren are busy surrounding it with playing cards.

"We're playing Kings," David calls, waving us over.

I force myself to pull away from Sebastian and join the rest of my guests.

"What's the upper age limit on these drinking games?" I joke as I take a seat on the couch next to Maren. Sebastian sits on a chair diagonal from me, which is probably for the best if I have any hope of concentrating on this game.

"Normally I'd say twenty-two," Hana replies, cracking open a beer. "But on nights my parents are babysitting? The limit does not exist." I knew I liked her.

Andre runs through the rules (with a few clarifications from Maren), reminding us what action each number and face card translates to.

"Nine is rhyme. Ten is categories," he says, rattling off the last few tasks. "Jack is GOAT-ed, of course—if you pull one, you can make up whatever rule you want. Queen is question master. King means you have to finish your drink."

"Your card goes under the tab of the can after your turn, and whoever cracks it loses," Theo interjects. He gestures to the can in the middle of the ring of cards.

"*And* has to drink the whole thing," Maren adds, helpfully.

"Everyone have a drink?" Henry asks.

"Now they do," David says, reaching across the table to top off my wineglass.

I catch Sebastian's eye and note a flash of concern. I'm surprised by the defensiveness I feel, like we're teenagers again and I need to prove I can keep up.

The game begins, and despite myself I *do* regret choosing to play it with wine pretty quickly. By round two I'm feeling more than a little buzzed, and I'm sure the color in my cheeks shows it.

"Six. Chicks!" Maren flips her card around, and us girls all reach for our drinks. In place of my wineglass I find a Solo cup of water. I shoot Sebastian an accusatory glare but he pretends not to notice.

My phone, which is facedown on the table, buzzes. I pull it toward me as Andre pulls a Jack.

"Make a rule!" Maren squeals. Hana laughs, snorting a little. At least I'm not the only one the wine is getting to.

The text from Sebastian reads: **Doesn't hurt to mix in a water.**

Thanks but you really don't need to worry about me, I tap out. **Just have fun.**

I am having fun, he replies before I can put my phone back down. Two more texts quickly follow.

I just want us to be able to have more fun later.

IDK about you, but if I drank that much wine I'd be asleep by 9.

If it's possible for my cheeks to redden even more, I'm sure they do. I try not to smirk at my phone as I type. **On second thought, I think I'll stick with water after all.**

As Sebastian reads the message, then returns his phone to his pocket, I notice with satisfaction that he looks as flustered as I do.

Andre strokes his chin dramatically and scans the room, pondering. "Superlatives," he says finally. "Each person has to give out a superlative for someone else in the room, high school yearbook style. If you accidentally repeat a person, or if you can't come up with something after five seconds, round's over and you have to drink."

There's a collective groan in response to this task and the relative brainpower it requires, but soon everyone begins looking around, plotting their moves.

"Your rule, Andre," Maren says. "Start us off."

"Easy," he says flirtatiously. "Maren: best smile."

Maren actually blushes. Yep, definitely time for us all to lay off the wine. "Why, thank you," she says, flashing the smile in question. She really does have a good one. "For Lina: best host."

Everyone raises their cups in agreement. I'm a little disappointed because I wouldn't have minded hearing Sebastian come up with something for me, but then I remind myself to chill. It's just a game.

"Thank you, thank you," I say, turning to David. "Most likely to become president."

Claps all around. David stands and delivers a presidential wave. "As much as it pains me to admit defeat: Henry's best dressed—for tonight, at least."

"Is someone recording this?" Henry quips. He considers the few remaining options, then goes for Hana. "Best laugh." She lets out another cute little chortle, affirming his choice.

"My husband's most likely to sleep through class," she says. "Or in our case, sleep through an infant's wails."

Theo throws his hands up. "It's a gift." His eyes dart between Andre and Sebastian. "Let's change it up a little. Sebastian: *Least* likely to end up back in Brantley Beach."

"Oh shit, T. That's a good one," Andre says, toasting Theo's cup with his. "If this really were high school, he would have been most likely to get as far away as possible."

Theo and Andre both laugh, as if Sebastian's disdain for our hometown is the funniest thing ever. As if it's as harmless and obvious as Maren's beautiful smile or Hana's adorable laugh. Sebastian's good-natured smile doesn't reach his eyes. My body tenses, but I keep my face stoic, even as I notice signs of alarm in Maren's and David's expressions.

"Andre's still biggest flirt—all these years later," Sebastian says, finishing the round.

Maren rolls her eyes. Andre bows, then delicately slips his card into the stack beneath the tab of the beer can. Just as he's about to release the card, the can lets out a hiss of air, followed by a definitive *crack*.

"Fuck! I knew it was gonna be me." Andre pops the tab the rest of the way and starts chugging.

Suddenly I feel stone-cold sober. I sense Sebastian's gaze boring into me, but I ignore him and head to the kitchen for more water.

I position my cup under the water dispenser on the fridge door. While I wait for it to fill, I feel a hand on my shoulder.

"Hey," says Andre. "I hope that superlative thing didn't weird you out."

I glance over at the living room. Sebastian is mid-conversation with David and Henry. Maren, Theo and Hana are out on the balcony.

"It really was just a joke," he adds.

"There was some truth to it, though," I say, turning to face him. "He's back in town because he feels like he has to be, but you and I both know it would be far from his first choice."

Andre rubs the back of his neck "I probably shouldn't say

this, but honestly? We were kind of relieved he called the wedding off."

I raise an eyebrow and ask, "Because of Claire?" I hate the petty jealousy I hear in my voice. I know that Claire isn't my enemy. In fact, she seems like a rather lovely person. But I'm only human.

"It's not so much that we didn't like her. She was a great girl. Super confident and successful. Fun to be around." Andre glances toward Sebastian as he says, "It was more so that we didn't love who he was with her."

"He acted different when they were together?"

"Yeah. He never seemed fully relaxed. Like he was putting on this perfect-guy act instead of just being himself. Which, sure, maybe he'd put on that front in the past, in school or at work, but around us? It felt like he was building his walls up higher and higher, shutting us out." Andre takes a sip of his beer, shaking his head. "He puts a lot of pressure on himself. Always has."

I nod, because I know this to be true. Sebastian has always been solid, the one everyone could rely on. It wasn't until later that I realized you can find cracks even in the toughest-looking armor if you're willing to look closely enough.

"And what about now?" I dare to ask. I feel Sebastian's gaze on us, but I keep my eyes on Andre, awaiting his answer.

"Now? Now I feel like we're starting to get the old Sebastian back," he says, one corner of his mouth turning up. "And I'm pumped. I really fucking missed that guy."

I smile back. I did, too.

I'm standing outside with Maren, waiting for her Uber. Theo and Hana reluctantly left around eleven to relieve Hana's parents from babysitting. They offered to add a second Uber stop for Andre, whose eyes practically popped out of his head when Maren planted a chaste yet decisive goodbye kiss right on his mouth. David and Henry announced they were calling it a night about an hour later, and I felt certain they'd make it to London to visit Maren before I would. Sebastian is still inside, cleaning up.

I blink back tears as Maren hugs me fiercely. She speaks into my hair. "It's funny."

"What?" I ask.

"How we were convinced all those high school summers were supposed to be monumental, and in a way they were, because everything *feels* monumental when you're fourteen, fifteen, sixteen." She pulls back to look at me. "But honestly? I feel like we're just getting to the good stuff now."

"That's deep, Mar," I say. "Maybe *you* should have been the writer."

"It's true! God, think about all those nights we stayed up for hours in my room, spinning dilemmas out of nothing. We were itching for things to happen to us, and I don't just mean getting attention from boys. I wanted to travel and design, you wanted to write. If I could go back in time I'd tell those girls that the real fun would start when they stopped waiting around for something to happen and finally just went for it."

I smile, because I've been thinking about those girls—high school Lina and Maren—a lot lately. They feel so real to me; if I were to drive over to the Murphys' house right now and walk up the stairs, I wouldn't be surprised to find the two of them there, sitting cross-legged on the pink waves of Maren's comforter. Eyes wide, voices hushed.

Sebastian loomed over that time in my life, so much so that whenever memories of it broke through to the surface over the years I typically pushed them right back down. But the more I let myself think about those two girls, the more I start to wonder if any of it really had much to do with him at all. High school Lina had been filled with desires; maybe Sebastian just happened to be the moving target she directed them toward. And maybe that said more about me than it did about him.

"I don't think he's as much of a flight risk as he used to be," Maren says now, "but you should still be careful." I'm startled by the subject change and the sudden seriousness in her glacial eyes. "I'm all for second chances but if he breaks my best friend's heart again . . ."

"You'll put a hit on him?"

We both laugh, but then Maren gets quiet.

"Let's just say I'd do anything to protect you, within the limits of what's legal." She smiles. "Just promise me you'll try to protect yourself, too."

I nod. Regardless of what Andre said, she's right to be wary. What if Bubba gets better—or, God forbid, what if she doesn't? Who's to say Sebastian won't be on the first plane back to California?

But I also know that I'm too deep into this to turn back now. I have no idea if more heartbreak is on the other side, but I have to see it through.

"I'll be careful," I say, not fully believing myself.

Maren's phone buzzes. We hug once more in the headlights of her approaching Uber.

"I love you," I say. "Message me when you land tomorrow?"

"Duh," she says, blowing me a kiss before ducking into the car.

Back upstairs, I open my apartment door and find Sebastian at the sink, handwashing wineglasses. I think of one shift during my first summer at the restaurant, when the ancient dishwasher finally crapped out. Omar said he couldn't get a technician to come until the next day, so we'd need to handwash everything. Sebastian had gathered the staff in the kitchen and rallied us around what he called the First Annual Dishwasher Derby, complete with rules and a point system (which, I remember thinking, was unnecessarily complicated). It turned out to be the most fun shift I worked all summer, and the Dishwasher Derby did, in fact, become an annual tradition after that.

"What are you thinking about?" Sebastian asks, rinsing the last glass. Carefully, he places it in the drying rack next to the sink.

"Dishwasher Derby," I say, smiling. I'm still standing near the door.

He laughs, turning off the tap. "My mom says the staff still does it." He dries his hands on a towel and turns toward me, leaning against the counter. He lowers his voice. "Anything else?"

In three slow steps I'm in front of him, close enough to see the faint shadows of water droplets on his T-shirt. I tip my head back as he tilts his down, our eyes meeting. He smells like beer and dish soap. I'm very into this combo.

Maren's words from earlier echo in my mind. Not the warning—the part before that. *If I could go back in time I'd tell those girls that the real fun would start when they stopped waiting around for something to happen and finally just went for it.*

"This." I graze Sebastian's jawline with my fingers and stretch up on my tiptoes, pressing my lips softly to his. He pulls me close, leans into the kiss. Then he transfers his mouth to the curve just below my ear.

"Well," he whispers, cradling my chin. "*I'm* thinking how glad I am that you switched to water."

"Oh yeah?" I manage to speak as he trails feather-light kisses down my neck. "Why's that?"

"Because I would have tucked you in or held your hair back if you needed me to, Mariano." His voice is a low growl against my throat. "But I'd rather do this."

"Well, then. I guess it's a good thing I'm so responsible." I pull his face back to mine and flash him a wicked grin. Then his lips are on mine again, possessive and all-consuming.

I've just slipped my hands under the hem of his shirt, pressing my palms to the warm skin of his stomach, when my own stomach growls.

I pull back, mortified.

"Hungry?" he asks with a smirk. I don't miss the double meaning in his playful tone, but I'm too embarrassed to play along.

"Sorry!" I drag a hand down my face. "I was so busy getting everything ready for tonight that I basically had cheese for dinner."

"Let's order something," he says, already pulling out his phone. I notice he doesn't seem at all bothered that I just totally ruined the moment, his mussed hair and crooked shirt the only reminders of what we'd just been in the middle of.

I spin toward the fridge and peer inside. I didn't have time to do a full grocery shop today, so aside from leftover hunks of cheese and cured meat, there's not much: eggs, milk, a single Jersey tomato, half of a red onion, a half-wilted bunch of parsley I bought last week but never had a chance to use. And of course the longstanding assortment of sauces, condiments and spreads that stand at attention along the door. "Yeah, we should probably order. I don't have much right now."

Sebastian grabs the door, opens it wider. "I don't know about that, Mariano. I think we have plenty to work with here."

His resolve transports me back to the occasional slow closing shift, when Omar would let us all hang in the kitchen while he whipped up whatever creative concoctions he could come up with. Sebastian and the other cooks would challenge him to incorporate seemingly incongruent ingredients—whipped cream and hot sauce, pickles and Smucker's jelly packets, you name it—like they were building a *Chopped* mystery basket. He always pulled off something delicious and yet I remember we were shocked and impressed every time. I should have realized then how talented he was.

"All right, Nikolaou," I say, taking the produce out of the fridge. "Let's do this."

* * *

An hour later we've made a pretty damn good roasted tomato quiche and a huge mess.

I can't remember the last time I've had so much fun in the kitchen. Growing up and in the years right after college, when I'd still lived at home, cooking and eating had been a communal event that I'd shared with my parents, a social activity as much as it was a practical one. Working at Bubba's echoed that. But in more recent years it had become quite solitary—enjoyable, but not joyous. I still loved cooking, and I did what I could to make it less lonely. Some nights I'd FaceTime my mom, phone propped against a mixing bowl, and we'd make dinner at the same time—together but not. Or I'd pour a glass of wine and listen to a podcast. Cooking with Sebastian, though? That was . . . something else entirely. Fun and messy and creative and sexy. I already want to do it again.

"What are you smiling about?" Sebastian asks, planting a kiss on my forehead as he moves to clear my empty plate. I grab his arm, stopping him.

"You," I say. I stand and take a step toward him. He's still on his stool, and I nestle myself in the space between his legs. "Let's clean up tomorrow."

When he starts to protest, I cup his face in my hands, steadying him. "My apartment, my rules." For once, my voice doesn't tremble.

He raises a brow, eyes glimmering with mischief. "All right, Mariano. I'll follow your lead."

I wrap my arms around his neck, breathing in everything about this night—the laughter, the messy kitchen, the man in front of me—and think: *It's about time.*

Chapter 25

Now

I wake up with a dull headache.

Half my face is pressed against my pillow, so I force the eye on the exposed half open. I'm facing the window, light spilling in through cracks in the blinds. I squint, and a water glass on the nightstand comes into focus, beckoning to me. I reach forward but don't get far, which is when I notice the long, tanned arm draped across my waist, pinning me in place like a locked seatbelt.

Sebastian.

I smile into the pillow, then snuggle closer to him. The water can wait.

I wake again an hour later with a much worse headache. I must have rolled over in my sleep, because this time half my face is pressed against Sebastian's chest. My body always runs cold when I sleep, and his skin feels like hot pavement in comparison. The light smattering of hair on his chest tickles my nose. Indulging myself, I let my eyes travel over his perfect body.

Then I give him a nudge.

He groans, but his eyes remain closed. With his left arm, which is braced across the small of my back, he pulls me closer to him. "Coffee?" he asks.

"Mmm. For sure. But water first."

We split the glass on my nightstand, and then Sebastian pads to the kitchen to pour two more. I hear him switch on the coffee maker before he returns. He has no shirt on, a pair of joggers slung low across his hips, exposing a part of his waist that sort of makes my throat close if I look at it for too long.

"I'm realizing there's a reason we didn't play those drinking games with wine in high school and college," I say, pushing myself up to a sitting position. I reach for one of the glasses he's holding and gulp it down.

"If I remember correctly, you weren't a huge fan of Natty Light, either." I roll my eyes at this. He sits facing me on the bed, then pulls me onto his lap. "Even when you're hungover, you look pretty."

I laugh in a way that sounds like the verbal manifestation of a blush. My hair is a mess, I'm not wearing a stitch of makeup and I *am* wearing a pajama shorts set that I bought at Marshalls ironically, because the pattern had reminded me of an ugly tablecloth my grandmother had owned. I'm not exactly used to impressing overnight guests. I make a mental note to finally take Maren's advice and order some lingerie. I'm also flattered that Sebastian apparently likes me this way.

"You're no slouch, either," I say, our noses brushing. He kisses me, and I think, *This is what morning Sebastian tastes like.* It may be my favorite Sebastian flavor yet.

Sebastian pulls on a hoodie (to my dismay), so I change into my coziest quarter zip and matching shorts—my at-home uniform. I pour our coffees while he cuts the pastries into smaller pieces so we can both try a little of everything. He's like me, apparently, in that he doesn't want to commit to just one. Then we relocate to the balcony. We eat our breakfast on the love seat, laughing as we string together highlights from the previous night. Just beyond us, speckles of reflected sunlight dance across the waves as they roll in. I can't remember the last time I felt so content.

Sebastian has been helping his mom manage this summer's staff—mostly high schoolers, just like we were—and as he tells me an animated story about their antics, it's so apparent how much he loves working at the restaurant that I register that familiar, hopeful feeling again.

"I wish I could stay here all day, but I should get to the restaurant," Sebastian says, frowning. "I'm doing inventory and payroll tomorrow. It's not, like, an ideal schedule, I know."

"I forgive you," I say, with a dramatic lip pout. "But only because you brought me pastries."

"I'm nothing if not a gentleman," he says, eyes darkening as he turns to kiss me. I'd have been happy with a goodbye peck, but his lips move against mine like they have an agenda, and soon my hands are in his hair. I shift onto his lap, and then in one fell swoop he stands, lifting me with him. I tighten my legs around his waist as he carries me to my room, kissing me the whole way.

"What about the restaurant?" I ask, breathless, when he drops me on my bed. I help him pull his hoodie over his head, then grab at my own sweatshirt.

"I can be a little late," he murmurs, reaching for the clasp of my bra. "The owner loves me."

I wrap my arms around him and try not to think about how she might not be the only one.

Chapter 26

Now

I hustle through the double doors to my office Monday morning, attempting to conceal my face with a tumbler of coffee and my laptop. I flip my phone to selfie mode and smooth my hair, praying David is on a call or absorbed in an email, too distracted to notice my frazzled entrance, but who am I kidding? Nothing gets past him.

"Well, well, well," he says, rotating his chair toward mine and examining his watch. "Nine nineteen a.m. Angelina Mariano, did I just witness a walk of shame?"

He's right, of course. Sebastian hadn't explicitly said he was going to come over Sunday evening after his shift, but I'd felt hopeful enough to turn my normally efficient weekend grocery run into a leisurely spree (first stop, my favorite Italian deli for arborio rice, dried porcini mushrooms, a craggy wedge of fresh pecorino and a semolina loaf; next, the liquor store; and finally the supermarket for my usual list). I figured if I didn't hear from Sebastian and wound up eating risotto alone, it wouldn't be the worst way to spend a Sunday night.

But a text from Sebastian came through at 4:00 p.m. after

all. He'd just gotten off and was stopping home to shower and change. He could be at my place by 5:00. I told him to come hungry and started soaking the mushrooms.

The buzzer rang as I was plating. I pressed the button to let him up, and when I opened my door a minute later he stepped inside and started kissing me before I could even say hello.

He pulled back long enough to say, "It smells amazing in here," then resumed the kissing, steering us backward until my back was flush with the counter. Then he lifted me so I was sitting on it. I wrapped my legs around his torso, pulling him closer, and clutched a fistful of his curls in my hand.

"The food will get cold," I said, even as I was slipping my other hand beneath the hem of his shirt.

He grabbed my wrists gently, stopping me, and said against my mouth, "You're right. Let's eat first. I'm starved."

I sat with the intention of wolfing down my meal, but one bite in I slowed my roll. This food, this wine, they were meant to be savored. Sebastian raised the fork to his mouth and the way his eyes widened told me he agreed.

So, we didn't rush. We ate and we drank and we ate some more. And then I led Sebastian to my room and we took our time there, too.

We both had places to be in the morning: I started work at nine, and Sebastian needed to get some work done at the restaurant before driving his mom to a doctor's appointment. But morning Sebastian has proven to be the most difficult Sebastian for me to resist. And then he insisted on making me breakfast, which was even *harder* to resist.

Now, I'm uncharacteristically late for work—not that anyone but David will probably notice—and already counting the minutes until I get home later and Sebastian picks me up for dinner.

I don't tell all of this to David, though.

Instead, I roll my eyes and sit. "Can't a girl be late for work for the first time in her entire career without an interrogation?"

"That's precisely *why* it's interrogation-worthy." He crosses his arms, that knowing smirk still plastered on his face as I start scanning emails. "Good for you, by the way. He actually seems like a decent guy. I liked his friends, too."

Relief washes over me, and I bite my bottom lip, trying not to smile. David's approval would mean a lot to me no matter what, but given Maren's lingering hesitation it carries even more weight.

I'm about to say something to this effect when an email catches my eye. It's from an email address I don't immediately recognize: trina@dg.com. Realization hits me when I notice that it's actually a reply. Subject line: Re: Shore Life inquiry.

Date: August 12, 2024
From: trina@dg.com
Subject: Re: Shore Life inquiry
Ms. Mariano,

Thank you so much for reaching out earlier this summer regarding Diamond Group's potential expansion to the Jersey Shore! Apologies for my delayed response—at the time of your original email it was a bit premature to share any details (you know how these things go, I'm sure!) but I'm thrilled to now be able to confirm that Diamond Group's next venture will in fact be in the area, specifically Brantley Beach!

On Friday Diamond Group was approved to purchase and renovate the building at 11 Ocean Avenue, which currently houses the boardwalk eatery and snack bar Bubba's (upon the current owner's retirement at the end of the summer). The new concept from acclaimed New York City restaurateur Chip Diamond will preserve the charm of Bubba's while building upon Diamond Group's legacy of excellence and innovation, with a target opening of May 2025.

I'll circle back with an official press release in the

coming weeks, and of course we'd love to have you at the restaurant next year. Please do not hesitate to reach out with any questions in the meantime!

Best,
Trina Stanford
Director of Communications
Diamond Group
New York, NY

"Earth. To. Lina," David says in a tone that tells me it isn't the first time. "What the hell?"

Words escape me, so I rotate my monitor toward David so he can read the email himself.

"I thought Sebastian was going to convince his mom to hold on to the restaurant," he says carefully.

"Yeah. I did, too." But as I say the words I feel a tremor of doubt. Sebastian had told me he was waiting until his plan for the café was perfect to pitch it to Bubba. I'd taken for granted that Bubba would fall in love with the idea, just like Sebastian had. Like I had, too. What if it didn't go over well? My heart sinks for him.

David stares at the screen, his eyes scanning the message again. I reread it, too, hoping to spot a line I missed the first time, a typo—anything that suggests another way to interpret Trina Stanford's words.

"Maybe Bubba wouldn't budge," David muses, "or Diamond Group upped their offer."

"Maybe." I frown, a new doubt creeping in. "But Bubba wouldn't sign anything without him there. . . . It doesn't explain why he found out on Friday morning and then spent all weekend with me without saying anything." I roll the tapes on our weekend: He'd doubled down on all his big ideas for the café multiple times during our coffee tour, apparently despite knowing it wasn't going to happen.

What if the idea was never really a serious one, and he just didn't have the heart to tell me?

David blows out a breath. "Shit. I'm sorry, Leens. But I think you just have to talk to him, you know? There's got to be some sort of explanation."

I try to latch on to David's words, but I feel them float away until they're nothing but unintelligible whispers, out of reach. The words that replace them are loud and firm and leave little room for explanation.

Bubba is selling the restaurant.

Sebastian lied to me about it.

He'll stay as long as his mom needs him, but then what?

Least likely to end up back in Brantley Beach, Theo had said at my apartment. Sebastian's oldest friend—the person who knows him better than almost anyone—was shocked by Sebastian's return, and would be even more shocked if it proved permanent. Keeping the restaurant would tether him to this town forever. That he'd chosen to cut the cord probably surprised no one except me.

I close my laptop and repack my bag.

"Where are you going?" David asks.

"You're right, I've got to talk to him," I say, standing.

He nods toward our boss's office. "I'll cover for you with Mandy."

"Thanks." I hadn't even thought about Mandy, actually. She'd been so disappointed when the Nikolaou-Cunningham wedding feature fell through, and with it her dream of a Kleinfeld Bridal–sponsored cover. The money bags in her eyes had disappeared, and she hadn't mentioned my promotion again since. I'm just as stuck as ever. I just can't bring myself to care as much as I normally would.

I get in my car—I drove today to save time and had miraculously found a street spot—and head to Bubba's. Over breakfast this morning Sebastian told me that he was going to get a few hours of work done before driving his mom to a one o'clock doctor's appointment. I maneuver around a family of four unloading so much gear you'd think they were permanently moving into their pop-up beach tent and pull into Bubba's small employee lot. I spot Sebastian's Jeep in its usual spot.

Parker smiles in recognition as I approach the hostess stand, then frowns when she realizes I'm about to sidestep her. I beeline for the back office.

"If you're looking for Sebastian," she calls, "he's not here!"

I whirl to face her again, arms crossed. "I saw his car in the lot."

Parker shrugs. "I haven't seen him."

I glance at the shut office door again, skeptical. But I'm obviously not going to trespass, especially not in front of a teenager. Am I?

"He's probably at the surfing beach," says a teenage boy who has poked his head through the snack bar door. "It's his Monday thing."

Parker shoots me an I-told-you-so look and says, "Thanks, Wade."

"Thank you *both* for your help," I grumble on my way out.

The surfing beach is only a couple of blocks from the restaurant. I speed-walk down the boardwalk, growing angrier with each step. Was Sebastian planning to spend all day surfing, when he'd told me he'd be at the restaurant? And what about all the other Mondays we'd texted this month, when he'd told me he was working? David had said that maybe something had happened that made Sebastian and his mom change their minds about keeping the restaurant, but I was starting to wonder if he'd ever seriously entertained an option *other* than selling it. Maybe he wasn't working here much at all.

I hold one hand up to block the sun and look toward the jetty and the section of the ocean beyond it. Normally I avoid the surfing beach: The sight of those jagged, algae-slick black rocks reminds me of the day I slipped. Not to mention the feeling of Sebastian's skin against mine as he carried me. And how innocent and boyish he looked sleeping next to my hospital bed.

Yeah. Enough of *that*.

I push the memory away and scan the silhouettes that dot the waves. None of them look like Sebastian.

I hear a car door slam a little ways down, and then another. And there he is, clad in a black wetsuit, standing on the footbed of a car that is not his. He reaches up to unfasten his board from the roof rack as a gorgeous red-haired woman in a one-piece and denim cutoffs appears, opening the hatchback trunk of the car and sliding out her own board. Sebastian jumps down, board tucked under one arm, phone in the other. He types something while he waits for her, then they both head toward the water.

I'm still attempting to process the scene I've just witnessed when my phone vibrates in the pocket of my dress.

Sebastian: **Hope work is great. Have some cool updates. Excited to tell you later.**

What the fuck?

I shove my phone back in my pocket like it will burn me if I hold it any longer and book it back to the parking lot. I run through the new facts along the way.

As of Friday, Diamond Group owns Bubba's, and yet Sebastian continues to tell me his future plans for the restaurant.

He's lied to me on multiple occasions about his whereabouts.

He spends his Monday mornings surfing, not working. The fact that—at least on this particular Monday—he does so with a beautiful woman is just icing on the cake.

I am an idiot.

I steal one last glance over my shoulder. Sebastian and the red-haired woman are in the water now, wading through the glistening waves, boards atop their pretty heads. And I'm here, watching them from afar. It's a feeling more familiar than I care to admit.

I jog the rest of the way to my car, not looking back. I've seen enough.

Chapter 27

Then
Fourteen Years Ago

Boardwalk Night was a longstanding tradition. Held every year in late August, it was Bubba's way of thanking her seasonal staff for a summer of hard work—as well as a bargaining chip she brandished as needed. The threat of being barred from Boardwalk Night had a way of dissolving quarrels and complaints on the spot. And for good reason: Bubba worked her connections to close the boardwalk to the public for an entire night, giving us free rein. In other words, it was epic.

I'd spent most of last year's Boardwalk Night with Tina, Carly and Helen, playing mini golf, riding the Scrambler and gorging ourselves on Italian ices and fried Oreos. Sebastian and the rest of the high school guys on staff were never far from sight: We hung out next to them more so than with them, which felt pretty exciting at the time. As is tradition, the event officially concluded with what we called Skit, which was a sort of farewell medley of performances put on by the staff. That year we all dressed up and impersonated different versions of Bubba; I wore a Springsteen concert tee and denim cutoffs in homage to one of her signature off-duty looks. Unofficially, it ended around 3:00 a.m. at Helen's house, when her neighbors threatened to call the cops with a noise complaint.

This year's Boardwalk Night would be different, of course. Helen had graduated last year, Carly's last day was in July (she was spending this August at tennis camp) and Tina would probably dip early to hang out with her new boyfriend. Not that I minded: The only person I cared about seeing was Sebastian.

I was running late, so by the time I hopped out of my mom's car, most of the staff was already on the boardwalk, lining up for games and rides. No Sebastian, though. Once an hour had gone by, I started to worry. I checked my phone incessantly but didn't hear from him.

The group I'd been going on rides with decided to take a break for lemonade and funnel cake, which was when I overheard bits of a conversation between Ravi and Chris Cappelli, friend of Maren's long-ago flame Aaron Reingold and this year's snack bar manager.

". . . with Louros and Silva, probably." This was Chris. ". . . better get his ass over here in time for Skit or I'm bailing, too."

I snuck another look at my phone. Nothing. I shot him a message: **Marco?** Then vowed not to check unless I felt a vibration.

I didn't.

A pit of dread formed in my stomach, heavy and unsettling. I realized I hadn't seen Bubba at the restaurant today, either. Had something bad happened?

My darkest worries evaporated when Sebastian finally did show up, just as the rest of us were gathering in front of the Ferris wheel, the traditional backdrop for Skit. But he wasn't alone: Theo and Andre rounded the entrance behind him, in a fit of hysterical laughter about who knew what. Sebastian, in contrast, looked lost in thought.

I sprung up from where I'd been sitting on the ground

and jogged toward them, ignoring the quiver in my stomach. Non-staff members were strictly prohibited from Boardwalk Night, and it wasn't like Sebastian to so blatantly disregard his mother's rules.

"You made it!" I said, smiling. I was relieved that he was okay.

Sebastian blinked several times, like I'd broken him out of a trance. "Hey, Mariano," he said finally.

Normally, Sebastian would greet me with his megawatt smile and a hug, maybe even lift me off my feet and spin me around while I half-heartedly begged him to put me back down. But now he kept his distance, hands shoved in his pockets. Still, we were close enough that I could smell the alcohol he'd been drinking.

"Where do you want to sit?" I asked, still trying to sound upbeat even though he clearly wasn't. "I was up in front with Ravi and Chris but I can grab my bag and move wherever."

"Actually we're just passing through," he said, gesturing to Theo and Andre, who were now passing a joint back and forth. "Might hit some rides."

I squinted at Sebastian, who continued avoiding my eyes altogether. What was going on with him? Showing up late was one thing, but arriving with a cross-faded entourage just to take advantage of the free rides was another. Bubba would be livid.

"You're not actually going to skip out on Skit, are you?" I asked, my tone more serious now. "I mean, will it be dumb? Definitely. But you can't miss it!"

Sebastian raked a hand through his hair, which looked even wilder than usual. "Yeah. I'm just not in the mood tonight."

I frowned. I felt certain that Sebastian would regret missing out on the tradition, especially considering he was about to be a senior and probably would only have one more summer here before trading his Bubba's shifts for a nine-to-five internship like most college kids did. But something told me not to push it. What mattered more was talking about the kiss. I needed to find out if it meant as much to him as it had to me.

"All right," I said carefully. "Will I at least see you at Chris's later, so we can talk?" Chris had volunteered to host the traditional post–Boardwalk Night soiree. We could have the conversation we needed to have there.

"I don't know, Lina." His eyes met mine. There was no sign of the warmth and affection that had been there last night, before he kissed me. Worse, there was an unfamiliar edge to his voice. He rarely called me by my first name. It made me feel like a child getting disciplined. "Didn't realize I had to clear my schedule with you."

I took a step back, and I'm sure my face spelled out exactly how much that sentence shocked me. "You don't. Obviously. I just—"

"You don't need to be so obsessed with me," he said, cutting me off. Behind him, Andre and Theo both stifled a laugh, like this was part of an inside joke they'd all heard and told many times before. My eyes went wide, and Sebastian took a step toward me, rushing to correct himself. "I didn't mean that. I just meant you're so worried about what I'm doing or not doing, and it's kind of . . ."

I forced myself to hold his gaze. I felt more humiliated than I ever had in my life, but still I wasn't going to let him off the hook. If he was going to hurt me like this, I at least wanted to experience the pain in full. "It's kind of what, Sebastian?"

He threw up his hands in frustration. "It's just kind of *a lot* right now. Okay?"

Correction: *Now* I felt more humiliated than I ever had in my life.

I nodded slowly, tears stinging at the corners of my eyes. To Sebastian's credit, his indifferent expression shifted, and I could see the regret written all over his face. But whether he regretted the actual words or just the fact that he'd admitted them out loud, I didn't plan to stick around and find out. I whirled around so I could head back to my spot, and that's when I realized we had an audience. The whole staff had witnessed everything.

"Lina," Sebastian called after me. "Lina! Hang on, please."

As I wove through the group, ignoring their wide-eyed stares, I heard one of the bussers just walking up call out, "Hey, Nikolaou made it!"

Chris and Ravi called my name, but I walked right past them, not looking back.

I didn't have a destination in mind at first. I just knew that I couldn't imagine facing my mother in my wrinkled sundress and tear-streaked makeup. So I kept walking, Sebastian's words playing on an endless loop in my mind.

Eventually I turned onto Maren's street. I didn't want to wake up the Murphys, so I sent her a text and waited outside until she opened the front door. She took one look at me and waved me inside, no questions asked.

Chapter 28

Then
Fourteen Years Ago

The irony of having a crush on someone is that, most of the time, they wind up crushing you.

For the next couple of weeks I limited my interactions and conversations with Sebastian to only those that were absolutely essential for me to do my job—without coming off like a complete jerk to everyone else. "Excuse me," if I needed to get around him in the dining room. "Thanks," if he brewed a fresh pot of coffee before I got to it. If we were tasked with rolling silverware or setting tables together, we did it in silence. I started riding my bike to and from work again, or, if the weather was bad, one of my parents drove me.

At work and outside of it, I struggled to process what happened on Boardwalk Night. I felt heartbroken, but at the same time I wondered if I'd even earned the right to that heartbreak. Sebastian and I were never dating. He hadn't cheated on me or even dumped me. He'd kissed me once, then immediately regretted it—that much was clear. There was no easy terminology for what he'd done to me—what I'd *let* him do to me—and that only made me feel more pathetic.

At first I worried that Sebastian would try to make amends.

That he'd corner me with pity in his eyes, apologizing for humiliating me while in the same breath saying he'd known how I felt about him all along and was flattered and all, but he didn't feel the same. I didn't want to give him the satisfaction.

I just wanted to get through the end of the summer.

But it turned out I didn't have anything to worry about on that front. Sebastian's whole demeanor changed during those final weeks. He didn't seem to want anything to do with me, or anyone else at the restaurant, for that matter. I didn't know what was going on with him—if it had to do with me or something else. But the humiliation I felt overshadowed any desire I might have had to find out.

Maren was even less sympathetic. In her eyes, Sebastian was public enemy number one. I'd come out of my shell that summer, only to close right back up. She was wracked with guilt for ever encouraging my infatuation with him.

When Chris Cappelli asked me if I wanted to go out with him sometime, I was surprised. We were running through our closing tasks on Labor Day, which was our last shift before school started back up for the fall. Sebastian was there, too, but in the kitchen helping Omar close up and, I hoped, out of earshot.

Chris was pretty cute, I realized, with a neat crew cut of light brown hair and big brown eyes to match. Last year he hadn't been much taller than me, but he'd shot up this summer. Why hadn't I noticed him before? I knew the answer, of course: I'd been so consumed by my attraction to Sebastian that I'd probably failed to notice a lot of other guys—including some, like Chris, who might have even been interested in me.

My ears rang with Sebastian's words. *You don't need to be so obsessed with me.*

"I'll get back to you," I told Chris. He was a nice kid. I didn't want to string him along if my heart wasn't ready. I certainly knew what that felt like.

I planned to leave my shift that night without saying goodbye to Sebastian, but he ran into me just as I was finishing clearing out my cubby.

"Sorry," I muttered, maneuvering around him. I'd stuffed all the belongings I'd accumulated over the summer into my backpack: a couple of overdue library books, a thrifted camera and way too many of those silicone bracelets shaped like animals that everyone was obsessed with that year.

He caught my arm, stopping me, and said, "Wait."

I looked up at him, my skin prickling at his touch. His eyebrows were knit together, and his expression looked almost pained.

"I heard you talking to Chris," he said.

My pulse started racing, but everything else seemed to slow down as I waited for him to elaborate. Despite how hurt and angry I still felt, some foolish part of me—the part that would always have hope—wondered if he'd tell me to say no. If realizing someone else wanted me would make him want me, too.

"You should go out with him," he said instead, and my heart shattered.

"Thanks, but I don't need your relationship advice," I said, tugging my arm away. But instead of taking the hint, he stepped even closer.

"Of course you don't," Sebastian said. His voice was infuriatingly gentle. "He's a good kid, that's all I'm saying."

"Is that all?" I asked.

He held my gaze for a few excruciatingly long beats. Then, with a single, nearly imperceptible nod, he said, "Get home safe."

"Goodbye, Sebastian."

By the end of that week I officially had my first boyfriend. Chris and I held hands between class periods, and Maren and I joined his friends' table for lunch.

During our five-month courtship we did things like go to the mall for frozen yogurt and make out while pretending to watch action movies in his basement. We even went to the homecoming dance together, meeting at the Murphys' beforehand to take pictures with Maren and her flavor of the month, an artsy freshman she'd met during our short-lived stint in photo club.

I still thought about the falling out with Sebastian more than I wanted to (sulking to Taylor Swift's "Teardrops on My Guitar" had become a guilty pleasure that even Maren didn't know about), but it stung a lot less now that I knew *someone* wanted me back. It also helped that avoiding Sebastian during the school year was easy, since we'd only ever acted like friends in the summer. We were in different grades, different social circles, different extracurriculars—different worlds, really. The occasional times we did cross paths in the hallways or the cafeteria, I offered him no more than a polite smile and nod to give the appearance of being unbothered, and he'd just stare at me in return, those mossy eyes more inscrutable to me than ever.

By February, Chris and I had amicably broken up, agreeing that we were better off as friends. I was grateful to have the experience of a relationship under my belt—albeit a very high school one—and to have gotten out of it relatively unscathed. We'd barely rounded second base, and no one had cheated. No harm, no foul.

Around that time is also when the halls began teeming with gossip about the seniors' college admissions results. I learned that Sebastian got into his first choice, the University of California, Santa Barbara, from Carly, who worked on the student newspaper with me and who was kept loosely in Sebastian's orbit thanks to her on-again, off-again flirtation with Andre. By next year Sebastian would be as far away from Brantley Beach as possible, just like he wanted.

Chapter 29

Then
Thirteen Years Ago

The week before Memorial Day, I biked to Bubba's to pick up the fresh navy polo that would be my uniform for the summer. I'd be working weekends starting that Saturday until school let out in late June and I could take on shifts during the week.

It was a Monday night and, aside from a couple of regulars, the restaurant was dead. I waved to Maria, an off-season hostess who spent the summers watching her grandkids, and headed for the back office.

"Lina! Welcome back, sweetheart," Bubba said when I knocked on the doorframe. She waved me inside and lifted a cardboard box onto her sticky note-strewn desk.

"Thank you, Bubba," I said, flipping through the shirt tags until I found my size. "I'm excited to be back."

"I can't believe you're almost a junior! How's school going this year?" She smiled her big smile. Sebastian's smile. It took everything in me not to look away.

"I know, it's crazy," I said, shaking my head. "School is good! Really good. I'm still liking the newspaper. Starting to think about colleges. My parents want to take me on some visits this summer."

"That's fabulous, Lina. The hard part will be narrowing it down, I'm sure. Any school would be lucky to have you!"

It meant a lot to hear her say that, but I waved her off.

"Although I will say, New Jersey has no shortage of good schools," Bubba continued. "All the kids seem to forget that, my son included." She said this in a teasing way, but I could see in her eyes that there was some truth to the hurt it implied.

"You'll have to work him to the bone this summer as punishment," I joked, just to keep the conversation light. I doubted she knew Sebastian and I weren't exactly on speaking terms.

"I wish," she said with a sigh. I raised a brow. "Sebastian won't be back this summer, honey." I only processed bits and pieces of what she said next, that's how rattled I was by this news. *Took a job on campus. Instructor at a kids' rec camp. Probably surfing all day. Flying out at the end of the month.*

I hadn't admitted it to myself until then, but I'd been holding on to more than a semblance of hope that once we were back at Bubba's for the summer Sebastian and I would find a way to fix what had broken between us. I would have resisted any reconciliation attempts last summer, but that was when the sting of what he'd said to me on Boardwalk Night was fresh. So much time had passed, and summer had a way of resetting things. But now we wouldn't get that chance.

The landline rang on Bubba's desk, and she scrambled to get it, mouthing an apology.

It's okay! I mouthed back. I whispered a thank-you as I backed out of the office—and slammed straight into a hard body.

"Whoa!" Sebastian grabbed my shoulders gently, steadying me. Then he bent down and picked up the shirt I'd dropped.

"Ow," I said, rubbing the side of my face that had connected with his chest. "What are you doing here?" It was the most I'd said to Sebastian since last summer.

"It's kind of a family business," he said. I grabbed the shirt and glared at him.

"Your mom said you aren't coming back this summer."

"I'm not," he said, pushing his hair out of his face. "Just helping out as much as I can before I leave."

"Well, if I don't see you before then I hope the move goes well." I flashed him a clipped smile and started for the door, but he caught my arm.

"Lina, is that seriously the last thing you're going to say to me?" His eyes reminded me of a forest, vast and dark.

I quickly maneuvered out of his grip and peered up at him. "What do you want me to say, Sebastian? That it will be weird without you here? Of course it will be. But honestly it was going to be weird if you were here, too, just in a different way. So."

"It doesn't have to be weird between us, you know," he said in a low voice. He sounded almost sad.

I laughed humorlessly. "I'm not the one who made it weird, remember?" Sebastian flinched. Some quiet voice inside me warned that he was trying to reach out again and that I might not get another chance to meet him halfway. But a louder voice took the fact that he was leaving as confirmation that what I needed to do more than anything was protect myself.

"Okay, Mariano." He straightened, and my heart sank a few more levels. I didn't want him to give up, but I also couldn't seem to stop pushing him away. I was a walking contradiction. It occurred to me that all those months dating Chris Cappelli I'd never once felt the flustering combination of want, resistance, hope and confusion that I felt every time I was around Sebastian. What that meant I couldn't say.

He looked at me a moment longer before saying, "I guess I'll see you around, then."

"Have a great summer, Sebastian." I spun around and headed for the door.

Outside, Maren was leaning against the bike rack, tapping around on the screen of her brand-new iPhone 4—she was the first of us to get a smartphone. I almost forgot that we'd planned to meet for a ride to Twisters, which was opening for the season that night.

"Everything okay?" she asked when she looked up and saw my face.

I nodded, pulling out my bike.

Maren dropped her phone in the basket of her yellow beach cruiser. As we began pedaling north on the boardwalk she asked, "Did you see anyone inside?"

"Nah," I said. "No one worth talking about."

Chapter 30
Now

Back at my apartment, I email Mandy to let her know I'm working from home for the rest of the day and allow myself exactly ten minutes to freak out over this morning's revelations. Then I sit cross-legged on the couch, crack open my laptop and spend twenty more minutes re-freaking out with David via Slack messages. He concedes that the new developments aren't ideal but insists I still need to actually talk to Sebastian, and before I can argue he says he's hopping on a call and sets his status to *unavailable*. Classic.

After struggling for an hour to write an un-snarky story about how the traditional rehearsal dinner is giving way to the unstructured welcome party, I pivot to editing a guide to the best bridesmaids' gifts on Etsy that I'd assigned to a freelancer. As much as I love writing, I sometimes crave the more removed process of fixing up someone *else's* writing. Writing is personal. Vulnerable. Editing, in my experience, is just work.

I publish the gift guide, then assign out a few more breezy stories to fill my editorial calendar for the rest of the month. If Mandy isn't going to let me write about anything else, I can at least put my freelance budget to good use.

The world of getting-ready robes and modern mirror seating charts miraculously distracts me from thoughts of Sebastian until nearly 5:00 p.m., when my phone buzzes and a bubble with his name appears on my glowing screen. I pick my phone up delicately, like it might bite, and swipe open his message.

Still good for dinner at 5:30? Just wrapping a few things up, then can come get you.

I wonder what things he's wrapping up and if they involve a certain red-haired surfer.

I debate canceling on him, but I know that would just delay the inevitable. I doubt Sebastian can sufficiently explain away all of the alarming things I've learned in the hours since I last saw him, but I also know that David is right: I owe him the chance to try.

I type and delete several responses, all of which sound either suspiciously clipped or overly enthusiastic. I settle on simply hearting his message, then flip my phone facedown on the table and trudge to my room to make sure I don't look as confused and angry as I feel. I step out of the black linen shift dress I'd worn to the office—the same one that Sebastian had zipped for me this morning—and pull on a pair of white cropped jeans and my favorite silky tank top. I change facing the closet to avoid looking at the bed, but the images bubble up anyway: of Sebastian's tanned skin against white sheets, of his curls and my waves splayed across the same pillow. God help me.

I run a straightener through my hair. Touch up my mascara. Apply lip gloss. Familiar tasks that distract me from the questions I don't want to ask. The answers I don't want to hear.

The buzzer sounds at 5:15. I tap the button on the intercom to let Sebastian up.

When I open the door, the sight of him momentarily jumbles my thoughts. Sebastian Nikolaou is here to see me. To take me to dinner. He looks as handsome as ever, in a white button-down with the sleeves cuffed in a way that shows off his infuriatingly appealing forearms, chino shorts and his usual Vans, now yellowing from almost a full summer of sand and sun. His face looks tanner than it had this morning, his nose slightly red. *Would he deny the reason if I asked?* I wonder. He smiles softly, green eyes roving over me in a way that makes my skin heat.

"You look so pretty," he says, closing the distance between us. He cups my cheek with one hand and pulls me toward him by my waist with the other, then presses his lips to mine. For a moment I forget all about my anger and confusion, giving myself over to the feeling of kissing him, a feeling that still exhilarates me but now leaves an ache in its wake. I pull back.

"I need to talk to you," I say quietly, forcing myself to meet his gaze. Those green eyes immediately swell with concern.

"Okay. Let's talk."

I lead him to the couch and reach for my phone. After pulling the email up, I hand it to him.

He must only read a sentence before realizing what it is. He looks at me with wide, pleading eyes. "Lina, I can explain."

"Your mom is still selling the restaurant," I say, matter-of-factly.

He exhales, and any shreds of hope I have that he'd deny it disintegrate with each second that passes.

"Yes," he admits. "But it's not what you think. My mom and I negotiated a new deal with Diamond Group—one that would let me stay involved. We aren't just handing it over to them—not anymore."

I shake my head. "I've seen these kinds of deals before, Sebastian. They'll keep your picture on the website, list you as some sort of advisor on their payroll. They'll meet with you a few times a year and pretend to care about your input so they can keep the story of a family operation going, but you won't have any actual say or power."

"No," he says, his voice firm. "They know I have ideas—good ones—and they want to hear me out. I know this restaurant, and I know this town. They see the value I bring."

"You *do* bring value—plenty of it. So what do you need them for?"

"Isn't it obvious?" He throws his hands up in exasperation. "Money, first of all, for new equipment, better ingredients, building repairs, more staff, the list goes on. A PR team to spread the word and bring in more customers. Connections to more vendors. I want to bring this restaurant into a new era—I want it to make money again—but I'm not arrogant enough to think I can do it on my own, especially while I'm also taking care of my mom."

I register the logic in his words, but another truth bubbles to the surface.

"But why not just tell me all this?" I ask. "Why act like you were working on this grand plan to keep the restaurant if that was never really the case? Why tell me you're working while you're *surfing*?" I cringe at the words as they escape my mouth. I sound young and petty and desperate, but I can't help it. I *feel* young and petty and desperate.

His eyes narrow in confusion, which only angers me more.

"I stopped by the restaurant earlier to talk to you." I don't tell him the part about how I followed him to the beach and saw his lovely surfing buddy.

Sebastian exhales. "I'm not really sure why I didn't just tell you the whole truth about the Diamond Group deal. Maybe I thought you would be disappointed in me for not having the confidence to walk away from them altogether. The situation is . . . it's complicated. And I'm still trying to figure it out myself." He leans closer to me, and when I pull back hurt flickers across his face. "But I didn't lie to you about working today," he continues. "I *was* working, just not at the restaurant. On Mondays I've been working on plans for the café—driving up and down the Shore to check out competitors, casually meeting with potential vendors, drafting a budget. I just don't advertise all that to the staff. They've mentally prepared for this summer to be our last season, and I don't want to get their hopes up."

Still no explanation for Surfer Girl, and I'm too proud to ask about her.

But you were willing to get my hopes up, I think. What's left unsaid hangs in the air, and in the silence that follows I realize I could have made the exact same accusation fourteen years ago, on Boardwalk Night. All this time later and we're still making the same mistakes.

"You knew," I say finally, my voice small.

When I don't elaborate, he asks gently, "Knew what, Lina?"

I meet his eyes. "You knew how I felt about you back then. What you said to me on Boardwalk Night made that crystal clear. So I guess I just want to know—why? Why cross the line with me in the first place, if you knew how I felt? You had to know that giving me an ounce of hope would only crush me that much more in the end. Why be so cruel?"

He winces, then squeezes his eyes shut completely, as if trying to erase whatever image had flashed in his mind. He shifts closer to me on the couch, hurt flashing across his eyes again when I inch further back into the cushion.

"I don't regret kissing you, Lina. But I do regret everything about that night on the boardwalk. I was in a god-awful headspace, but it's no excuse for the way I treated you. I would give anything to take back what I said. Sorry doesn't even begin to cover it."

"Tell me about the headspace," I say, hating the way my voice trembles. "I want to try to understand."

He lets out a long breath, and I'm reminded of something my mom once said to me years ago, when I'd found myself at the center of some middle school girl drama and desperately wanted to avoid confronting it. *Sometimes the truth is hard to hear but easier to live with.* I can tell that whatever Sebastian is going to say next won't be easy for him, but I also know that, for there to be any chance of us moving forward, I need to finally hear it.

"The night we kissed in the snack bar," he says, and I nod, allowing myself to go back to that night—a night that I haven't let myself go back to in a long time. "It was the same night my dad told my mom and me that he was leaving us. We were completely blindsided."

My body tenses as I absorb this new piece of information and match it up with what I remember. Sebastian's dad *had* unexpectedly picked him up that night. It was the reason Sebastian didn't drive me home like usual—the reason we didn't get a chance to talk about the kiss and what it meant.

"Your dad left . . . that night?" I ask, trying to get a handle on the timeline. "So, before your senior year?"

He nods, and my stomach twists. I'd assumed Sebastian's parents had split up later, when we were in college or maybe even years after that. Was I really so oblivious that I didn't realize it had happened while we were still in school together?

But then I remind myself of the facts. Mr. Nikolaou wasn't exactly a consistent presence in the first place. Sebastian and I were no longer on speaking terms. And Bubba has always been a proud and private woman. It makes sense that I wouldn't have connected the dots.

I think of Sebastian's withdrawn state at the end of that summer. His somber mood in the halls during the school year. His rush to California the following summer. It's all starting to make a lot more sense.

Across from me on the couch, Sebastian has gone still, his expression uncharacteristically grim.

"My dad traveled a lot for work, to cities all over the country," he says. "But my junior year, all of a sudden most of his conferences were in Philly. Not far at all." He lets out a heavy sigh. "Turns out he'd met a woman there. She had kids of her own, younger than me. He chose his new family over us."

"Sebastian," I say, shaking my head. "I'm so sorry. I had no idea."

I think about that long-ago conversation at Twisters, when Sebastian had confided in me about his dad's extended Philly trip. I'd assumed Bubba had been upset because Mr. Nikolaou prioritized work over his family. The reality had been even worse.

"It's okay," he says, smiling wearily. "No one really did. Mom made sure of that. She didn't want to deal with people talking about it while I was still in school. So we sort of just . . . didn't deal with it at all."

"You must have been crushed. And your mom . . ."

He nods sadly. "I was hurt. And confused. And angry. But my mom—God, it was so much worse for her. She was embarrassed, more than anything. She told my dad to get out right then and there, and once he left she just completely shut down and wouldn't talk about it. I knew my dad always resented my mom because inheriting the restaurant meant they'd never be able to leave Brantley Beach. But I had no idea how deep that resentment ran until that night."

There's so much I want to ask. Did he and his mom eventually process their feelings about what happened? Has he been in touch with his dad since then? But I bite my lower lip, stopping myself. I can tell there's more he needs to say first.

"I was supposed to meet you at the boardwalk the next night, but I felt like I needed to calm down first," he continues. "My mom had stayed home that day—something she never did—and I could tell she wanted to be alone. So I went over to Andre's. His parents were out of town, and he was having a bunch of guys over to pregame before this beach bonfire. When I got there he and Theo could obviously tell something was up, but I just waved them off and chugged as much bad tequila as I could stomach."

My stomach churns, because I know what happens next. I brace myself to relive the humiliation.

"I was still planning on going to Skit," he says. "I wanted to see you. Talk to you. You were the one person I thought I might feel comfortable talking to about what happened with my dad. I wanted to tell you how confused I felt—about everything." His eyes lock on mine, dark and anguished. "Including what happened between us."

I open my mouth to say something, then close it again uncertainly. I settle on: "I felt confused, too."

"Kissing you felt so right in the moment," he says carefully, and my heart sinks. "But thinking about it the next day, right in the middle of all the shit with my parents . . . it freaked me out, Lina."

His words from the boardwalk echo in my head: *It's just kind of a lot right now.*

"Because you knew I was 'obsessed' with you," I say, making a pair of pathetic air quotes with my fingers.

"It was an awful thing to say, Lina," he interjects. "Something I got from the guys. They'd been giving me a hard time about a few girls for a while at that point, including you. But Lina? I swear it wasn't like they thought I was better than you, or that it was embarrassing that you liked me. They just loved giving me shit because they were jealous of all the attention I got from girls—attention they thought was wasted on me. And the few times I did mess around with girls back then, it never turned into anything that remotely mattered."

"So you were just worried you'd given me the wrong idea," I say, the words tumbling out in a rush. "That's the reason you completely humiliated me. That's why you told me to go out with Chris?"

"No, Lina." My breath hitches as he tips my chin up until we're looking each other right in the eye again. "The reason I did those things was because I was more certain than ever that I wanted to get the hell out of Brantley Beach, and I had just kissed a girl who almost certainly would have become a reason for me to stay."

Oh.

"When we ran into you," he continues, releasing my jaw, "I was drunk, and I said terrible things that I didn't mean. I think I was just in the mood to hurt people, hoping it would it make me hurt less. As soon as I saw the look on your face I knew I needed to apologize—"

"But you didn't," I say, softly.

He nods. "Not right then, no. And I should have. I expected you to be angry with me, but you weren't—you just wanted nothing to do with me. And honestly? That was even worse."

"Because I had no idea what happened," I say, feeling a little defensive. "You acted like a jerk to me, but if you had told me what you were going through, I would have understood. I would have been there for you. You had to know that, right?"

"I know that *now*," he says. "But back then? I didn't *want* anyone to be there for me—or at least I thought I didn't. You'd always thought so highly of me. I told myself that I was leaving and maybe it was better this way. You hating me. Everything in my life was going up in flames anyway, so what was one more bridge burned? I was determined to leave everything behind, and at the time you just believing I was a jerk felt easier than admitting the truth. It sounds ridiculous now, but to my immature brain it seemed logical."

I let his words sink in. All this time I had convinced myself that Sebastian had revealed his true colors on that humiliating night. That the kind, magnetic boy I'd developed a massive crush on—and who was maybe finally reciprocating those feelings—was actually a huge jerk who had led me on, only to make fun of me right to my face. What if it hadn't been that simple?

"Lina. What are you thinking? Tell me."

I'm thinking a lot of things. Sadness for Sebastian and Bubba. Anger at his dad for leaving them behind. Frustration with Sebastian for shutting me out all those years ago. Disappointment in myself, for not realizing something bigger was going on. I don't know if things would have played out differently for us in the end. We were so young, after all. But we could have stayed friends. And it would have saved me a lot of self-loathing.

But then again, would it have? Because if I'm being honest with myself, I was in what you might call a self-loathing era. Sebastian's behavior on Boardwalk Night gave me someone to project my insecurities about myself onto. He wasn't the only one with an immature brain back then.

"I'm thinking I wish we met later," I say instead, which is actually another way of saying the same thing. "When we were real people."

Sebastian reaches out to brush his thumb along my jaw, smiling softly as he says, "We did. Earlier this summer."

I lean into his touch, tamping down the doubts and questions that remain. They don't feel like they matter as much as they did a few hours ago. All I can think about now are the answers I *am* getting—answers I couldn't have gotten back then, because I hadn't known the right questions to ask.

"I'm so sorry about your dad, Sebastian," I say. "You and your mom—you didn't deserve that. And it's okay that you didn't know how to process it."

He tugs me closer, and this time I don't back away. I let my body follows his lead until my legs are wrapped around his waist, our eyes inches apart.

"I wasn't ready for you then, Lina. But I am now." He reaches up to catch my jaw. My heart thrums in my chest, a metronome keeping time. And then he says, "I'm falling in love with you."

For once I'm at a loss for words. I respond by tentatively pressing my lips against his.

He grips me in place as he speeds up the kiss, palms skimming the bare skin above the waistband of my jeans. I lose my fingers in his hair and roll my hips toward him. We're close, but not nearly close enough. I want *more*.

He pulls my camisole over my head, breath hitching as he

takes me in. He tugs his shirt off next, skin glistening in the golden light coming in through my window. We discard the rest of our clothes in a flurry of shaky hands and shuddering breaths. It's messy and passionate and apologetic and forgiving all at once.

As he lowers me onto the couch, I'm overcome by how much I want him. Not just his body: I want his love, his acceptance, his honesty.

And I want to give him things, too.

I want him to know that we can be different this time around, if he fully lets me in. I want to assure him of the very thing I tend to doubt myself: That not everyone leaves. I want to start over.

The way he looks at me—eyes slightly wide and vulnerable—tells me that he wants to start over, too.

My phone is buzzing.

I open one eye. The phone is faceup, rattling against the glass top of my nightstand. Staccato vibrations, the kind that indicate a series of texts arriving in quick succession. Not my phone, I realize: Sebastian's.

"Mmm." Sebastian groans in my ear.

I roll to face him, then throw my leg over his hip. He pulls me closer, until my face is buried in his neck. I'm wearing his T-shirt. He's wearing . . . not much at all.

I have no idea what time it is. We've been wrapped up in each other for hours, our dinner reservation long forgotten.

More buzzing. I smile against his throat and say, "I think that's for you."

He grumbles again but stretches one long arm across me and grabs the phone.

"Everything okay?" I ask, thinking of Bubba.

He scans the screen. Smiles. "Very okay. Nothing that can't wait." He returns the phone to the nightstand, then crouches over me, grinning wolfishly. "Now what?"

I grin back and prop myself up on my elbows, so I'm right next to his ear. "Now?" I lower my voice to my best sexy whisper. "I'm thinking pizza. And a biiiig glass of water."

A laugh shudders through him. "Fair enough. You work on the first, I'll work on the second?"

I nod. He drops a kiss on my forehead and then heads for the kitchen.

I'm scanning the room for my own phone to call the pizza place when Sebastian's buzzes again. Reflexively I look over. It's still unlocked from when he checked it, and I let my eyes linger a little longer than they should. The first notification is a calendar reminder for something called a Q4 planning meeting happening tomorrow morning. I recognize the name of the supply chain company Sebastian worked for in the subject line. The rest are all texts from someone named Gina. There's a contact photo in the little bubble: A pretty redhead. The preview text says **Attachment: 5 photos.**

Another buzz. Gina says: **Can't wait to show you more tomorrow. ;)**

My stomach twists.

"Drink up."

I whirl around to face Sebastian, accepting the water glass with a forced smile. "Thanks."

I take a sip as he collapses on the bed. I want to climb on top of him. Ignore the sinking feeling in my gut and pick up where we left off before we fell asleep.

Instead I sit on the edge of the bed, my back toward him, and brace myself to ask the question I should have asked hours ago, before I let myself get swept up in the past. The question I know could change everything.

"Does your boss in Santa Barbara still think you're coming back?" I say to the wall. "Is that the plan, if all this doesn't work out?"

For a moment the only sound is the rustle of sheets as he moves to sit next to me. He runs a hand through his hair.

"I'm still figuring all that out," he admits, and my heart feels like it's wrenching in my chest. "That job . . . it's been so good to me during a really shitty time. I can't afford to let go of it until I figure out what I'm going to do next."

I nod, clarity lapping over me like the tide on the shore. He's talking about his job, but couldn't he just as easily be talking about me? The time we've spent together *has* been good, the way any convenient distraction is. It also isn't his real life.

"I don't think we should keep doing this," I say, hating the words as they tumble out.

Sebastian's eyes dart to mine, his expression pained. "Lina, please. This has nothing to do with how I feel about you." He reaches for my hand, but I pull it away. I can't afford for my judgment to be influenced by the feeling of his skin on mine. "I don't even know if I'll go back to California, but if I do we can still be together. Split time between the two."

I shake my head, thinking of what he said about Claire suggesting they try long distance, when they couldn't get on the same page about where to live. How all it would have done was delay the inevitable. Then I think of the messages from Gina on his phone. Maybe they're totally innocuous and maybe they're not, but they sent me spiraling. How would I stay sane if he moved to the opposite coast, surrounded by Claires and Ginas?

"You could come with me, then," he says, and the hopefulness in his voice breaks my heart even more. "We can figure this out. Together."

It's scary how easy it is to picture myself saying yes. To imagine changing my whole life to accommodate him. But then I think about how little that could leave me with in the end, if he decided I wasn't enough again.

I don't want to risk finding out.

"You don't know what you want, Sebastian. And that's okay. You already have so much going on. You should focus on yourself right now. And your mom. I can't just be another thing you're trying to 'figure out.'"

He drags a hand down his face, and when he looks back at me I can tell something has shifted. "You're afraid, Lina. You're afraid because there are some unknowns right now, so you're pushing me away. But what's going on with my family has nothing to do with us."

"Can you blame me? You don't exactly have a track record of balancing the two." I regret the words as soon as they've left my mouth.

He winces. "Wow. That was a really shitty thing to say."

I squeeze my eyes shut. "It was. I'm sorry. I shouldn't—"

"You're afraid," he repeats. "It's the same fear keeping you at that job, writing stories you don't even believe in anymore instead of taking a risk and going somewhere that actually values you. Instead of betting on yourself."

I bristle. First at the harshness of his words, and then at the truth in them.

So many people had warned me it would be next to impossible to make it as a writer in New York City, which only made me want it more. I'd thought I'd proven them wrong when I got the job at *Ever After*, only to have it all ripped away from me after just one year. I think about how scared and humiliated I'd felt when I was first laid off. The long, anxiety-riddled days spent applying for jobs, alone at my parents' house while they worked. The steady stream of rejection emails that followed. Wanting that life as badly as I had made losing it all the more crushing. Maybe Sebastian is right: Maybe I thought I could protect myself from all that potential heartache if I just stopped wanting in the first place.

It's the same defensive mechanism I can feel myself reverting to right now, and yet I can't seem to override it. With Sebastian, I'll want far too much.

"Believe it or not, I'm perfectly happy with my life, Sebastian," I say. "When I first took the job at Shore Life I thought I'd stay a little while, save some money, then start applying to jobs in the city again. But then the months turned into years, and you know what? I started to realize that maybe moving on from this place like everyone else just isn't in the cards for me. Maybe this is where I'm supposed to be, and maybe that isn't as bad as everyone seems to think it is."

"Of course you don't have to go back to the city if you don't want to!" He throws up his hands, exasperated. "Who are these people saying Brantley Beach is so bad? I don't understand where that's coming from."

I laugh, incredulous. "Um, you?"

Sebastian looks at me like I've just told him two plus two equals five, but then realization hits him. "Lina, that was fifteen years ago. I was a kid—a kid who grew up with a mom whose life was consumed by keeping a small business alive and a dad who resented her for it. I associated a lot of our family problems with being tied to this town, and I latched on to the idea that leaving it would fix them—or at least prevent me from ending up with the same ones. It's not because I thought I was better than you, or anyone else who comes back. Hell, everyone I care about is still here!"

Does that include me? I feel the doubt settle in. He could easily just be talking about Bubba and Andre and Theo and Hana. Yet again I find myself wondering where exactly I fit in. If I fit at all.

"Whatever the original reasons were, you were adamant about not wanting to end up here until a couple of months ago, and you're still not sure you want to stay now. And that's fine, Sebastian, it really is. But I hope you understand that I need to just remove myself from the equation. For my own sake."

Sebastian furrows his brow, the disappointment apparent in his eyes. "Is that really what you want, Lina?"

I suck in a few deep breaths, until I feel my heart rate resume a normal pace. I know that I'm lashing out because I'm angry and hurt, and that he's probably doing the same. But now that I've let those raw emotions bubble to the surface, what I'm left with underneath is a feeling of overwhelming sadness. Because Sebastian wasn't a bad guy back then, and he isn't now. We just can never seem to get the timing right.

"It's what I want," I say.

He places a palm on either side of my cheek. Then he leans forward, presses his lips to my forehead and says, "Then I'll go."

We sit like that for a few minutes, our foreheads touching, not saying a thing, until he gets up, dresses quietly and leaves.

Chapter 31

Now

The sound of the building buzzer wakes me from a fitful sleep. I groan, rotating my face deeper into my pillow.

Another buzz.

I thrust off the covers and say aloud, to no one, "Fine! I'm coming."

Arms crossed over my sweatshirt, I trudge to the hall, tap the microphone on the intercom and ask, "Who is it?"

"Delivery." A gruff voice. "Leaving it here." The microphone clicks off.

I groan again but slip on my flip-flops and pad out of my unit and down the steps, to the front entrance. I open the door to a large cardboard box paneled with *Jeni's Ice Creams* in loopy orange script.

Maren. I let out a pitiful laugh.

Jeni's is our heartbreak tradition.

In high school we nursed snubs from boys and mean-girl slights over cones at Twisters. But when our friendship became long distance in college, we discovered a shippable alternative in the midwestern creamery.

Wherever tragedies big and small appeared, the colorful ice cream pints followed. Like when my grandmother died three weeks into my freshman year and a box showed up outside my residence hall, frosty from the dry ice. Or the time Maren came down with the flu and had to miss her first big New York Fashion Week event. Even after college the shipments continued. The week I was laid off from *Ever After*, I ate bowls of Texas Sheet Cake for dinner three nights in a row.

And now, the morning after I told her my summer fling with Sebastian Nikolaou had come to an abrupt end, I'm receiving a breakup box.

I crouch to inspect it, wondering if she'd gone with my longtime favorite—Brambleberry Crisp—or a limited-edition flavor, or a combination of a few. A typed delivery note taped to one side flaps in the breeze.

L—he's an idiot. Also, check your email. Love, M

I pull my phone out of my back pocket and open the black hole that is my nonwork Gmail app. I scroll past DSW promo codes and Goodreads updates until I find one from an unfamiliar address, confirming a two-person reservation for afternoon tea at Fortnum & Mason this Saturday.

In *London*.

I tap into my WhatsApp thread with Maren. **Got the pity pints—now tell me what you did???**

I return my phone to my pocket, pick the box up with both hands and head back upstairs. She responds as I'm cracking open a pint called Frosé.

I knew you wouldn't let me buy you a plane ticket, but this res is much harder to get. If you don't show up I'll be pissed. :)

Maren wants me to have tea with her. In London. This weekend.

My thumbs freeze above the screen as I wait for the excuses to echo in my mind.

For once, I can't really come up with any.

Another message appears: **You've been wanting to come for years, Leens. What better time than now?**

I scan my apartment and realize Sebastian is everywhere: kissing me against the counter, sipping coffee on the balcony, carrying me into my room. There's no denying that I could do with a change of scenery. Then I think about work. I assigned almost a dozen stories and won't be getting drafts in until next week. Not to mention, I have yet to take a true vacation as a working adult. If Mandy gives me a hard time about the last-minute PTO request, I could remind her of that, maybe attach an article about millennial burnout to underscore my point.

I grab my laptop and start looking into flights.

Chapter 32

Now

"Like it?" Maren asks, beaming as she takes my suitcase handle from me. It's Friday night, and we're standing in the entryway of her Soho flat.

"Love," I say, taking everything in. I'm thirty-five hundred miles and a seven-hour flight from home, but the apartment I'm standing in doesn't feel foreign at all: It feels exactly like a place my best friend would live. The kitchen—filled with the delicious scent of whatever Maren has in the oven—is small but pretty, with a green-tile backsplash and white appliances on one side and a freestanding, wood-topped island on the other, a rack of copper cookware suspended above it. The kitchen opens into a living room with a leather love seat, a mosaic coffee table and an assortment of pillows and throws that don't match but somehow go together. There's no TV, the focal point of the room instead the array of colorful abstract artwork and designer fashion sketches on the walls. "It's so *you*."

I follow Maren down the narrow hallway, which is lined with more art, to the spare bedroom to get settled.

It's almost 10:00 p.m. (my usual bedtime) in London but

only 5:00 in my body clock, and Maren is a lifelong night owl. So, after I've showered and changed, I sit at the island, where she plates roast chicken and potatoes and pours us each a glass of prosecco.

"What are we celebrating?" I ask.

Maren places a hand on her chin, swirling her glass with the other as she dramatically ponders my question. "Us," she says finally. "We're celebrating the fact that no matter where we live or work, no matter who else comes in or out of our lives, we'll always have each other. That's no small thing."

I blink back the sting of threatening tears as we raise our glasses. "To us."

If the change of scenery isn't already enough to distract me from unwanted thoughts, our jam-packed itinerary certainly is. Maren wants us to get all the touristy stuff out of the way so that we can spend the rest of my weeklong trip like locals. So, that weekend we cover as much ground as we can—tours of the National Gallery and Tower of London, lunch at Borough Market, shopping on the closed blocks of Portobello Road, pints in Shoreditch, a West End show and, of course, our coveted afternoon at Fortnum & Mason, a high-end department store with a tea salon on the top floor, where we gorge ourselves on Earl Grey, scones and clotted cream.

Maren had warned me to prepare for London's gloomy gray days, but the weekend turns out to be one of the sunniest she can remember since moving here. We tie our jackets around our waists, marveling at the clear blue skies. She tells every shopkeeper and tour guide and server we meet that I brought the sunshine with me.

On Monday, Maren has to go to the office for a few meetings, so I spend the day perusing bookstores and boutiques. We meet up again for dinner at her favorite Indian restaurant, then roll ourselves over to a pub having trivia night.

The place is packed, the announcer already rattling off the team names. We're about to duck back outside when someone calls out, "You're all right! We'll take two more on our team."

Maren tugs me toward a booth in the corner of the pub right next to the bar, where the voice had come from. Two guys sit on one side, and a third stands and pulls up a chair, gesturing for us to take his side of the booth. I'd have been hesitant to join a table of strange men, but earlier that day a woman had helped herself to the second chair at my small table at the café where I'd grabbed lunch without uttering a word. I'd texted Maren about it, and she'd sent me a crying/laughing emoji in reply. Apparently, my hesitation to share a table in a public space is so very American.

"Thanks for letting us join you guys," I say, sliding into the booth after Maren. The men across from us look harmless enough, if a little nerdy. (As someone with her own nerdy tendencies, I'm allowed to think this.) One is bald, with a reddish-brown beard and round wire glasses. The other has light brown skin and pale blue eyes, and he's wearing an anime T-shirt.

"Isn't it a bit strange how every time we try to be accommodating, we wind up with Americans on our team?" This is the third guy, the one who had called out to us. He's now leaning against the counter and gesturing for the bartender to pour us a round.

"Pay no mind to Krish," says the bearded one. "He gets cheeky when he's nervous for pub quiz. I'm Rory. This here's Jordan."

"Pleasure," says Jordan. "We'll pray they have one of those Hollywood categories. I can never keep all those American actors' names straight."

Krish returns to his seat and deposits five pint glasses of pale gold ale on the table. I shift to get a better look at him. He's well over six feet tall, with golden-brown eyes and thick black hair that he pushes off his forehead, only for it to fall back again. Handsome. The smirk on Maren's face tells me she agrees.

"I'm Maren," she says, pulling one of the glasses toward her and passing another to me. "American, yes, but I've been living here for about six years. Lina's my best friend. She's visiting."

Krish asked, "Where in the States are you from?"

"New Jersey," Maren says.

"We grew up in a small town on the Shore," I add. Maren winces.

"Is that right?" Jordan straightens up in his seat. "I can't get enough of that show!"

It takes me a beat to realize he's talking about *Jersey Shore*, the one reality show I refuse to watch on principle. Maren's wince makes perfect sense now. I remember all the times I got this response in college from anyone not from the tristate area. I've been asked more than once if I personally know Snooki.

Maren scoffs. "Don't even get me started with those people. They're from New York!" She clinks her glass against mine. "You've got a couple of real Jersey girls here."

The guys let out a few hoots over this and raise their glasses to us. Then the announcer comes around, handing Krish a pen and an answer sheet.

The guys lean in, and Maren and I follow suit. Krish slings one arm across Rory's shoulders and the other across mine, scanning our huddle like he's about to deliver a pregame pep talk.

"Lina—you should know that this is no American trivia night. This . . ." Krish's voice is grave as he lifts his arms, gesturing around us. "This is pub quiz."

"It's proper serious," Jordan adds.

Rory nods. "We've got a reputation to uphold."

"Tell us, ladies," says Krish. "What are your specialties?"

I glance sidelong at Maren, finding a slightly wary expression that I'm sure reflects my own.

"Um," I say. "I'm pretty good with pop culture?"

"I'm not the worst at geography. . . ." Maren offers, sounding uncertain for perhaps the first time in her life.

The guys look at each other, the disappointment in their expressions palpable.

And then they burst out laughing.

"Oh, piss off!" Maren says, but she's laughing, too, and so am I.

"We're shit," Krish says between laughs.

"Total rubbish!" Jordan agrees.

"You just come for the cheap pints, then?" I ask once I've caught my breath.

Krish locks eyes with me and flashes a dazzling smile. "She gets it, lads."

Under the table, Maren squeezes my knee. I place my palm over hers and squeeze back. A wave of gratitude for my best friend washes over me because this night—this whole trip—is exactly what I need.

Krish is right: They're rubbish at trivia.

Which isn't to say they aren't smart. Quite the opposite: Over the course of the night, we learn that Rory is getting his PhD in environmental science, Jordan is an engineer and Krish is in specialty training—the UK equivalent of residency—for neurology. The Achilles' heel for this particular trivia team is that they can never seem to agree on which answer to put on the paper, and they often run the clock down while heatedly arguing about it. For ninety percent of the questions tonight, whoever the majority ruled against wound up being right.

I can't remember a night I've laughed this much.

After a crushing final round—Maren proved her geography chops after all by supplying the names of two Mesopotamian rivers, but we tanked the photo challenge and the debate over which artist to put down for the musical bonus got so contentious I wondered if Jordan and Rory would still be on speaking terms tomorrow—we all stumble to a wine bar across the street.

Maren, Rory and Jordan huddle around one of the two available high-top tables and quickly become engrossed in a good-natured argument about whether *Friends* or *Seinfeld* is the best American sitcom. (The boys groan when Maren also makes a pitch for *Sex and the City*.) Which leaves Krish and me at the other.

"Tell me, Jersey. What is it you write about?" Krish asks me. When we'd talked about our occupations earlier, Maren had wrapped an arm around me and exclaimed proudly, "She's a writer! A great one." I'd blushed but left it at that.

"I mostly write about weddings," I say, twirling the stem of my wineglass. "Sorry to disappoint, if Maren made you think I'm a literary genius or something."

I expect Krish to smile, nod and change the subject, but when I look up I see his expression has brightened. "A wedding writer! I imagine that'd be quite nice—to write stories about love every day."

I offer a weak smile. "It certainly beats the news cycle most days."

"Do you believe in soulmates, then?" Krish cocks his head. "Fate and all that?"

I think about it for a moment. And surprise myself by saying, "No. I don't think I do."

He eyes me curiously. "That's not very romantic for a wedding writer to admit," he says, mouth curled in a playful half smirk. I shrug, meeting his eyes.

"I don't either," he admits. *Good*, I think. Cynics love company.

He leans toward me across the table and lowers his voice. "What's so romantic about not having a say in who you love?" I narrow my eyes, wondering where he's going with this and if I'm sober enough for the journey. For me there's always been a distinct precipice right before I'm drunk and the world goes fuzzy. A moment when everything feels heightened and crisp. A clear sky before the fog settles in. "About having it decided for you? Choosing to love someone, despite knowing that there are a million other people out there you could potentially connect with . . . knowing that there are a million other ways to be happy, or a million other ways to have your heart broken, but committing to that one person anyway. I think that's as romantic as it gets."

"I feel like I've heard this on a podcast," I say, deliberately ruining the mood.

"Piss off," he says, but in a playful way.

"In all seriousness, I hear you with this lining of thinking. But also? You could just, like, not open yourself up to heartbreak in the first place. That actually seems like the safest option of all, am I wrong?"

"Who ever said we were talking about safety?"

We weren't, I think. But apparently I'm *thinking* about it.

Krish is still eyeing me when my phone buzzes on the table between us. He politely takes a sip of his beer and glances toward the bar while I check it.

My stomach flips when I read Sebastian's name in the bubble on my screen. I swipe to open the message.

Heard you're in London. No need to respond. Mom had some good news this week. I'm heading back to Santa Barbara for a while. Just wanted you to know.

I cycle through a jumble of emotions as I read over the text three more times. Excitement that he reached out. Relief that Bubba is doing better. Disappointment that he's taking the first chance to skip town. Validation that I'd been right.

I consider not responding, but my fingers have a mind of their own, crafting a message that's sensitive to Bubba but indifferent to her messenger.

I'm glad to hear about your mom. Please keep me updated

on how she's doing, and let her know I'll be here for her if she needs anything.

"Everything all right?" Maren asks.

I look up, startled to find her in Krish's place. Over her shoulder, I see that he's taken her spot with his friends at the other table. My rudeness must have scared him off. Great.

I shake my head. Hand her my phone instead of explaining.

"Jesus, Nikolaou," she murmurs. I just nod slowly. Then she says, "He likes you."

I shoot her a look. But then I realize she's talking about Krish.

"Well, easy for him to say. He barely knows me."

"Some would argue that's kind of the point."

The guys call to us from the bar, where they're ordering one last round. As I sip the water I'd requested instead of another glass of wine, catching Krish's eyes across our circle every now and then, I decide that maybe Maren is right. There's something to be said for liking someone in the moment and just running with that. Maybe for once I could under-think it.

I planned to slip into the guest room without waking Maren—and I would have succeeded if I hadn't stubbed my toe as I was rounding the corner into the hallway.

"*Fuck*," I hiss under my breath.

I jump back to avoid the pillow that sails through Maren's open bedroom door and into the hallway.

"How dare you try to sneak past me!" Maren whisper-scolds. "Full report. Stat."

I tiptoe into her room with my shoulders slumped, like a teenager caught climbing back inside through a window. Maren is sitting up in her bed, the wispy strands of her blow-dried bob sticking to her cheeks as she glares at me with a mix of admiration and suspicion. She eyes my slightly askew clothing and points to her dresser. Obediently, I open the middle drawer and pull out a soft pajama set, like I used to back in middle and high school when I'd decide to sleep over Maren's at the last minute. No matter that this time my own pajamas are in the next room, tradition stands.

Maren falls back on her pillow while I change, then holds up her duvet so I can slide in next to her.

"So," she says, raising a brow. We lie side by side, our faces half hidden by our pillow halos.

"So."

"So am I going to have to beg you for details?"

I sigh, thinking about how Maren and I used to spin a single look from a boy one of us liked into an hours-long postgame analysis. Why is it that now, when so much more is happening, there doesn't seem to be as much to say?

"He's hot," I say finally. "And funny. And actually a very nice guy." I shrug. "I think it'd be easy for me to be with him. Or . . . not him, exactly, considering the whole *he lives in London and is a doctor with no personal life* thing. But someone like him. I think I could be happy with someone like Krish."

Maren smirks. "Well, that's quite a wholesome conclusion to make from a one-night stand. Very on-brand for you."

I give her a shove.

After the last round at the wine bar, I'd surprised both myself and Maren by agreeing to go back to Krish's flat. Despite her earlier encouragement, when faced with the reality of my disappearing into the night with a stranger in a foreign country, my best friend's face pinched with worry. But once I'd assured her that I'd stopped drinking more than an hour earlier, confirmed she had my location on Find My Friends and reminded her that I was a twenty-nine-year-old woman who did not want to insult the universe by rejecting its generous offer of a very handsome, well-educated rebound with a British accent, she agreed to let me go.

Krish's flat was spare and tidy—more like a hotel room than

a home, which made sense given what I'd learned about his lifestyle during our conversation at the wine bar. He worked long shifts at the hospital, and he spent most of his free hours sleeping. Maren and I had crossed paths with the guys on a night when their schedules had all aligned—something that he said was becoming more and more rare these days.

He'd led me to the kitchen and held up two beverage options—a decanter of whiskey and a pitcher of water. He laughed as I eagerly pointed to the latter. After I downed the water that he poured for me, we had a brief but steamy kitchen make-out. Then we relocated to the living room and had a less-brief but equally steamy couch make-out, which turned into brief but fairly enjoyable sex. Then I called an Uber.

I recount all of this to Maren, who listens with rapt attention at first but gradually loses steam, her white-blond eyelashes fluttering with a sleepy heaviness. I yawn. Maybe we aren't running out of things to say, just energy to say them.

As I drift toward sleep, the cinema of my mind settles on a screening not of Krish's flat, but the ride back to Maren's. I'd spent the better part of it rereading Sebastian's text message. The evening had felt monumental: proof that Sebastian wasn't the only man on earth worth my attention, and that I could enjoy being with someone without my heart catching fire. And yet there I was, still thinking about Sebastian. I'd told myself not to get carried away and had done just that. All these years later and I still haven't learned my lesson.

I tell myself that I will now, though. When I get home things will be different. I'll be different.

"I'm sorry things didn't work out with Sebastian," Maren says, her eyes closed. My best friend, the mind reader.

"Go ahead. Say, 'I told you so.'"

Her eyes snap open. "I would never."

I squeeze her hand. "I know that. But seriously, I want you to know I'm okay," I say, realizing it's mostly true. "I'm sad, but I'm not crushed. It wasn't meant to be."

"Good." She sounds relieved. "And with a few more handsome distractions like tonight? You won't be sad for long."

I laugh, shaking my head. "Honestly? The whole Sebastian thing has made me realize I have bigger problems than my love life." My smile falters. "I feel stuck."

Maren scans my face, lips pursed in thought. "You're not stuck, Leens."

I raise a brow, skeptical.

"Being stuck means you *can't* move on. It's out of your control," she says. "What you are is more . . . stagnant."

"That sounds much better," I say dubiously.

She rolls her eyes, but in a good-natured way. "I think you just need to shake things up a little. Think about the things you don't like about your life that *are* in your control, and make a conscious choice to change them."

"You make it sound so easy."

"It's not," she concedes. "Leaving the comfort of what you know—it's hard. Remember my first year out here? I was so homesick I almost quit."

I do remember. Maren is so happy and settled now that I sometimes forget how much she struggled in the beginning. It's the reason I instituted our standing weekly FaceTimes and kept our WhatsApp chat active with voice memos and memes. I wanted Maren to always feel like she had a tether to home.

"How did you convince yourself it was worth sticking out?" I ask.

She considers this. "I guess I told myself that the discomfort wouldn't last forever. That one day I'd wake up and realize this big, scary thing I'd been doing had just become my normal, everyday life."

"I'm really proud of you, Mar."

She scrunches up her face, like the teary-eye emoji. Then we're quiet for a little, our words hanging in the air. I'm in and out of sleep when she speaks again.

"Also?" she says softly. "I reminded myself that I wasn't

actually alone. You, my parents, my grandparents—I had this whole support system rooting for me. It's easier to take a leap when you have people to catch you."

It's the last thing I hear before I let my eyelids flutter shut for good.

Chapter 33
Now

I decide to quit my job on the flight home from London.

If I'm honest with myself, I've been toying with the idea for a while. But ultimately it's Maren's words—and an email from Mandy—that drive the nail into that coffin.

I purchase the ten-dollar in-flight WiFi and watch as my inbox shoots up to four hundred unread messages. Avoiding my Outlook app all week felt like a good PTO boundary until now. I scan through PR pitches and invitations to local events to see if I've missed anything urgent. I haven't, but I do spot a message from Mandy, requesting a draft of my Q4 editorial calendar as soon as I'm back on Monday, including ten pitches for "Real Weddings." No mention of the promotion we're supposedly revisiting in September or factoring in time to focus on new verticals.

The thought of scouring the Instagram feeds of local photographers for recently engaged couples who would make good candidates for "Real Weddings" makes me feel physically ill. Ditto for returning to the office Monday and having to interact with Mandy and Jenny. I don't even want to face David, who will take one look at me and know that I'm hanging on by a thread.

But as much as I'd love to fire off a snarky reply to Mandy, then march into her office and quit on the spot, I know that this is real life. I need a plan first.

So, I spend the rest of the seven-hour flight drawing one up.

I decide I'll finish out the month at Shore Life, simultaneously getting my contacts in order and lining up some freelance work. After Labor Day, I'll put in my two weeks' notice. No turning back.

It's a big, scary leap, but I'm finally ready to take it.

About halfway through the flight an attendant pushes a beverage cart down the aisle, and I order a Bloody Mary to celebrate. I empty the plastic shooter of vodka and the mini tomato juice can into a clear plastic cup and sip on the concoction like it's a fine wine. My seatmates exchange a look that falls somewhere between amusement and mild concern. I don't care. I'm toasting to my freedom.

The second the wheels of the plane hit the ground I switch my phone out of airplane mode and message Maren to let her know that I landed. Then I call my mom, who confirms she's in the cell-phone lot waiting for me.

"Are you starving?" she asks. "If you aren't in a rush to get back, we could grab something. Or we could stop home. I have plenty of things I could make you." I smile into the phone. Everything changes, but somehow my parents don't.

"That sounds great," I say. "I'm not in a rush at all."

"Oh, good! Dad and I are *dying* to hear about your trip."

"Absolutely," I say. "I have a lot to tell you, actually."

My parents convince me to spend the night. When I tell them my plan to quit Shore Life and pivot to freelancing, they're nothing but supportive. Part of me had wondered if they'd try to talk me out of it—I wouldn't blame them if they thought forgoing the stability of a staff position was a little brash. But they're the kind of parents who always told me I could do anything I set my mind to and actually seemed to believe it. Unconditional confidence.

I email Mandy to let her know I picked up a cold on the plane and am going to work from home all week. She's a germaphobe so she doesn't question it. David, on the other hand, can tell something's up after three Slack messages and quickly wrestles the truth out of me over the phone. I make him swear to secrecy until the following Tuesday, when I plan to tell Mandy the news. Again I brace for pushback, but he doesn't even seem surprised. He admits he's been applying to other roles, too. We agree that we've both outgrown Shore Life. I know I'll be leaving with our friendship, and that's enough to make the last six years feel worth it.

One night turns into one week.

My parents are taking a bucket list trip to Italy next month, so I stay with them under the pretense of helping them prepare for it. I help them book tours and save shopping and restaurant recommendations to Google Maps. They joke that they should be paying me instead of their travel agent. We don't talk about why I'm really there, which I'm not certain of myself but suspect has to do with this being the place I stayed last time I was jobless. I remind myself that this time it's my decision, but still. After I quit I want to come home to a place where other people are in charge of me.

My parents have never been huge drinkers. A glass of wine with dinner on the porch in the summer, sure. Maybe two on a holiday or special occasion. So I smile when we sit down to dinner on Labor Day and my dad pulls a dusty bottle off the rack and starts twisting out the cork. He pours a glass for each of us, then raises his.

"To our baby, Angelina. You make us so proud every day."

I roll my eyes to reroute the tears I feel forming and nudge him. "Who knew quitting my job would make you guys so sentimental. Or maybe it's this trip you're taking."

My mom shoots my dad a playful glare. She's such a lightweight that just holding the glass probably makes her feel tipsy. "Could be that. We've only waited decades for it."

"I'm glad you're finally going, but I still don't get why you guys waited so long. You've been talking about Italy for as long as I can remember, Ma."

My dad waves a hand. "Your mother's all talk, Leens. I told her so many times over the years, say the word and we'll set the money aside and make it happen. She'd always come up with one excuse or another to put it off."

I straighten in my chair. This is news to me. Money was pretty tight at times growing up, and I figured my parents considered taking an extravagant trip like that to be selfish, irresponsible—something to dream about and nothing more. "Ma?"

My mother shrugs. Her cheeks are flushed red from the wine, like she's blushing. "I figured I'd get there eventually, but traveling just wasn't a priority for us, especially when you were young. I mean, we were lucky enough to be raising you in a place *other* people traveled to."

"Our lives are their vacation," I say, remembering a line my dad had said on more than one occasion when I was growing up. Usually it was said sarcastically, in a moment of frustration—while sitting in traffic driving anywhere south of our turnpike exit in the summer or circling to find parking at a local restaurant that we loved long before the tourists discovered it—but now the sentiment makes me smile.

My mom squeezes my dad's hand across the table, looking from him to me. "We had everything we wanted right here."

My dad pats my arm, linking us all for a moment, and says, "Still do."

The first tear finally spills over the threshold, and then

there's no use fighting any longer. I don't even lift my hands to intercept them as they fall.

My mom scoots her chair closer to mine and pulls me to her chest. "Talk to us, honey," she says into my hair.

The errant tears transform into ugly sobs. I force myself to wait until I can take a few slow breaths. My parents are patient people: I know they'll wait until I'm ready.

"I always thought," I say slowly, "the goal was to move on from here. A nice place to go home to, sure, but not somewhere to stay forever. I was so proud when I got the *Ever After* job. I was going to have this big-time career—this big-time life—in New York City." I squeeze my eyes shut, focusing on the feeling of my mom stroking my hair. "When I got laid off, I felt like such a failure."

"You're not a failure, honey," my dad says. "Not even close."

I continue anyway. "And then a month later Maren called to tell me she was staying in London after her internship ended. It felt like everyone else was moving on, and I was back to square one."

"Lina," my mom says, cupping my face with her hands until we're eye to eye. "Do you remember what you used to say you wanted to be when you grew up?"

I raise a brow. "A vet who could read pets' minds?"

My mom rolls her eyes. "After that."

I shrug, and my mom finally releases me. "Let's see. If I'm not mistaken I believe it went something like, 'Mom, I'm going to be a writer. And Maren's going to design clothes for famous people. We'll both probably work too hard to have boyfriends for a while but we'll have each other so it's fine.'"

"I personally was thrilled with the no-boyfriend part," my dad adds, helpfully.

"You're doing exactly what you said you would. Is it a little less glamorous than you pictured? Sure. Adulthood can be disappointing that way. But you earn money doing what you love.

You've got a great apartment. You have wonderful friends, you have family, your health." A series of affirmative nods from my dad. "From where we sit, you're doing just fine. And you know what, Lina?" My mom takes my hands in hers. "Maybe you're just not feeling a hundred percent happy, because you want even more. And that's okay. Because I have a feeling those other things you want will come when the timing is right. You're just getting started."

My mom squeezes my hands, and I squeeze back. Tonight I'll eat eggplant parm, watch *Dateline* with my parents (they've always disapproved of my reality TV habit, which feels a bit pot-and-kettle) and fall asleep in my childhood bedroom. Tomorrow, I'll leave the job that's been my safety net for the last six years and figure out what comes next.

Chapter 34

Now
Nine Months Later

I inch my car onto the exit ramp for Newark Liberty International Airport, cursing myself for offering my pickup services in bumper-to-bumper traffic. Next time Maren decides to book a last-minute flight home the Friday before Memorial Day Weekend, she can Uber.

She messaged me a week ago with a screenshot of her flight confirmation, saying the price tracker she used had alerted her that tickets were seventy percent cheaper than usual, which had to be a sign: She'd come home and kick off the summer with me in Brantley Beach.

My road rage instantly subsides when I enter the chaotic arrivals level and spot my best friend. Who am I kidding: I'm ecstatic. I spot an opening between two Ubers and whip into the space, avoiding eye contact with the traffic guy attempting to usher us all along. (My pride shudders at the thought of looping around.)

I pop the trunk so Maren can toss her suitcase in, then she jumps in the front seat, pulling the door shut in one swift motion. I peel out like a getaway driver.

"Impeccable timing," Maren says, catching her breath. Then, with a squeal, she leans across the console and side-hugs me.

I squeeze her back. "I hope you peed when you got off the plane, because we're going to be here a while." I nod toward the sea of taillights ahead of us. "Do me a favor? Text David and let him know we're going to be late."

Renting a house for the long weekend with David and Henry was Maren's idea. Of course, by the time she suggested it nothing was available—most rentals in the area were booked weeks, if not months, in advance of holiday weekends. But Henry's aunt is renovating an Airbnb that technically won't be ready until next season. She said we could stay there for free as long as we didn't mind that half the house was still under construction. The selling point for me was that it's on the harbor side rather than near the beach. It may be one of the biggest beach weekends of the year, but with Bubba's reopening for the season I plan to stay far away from the boardwalk.

I've managed to avoid any major Bubba's-related news for the last nine months—quite a feat, considering most of my freelance work is in the dining space. When I reached out to all my PR and culinary contacts from the new email address I'd set up, I intentionally left out Trina Stanford of Diamond Group. Any updates she's sending to my Shore Life address are going into the void, which is more than fine with me. All I know is what my parents have told me: that Bubba's has been closed for renovations since September and is reopening this weekend under new management.

It's also been nine months since I've heard from Sebastian. I assume he's been in Santa Barbara since the single text he sent me while I was in London. I have no idea if he'll be back for the reopening this weekend, or if he's still involved with Bubba's at all.

I'd be lying, though, if I said I wasn't hurt by the fact that he hasn't reached out. I can accept the fact that he didn't want to have anything more than a summer fling with me, that he was less than truthful about his commitment to keeping the restaurant, and even that he hightailed it to California the first chance he got. But what I have trouble accepting is his decision to not even text me the occasional update on his mom.

In October, once I realized I wouldn't be getting any updates from Sebastian, I went over to her house to check in myself. I'd texted her and asked if I could come by under one condition: I didn't want to talk about Sebastian. She agreed, and I've been meeting her for lunch or coffee about once a month ever since. For the most part, we keep our conversations to safe topics: her health (she continues to respond well to the new treatment she began in August), my freelancing and general town gossip. A perfect arrangement.

When Maren and I pull into the circular driveway an hour and a half later, I immediately feel guilty—because, fully renovated or not, this is a *really* nice house.

Henry meets us outside to help with our bags.

"Ohmygod, this is incredible," Maren says, pulling Henry into a hug.

He greets me next. "Seriously," I say, "your aunt did not have to do this."

Maren squeals. "I'm pumped she did, though!"

Henry makes a *no-big-deal* gesture with one hand. "Don't thank me yet. David's in charge of dinner."

"Aw," I say, closing the trunk, "he's a great cook!"

"Yes, well," he says with a sly smile. "The food will be delicious, but I'd avoid the kitchen for the next hour unless you want to be Gordon Ramsay'd."

Henry shows us to our room. Three of the five bedrooms are out of commission, so Maren and I are sharing a kids' room with two twin beds, fading white carpet and seashell wallpaper.

"They haven't started on this one yet, so it's a bit outdated," Henry says. "But I kind of love the classic beach-house feel of it."

I couldn't agree more. "It's perfect."

Maren and I change and unpack, then bound down the staircase like elementary schoolers. We say hello to a frenzied David, who pours us both a glass of rosé before shooing us toward the wraparound porch so he can finish cooking (and stress-scolding Henry). We sit at the big eucalyptus dining table and watch the boats in the harbor, sipping our wine. Maren catches me up on the latest with her job (she was promoted again a few months ago) and her various suitors, and I tell her about stories I'm working on for a mix of local and national outlets: a history of saltwater taffy and its Atlantic City roots for *Food Network Magazine*, a roundup of the best new ice cream shops down the Shore for NJ.com and an essay about cooking through my grandmother's handwritten recipe box with my mom for Food52. Maren says how proud she is of me, and for once I don't deflect. I'm proud of me, too.

Henry joins us a little while later, and we help him set the table.

The meal is incredible. The stress on David's face lessens with each course. A watermelon salad with feta and mint. Scallops in a saffron sauce. Lobster tails. Somewhat reluctantly, David had agreed to let me be in charge of dessert, so we finish the meal with espressos and a fancy blueberry cobbler, one of my favorite summer dessert recipes from New York Times Cooking (the next target on my freelance list), based on a dish from Chez Panisse. I ignore a ricochet comment from David about having California on the brain.

As we scrape our bowls clean and watch the sun set over the harbor, I feel overcome with a sense of peace. My mom was right: I have so much to be grateful for. Good food. Great friends who have stuck around regardless of where we've worked or lived. A beautiful place to call home. The beginning of a writing career I can be proud of. I'm finding my way.

The only thing still missing is a partner to share it all with. Someone who sees all of me—the good and the bad—and accepts me anyway. I want what my parents have. What David and Henry have. But I can wait for that.

Because in the meantime, I've been learning to accept myself. And that's more than enough for now.

I wake up the next morning around eight. Maren's bed is empty, so she must already be downstairs. This doesn't surprise me: It's early afternoon in London.

I locate a full pot of coffee in the kitchen and pour myself a mug, then find Maren on the porch. She's stretched along the bench swing, a mug of her own in one hand and a memoir in the other. When she sees me she scrunches her feet in so I can join her.

"Sleep okay?" I ask.

"Nope. I never learn my lesson with those late-night espressos. You?"

"Honestly? Yes. I slept better than I have in a while."

"Good." She peers over the top of her book. "You looked like you needed it more than me anyway."

I respond with a shove.

My book is upstairs, so I open Instagram, happy to aimlessly scroll for a bit. But when the very first post loads, my thumb freezes.

It's a photo of Sebastian in front of the restaurant, which confuses me at first—I unfollowed him months ago. But then I look at the handle: It isn't his personal account that posted, it's the professional one for Bubba's.

In the photo he's leaning against the side of the restaurant, smiling softly, hands in his pockets. The look in his eyes tells me that whoever took it may have caught him off guard slightly. It's a great picture of him. The caption reads: We're back—and we've got a great season in store for you. Our new café is open this morning! Official restaurant opening @ noon. Kick off the summer at your favorite place.

WE'RE READY FOR YOU! #BUBBASNJ #JERSEYSHORE #RESTAURANT #LOCALSUMMER.

I smile despite myself, because it's a typical Bubba's caption, probably written by Bubba herself. I remember the summer after my senior year of high school—my last summer working at the restaurant—when a few of us convinced her to create a business Instagram handle. A Facebook page wasn't enough anymore, we'd insisted. She'd resisted at first, then reluctantly agreed to give it a shot that season, populating the feed with grainy, sepia-toned food pictures reposted from diners, candids of the staff and horizontal shots of the boardwalk. She loved reading us the few comments that rolled in under each post, mostly from longtime customers who were just starting to use social media themselves. It wasn't exactly groundbreaking social content, but it was authentic.

I'm surprised that Sebastian does still appear to be involved, and that Diamond Group would approve of such an unpolished post. I assumed Trina Stanford would have installed an official social media manager to overhaul the account by now.

I notice three dots below the post, indicating that it's a carousel. I swipe to the second picture, which shows Omar in the kitchen, holding up a burger. This one surprises me even more: Did they decide to keep Omar, after all? I notice Omar is tagged—I didn't realize he had an Instagram—and click into it. My chest pounds when I read his bio: "Chef and co-owner @bubbasnj." I toggle back to the Bubba's post and swipe to the first photo. I click on Sebastian's handle. He's not private anymore, so even though I don't follow him I can see his full feed. His bio confirms what I'm already suspecting: "Jersey kid. Surfer. Co-owner and GM @bubbasnj."

But it's the third and final photo that causes me to audibly gasp.

"What is it?" Maren sits up, startled.

I'm silent, my thumbs hovering over the screen.

"Show me, Leens!" Maren reaches a hand toward my phone. I let her take it.

"The Jetty," she says, reading the sign in the picture—a picture that looks just like the sketch Sebastian had shown me in the snack bar last summer. "Wait—they went with Sebastian's café idea? This looks cool." She swipes backward through the rest of the carousel.

I nod. And then I wait as she taps around some more—because she's my best friend, and I know she'll do exactly what I did. I watch as she puts the pieces together.

"Oh. Oh, shit." She looks at me. "So Bubba didn't sell the restaurant to that New York group."

It's a statement, not a question, but I shake my head anyway.

"She sold it to . . . Sebastian and Omar."

I nod.

"And he's calling the café The Jetty." She looks back to the screen. "I mean, that's clearly . . ."

Reflexively, I run my hand along the scar on my thigh. I'm transported back to that day, the sensations eerily clear. Sebastian's arms bracing my body as he carried me. The back-seat fabric of his Jeep sticking to my skin while Maren stroked my hair. The vulnerability of his face as he slept in my hospital room.

"It might not mean anything," I say uncertainly. "The name—it could just be a coincidence. Right?"

Maren doesn't look up from my phone. "There's a Story, too. Can I click on it?"

"Only if you let me look, too," I say, hunching over her shoulder.

"It's not even eight thirty," David says, startling us both. We look up and find him squinting groggily at us. "Did I miss something already?"

Maren responds by patting the remaining sliver of cushion on the swing. David sits obediently, and we all huddle our heads together as Maren taps open the Story, pausing it with her thumb.

It's a screenshot of a digital article about the restaurant opening. Maren taps the "read more" link. She scrolls through a Q&A between the writer and Sebastian, stopping short when she gets to a question about the inspiration behind the new café's name.

Sebastian: I like what jetties symbolize. They're these man-made structures that protect the shoreline from erosion. You can also use them as walkways, or to dock ships. I want the café to serve a similar purpose in the community here. A place that preserves our legacy and keeps us connected. A kind of second home.

Interviewer: Sounds a lot like the role your mom's restaurant has played in the community for decades.

Sebastian: Exactly. (Clears throat.) And, yeah—it's also a word that makes me think about someone I really care about. Someone who has always felt like home to me.

My stomach flips.

"Keep scrolling!" David hisses.

Maren obeys.

Interviewer: That's quite a tribute. What does this "someone" think about everything?

Sebastian: I don't know yet. (Smiles.) I hope she'll be proud. Maybe if she reads this, she can tell me herself.

"What are you going to do?"

David's question jolts me back to the present. I'm still silent. Processing. I look to Maren but her eyes are on the harbor, expression unreadable.

"Let me ask you something, Lina," David says, squeezing my hand. "Why did things end between you two?"

"Because," I say, unsteadily, "it seemed like being with me—being here, in general—wasn't his real life. It was just temporary. Convenient for the summer. Just like our friendship always was." *Yes*, I think, gaining confidence. *That's right!* "I saw the writing on the wall. For once I didn't want to be the one who got left behind, so . . ."

"So?"

"So I ended it. Before he had the chance to."

This is the story I've been telling myself for months, but said aloud, I have to admit it carries more than a whiff of self-sabotage. David raises an eyebrow, nostrils flared, like he can smell it, too.

"But he's back now," he says. "For good, it seems."

"Does that really change anything, though? He's back, great—it's not like he came back for me."

"You don't know that! I'm sure a lot of factors were involved, but if you think you weren't one of them—a big one—I think you're selling yourself short."

"If he cares that much, he could have told me last summer. He didn't exactly put up a fight. And I haven't heard from him in nine months!"

Maren, I notice, remains uncharacteristically quiet. I can tell she's chewing the inside of her lip, a lifelong nervous habit. And, in many cases, a hint that she's hiding something.

Finally she says, "Right. So, about that." I raise a brow and try to ignore the sinking feeling in my stomach.

"I'm gonna make some more coffee," David proclaims. He gives my shoulder a gentle squeeze before disappearing into the house.

"Mar," I say once we're alone again. "What am I missing here?"

She grabs a cushion and buries her face in it. Whatever she says comes out muffled.

I pry the cushion out of her hands. "Try again."

"There's a reason Sebastian never reached out," she says.

We're sitting on the swing facing each other, and her eyes shift to our bent knees. "I think it had to do with a conversation we had."

"I don't understand," I say. "When?"

"Like, two months after London."

"You called him?" I ask, surprised.

She shakes her head. "He called *me*. He was worried about you. He wanted to know how you were doing."

My head spins as I turn over the new information. Sebastian had tried to check in?

"What did you tell him?" Maybe hearing how heartbroken I was from Maren scared him off all over again.

"I told him the truth," she says, finally meeting my eyes. "That you were doing better than you had been in a long time."

I narrow my eyes, trying to think back. That phone call must have happened in October. I was only a couple of weeks into freelancing, but already it was going better than I'd expected, my inbox full of assignments from local and national editors. I worked late most nights, packing my weekends to make up for it: home-cooked meals with my parents, lunches with Bubba, movie nights with David and Henry. I'd even met Hana for coffee and agreed to go bowling with one of her brother's single friends. There wasn't necessarily a spark, but it had felt good to put myself out there.

I was far from having everything figured out, but I realize Maren is right: I'd been doing pretty well, all things considered.

"He told me he missed you, and that he was thinking of calling you," Maren continues.

I shake my head. "He never called me, though."

She purses her lips, and my stomach twists with realization.

"You told him not to," I say softly.

Maren nods, her gaze drifting to the harbor.

"Why?" My voice breaks on the word.

"I asked him what the point of calling you would be, and he said he wanted to tell you that he still had feelings for you." I suck in a breath, my heart thrumming in my chest. "But when I pressed him for a concrete plan—what he wanted, and how you fit into it—he couldn't give me one. He said he still had a lot he was trying to figure out." Her eyes shift back to mine. "It really pissed me off, you know? So I said that if I were him, I wouldn't bother calling, or ever speaking to you again. I told him that if he cared about you as much as he said he did, he'd finally let you go."

The reality of Maren's betrayal sets in, and I'm momentarily speechless as I try to fit this new puzzle piece into the picture I have of the last nine months. Sebastian had wanted to reach out. Had held on to hope for the future. But the person who knows me better than anyone had advised him not to—without ever confirming what *I* wanted.

Maren reaches for my hands. "Please say something, Leens."

"Why didn't you tell me about that conversation?" I think of all the opportunities she's had to tell me in the time since they talked, all the FaceTimes and messages we've exchanged with this secret between us.

She shakes her head. "I should have. I knew I shouldn't have gotten involved, especially not behind your back like that. But I was just so *angry* at him. For sucking you in again only to let you down, but also for not seeing this fucking amazing person who has always been right in front of him." She leans toward me. "I told myself I would tell you eventually, but then you hit your stride freelancing. You were *thriving*. I didn't want to throw a curveball at you. I know you hate me right now, Leens, but try to see it through my eyes."

I feel hurt and confused and angry, but I squeeze my eyes shut and try to do what she's asked. I think back to our conversation in London, when I told her how stuck I felt. What I'd been doing wasn't working. If Sebastian had reached out to me back then, who's to say I wouldn't have gotten sucked right back into his orbit? Good intentions aside, he still didn't really know what he wanted.

Then another thought hits me: If someone had treated Maren that way, would I have handled it any differently?

When I look at Maren again I can see that she's blinking back tears. I reach across the swing for her hand.

"I could never hate you, Mar," I say as she turns toward me. "You know that."

"But you're really mad," she says.

I cock my head. "I'm a *little* mad."

Her face falls. "I'm a terrible person."

"Hey," I say, pouting my lip. "Don't talk about my best friend that way."

She smiles weakly.

"I really wish you had trusted me to make the decision myself, but I get it," I say. "You were just trying to protect me."

Maren lets out a sigh of relief and throws her arms around me.

"I'm so sorry," she says into my shoulder.

"Any more secrets you need to get off your chest?"

"None. Ever again." She pulls back to look at me. "I think you should talk to him, though."

I give her a quizzical look. "Nothing has changed, Mar. Everything you said is still true. What makes you suddenly think this time would be any different?"

"Actually? I'd argue a pretty big factor has changed."

I squint at her.

She nudges me playfully and says, "You."

Me.

I've changed?

I let the thought wash over me like a wave.

A lot *has* changed in the last nine months. I took a huge career risk. It's a hustle for sure and trying to figure out how to do my taxes as a freelancer nearly sent me begging to Mandy for my job back, but I've never felt so professionally fulfilled. I took an epic trip with my best friend. I strengthened my relationships with friends and family. I've been more present than I've felt since I was a kid. I'm not stagnant anymore—I'm moving forward.

Ever since I met Sebastian, I've let him be in the driver's seat. If he decided he wanted to be with me, then we'd be together. The proverbial ball never left his court. So I blamed what happened last summer on the fact that he wasn't ready for me, just like when we were teenagers. But the truth is that I hadn't been ready for him, either.

I jump to my feet, pulling Maren with me. "Can you lend me something to wear?"

My best friend smiles. "I thought you'd never ask."

Chapter 35

Now

Sebastian

"Today is not going to go perfectly, so just get that out of your heads right now," I say to the blinking group of polo-clad teenagers huddled in the kitchen in front of Omar, James (our new head barista) and me. "What matters is that we show people the restaurant they love hasn't gone anywhere, it's just gotten even better. And the way we do that is by working as a team. So, if you need help, ask for it. And if you *can* help, offer it."

I catch Omar stifling a smirk, but he nods. Part of the agreement we came to when we decided to take over the restaurant together was that Omar would have the final say on menu development and culinary operations, while I'd oversee the finances, vendor relationships and staff—and that means no eye rolling in response to my pep talks, hokey as he may think they are.

"I have a question." Parker raises her hand.

"Shoot."

"Can I *please* help out with the IG account? This sounds like something my grandma posted."

She holds out her phone, and I squint as she swipes through

a carousel of photos from training this week. I purse my lips and think, *Mom.* She'd insisted she'd be hands-off this weekend and let Omar and me take the reins, but I'm not surprised she finally broke my no-posting-until-we're-open rule. She's been trying to get me to take press calls for months, and I've only agreed (begrudgingly) to one. She assumes it's because I'm nervous about how opening weekend will go. But the truth is, the only journalist I've wanted to call since officially taking over the restaurant is one who definitely doesn't want to hear from me.

"Why are we even bothering with IG?" Wade pipes up. "We should be focused on TikTok."

I take a deep breath and think—not for the first time—that my mom has the patience of a saint to spend her summers surrounded by teenagers.

"Let me worry about marketing for now," I say with a smile. "Once we get through opening weekend, I'm down to have you guys take the lead on some fun social ideas."

Parker and Wade exchange a handshake that involves a complicated series of snaps and fist bumps, and then I dismiss everyone to their stations. We open in thirty minutes and still have more prep to do than I'd like. I'm about to head into my mom's—*my*—office to respond to a few vendor emails when my phone buzzes. It's Gina from Manasquan Roastery: **I'm out back!**

Thank God.

I shove open the heavy door to the parking lot and jog over to help her unload the crate of coffee and espresso beans from her car.

"Sorry I'm late," she says, throwing her long red hair over her shoulder. "This should get you through the day, but like I said, if you need more just call me. It's hard to estimate with a brand-new location."

When I'd first pitched her and her brother Logan my idea

for The Jetty, they'd been skeptical. They'd partnered with other existing businesses on the Shore, but never a new, unproven one. But after a few casual conversations (usually over beers with Logan or while surfing with Gina), I'd convinced them to take a chance on Omar and me.

I thank her and head back inside, then through the former snack bar entrance that now leads to The Jetty.

I'd come up with the name years ago, long before the other details fell into place. Back when all I had were a few initial sketches and an idea for a boardwalk counter that sold café-quality coffee drinks instead of just hot dogs, French fries and soda. I wanted the name to feel beachy without being too on the nose. The Jetty felt like the perfect name for a place designed to call out to the constant flow of beachgoers: Hey, why not drop anchor and stay a while? Grab a stool and a coffee, let's chat.

That's the practical reason I gave my mom and Omar, anyway. The bigger reason, of course, is that the name reminded me of *her*.

I'd be lying if I said I'd always had a thing for Lina Mariano. At first I lumped her together with all the other teenage girls who had cycled through summer jobs at my mom's restaurant. Sweet and helpful, sure, but not anyone I could see myself connecting with on a particularly deep level. We got much closer the next summer, after the jetty accident. I'd been surfing with some friends, and we knew she and her friend Maren were there, watching. It was the summer we'd all suddenly become hyper-aware of when girls were in our proximity. I remember keeping an eye on them. I knew how slick those giant gray rocks could get—I'd stumbled on them myself a few times. When she slipped, my chest constricted in panic. I ditched my board right there in the water and swam to her. I felt strangely protective of her after that, and even more so as I got to know her better. She had this innocent way of looking at the world that made me want to build a moat around her, safe and secure. The irony that I'm the one who wound up hurting her isn't lost on me.

When I kissed her I'd felt something I hadn't expected to feel. It had excited me. Scared me. I'd had plenty of attention from girls, but I wasn't nearly as experienced as everyone assumed I was. And those girls didn't know me—not really. But Lina did.

I'd felt horrible about how I'd treated her, but then again I'd felt horrible about a lot of things that school year, thanks to what had gone down between my parents. Horrible had become my new normal.

It wasn't until the following summer—my first one away from Brantley Beach—that I found my thoughts drifting to Lina Mariano almost daily. I'd gotten a job with the department of youth recreation on campus, teaching surfing lessons, lifeguarding and overseeing ropes courses. Whenever something remotely interesting happened—like when one of the less-athletic fifth graders stood up on his surfboard for the first time, or that time a group of campers pitched and organized a full-day beach cleanup—the first person I wished I could tell was Lina. I'd imagine her laughing and smiling at all the right moments, how her big brown eyes would sparkle with wonder.

I got the idea to develop the photos the first semester of freshman year. Maren had given Lina an old film camera one day that last summer we worked together, and Lina had worn it on a lanyard around her neck that whole week, snapping pictures of the staff and occasionally letting me take some of her. She'd been so disappointed when it ran out of film and she'd found out the model was so outdated, nowhere nearby could print the photos, let alone sell her another roll. But I'd popped the film out, taking care not to expose it, and held on to it. When I found out my roommate was planning to declare a film-and-media-studies major and had access to the darkroom on campus, I asked if he'd mind taking a stab at developing the pictures. He said not to get my hopes up but he'd give it a shot.

The pictures were like a salve for me, homesick as I was and yet unwilling to admit it. I thought about mailing them to Lina so many times, along with a long-overdue apology letter. But I never quite landed on the right words—and anyway, I couldn't imagine parting with them.

Eventually, as I got better at building the barrier that kept my homesickness at bay, I thought of Lina less and less frequently. She became a reminder of *then*, like mornings spent surfing with Andre and Theo, and working at the restaurant, and having what I thought were two happily married parents. Remnants of a past life I was no longer living.

Until, of course, she showed up at the clerk's office the same day as me.

Pieces of my past had already been flooding into my present, ever since my mom had told me she was sick and needed to sell the restaurant. But the dam broke that day. Claire and I finally admitted we weren't on the same page about what came next for us. We'd agreed to give it one last shot when I came across the mistake on the marriage license application. I think I actually laughed out loud. If there's a God looking out for me, he has a sense of humor.

Lina coming back into my life was the last thing I expected. And when I finally let go of my baggage enough to realize what I had right in front of me, I was all in.

Of course, I still managed to royally screw the whole thing up. No surprise there. And last year, when I worked up the courage to call the person who knows her best to find out if I had any shot of fixing things, she made it clear that I'd run out of chances. Lina Mariano had moved on, and the last thing I wanted to do was hold her back.

Now *I'm* back to unproductively thinking about the same girl daily. Only difference is this time instead of just thinking about her laugh or her smile, I'm thinking about how soft her skin is, and the way her lips taste first thing in the morning, the little groan she makes when—

Yeah. Not productive at all.

After I shelve the coffee beans and do one last round of check-ins with every station, I unlock the front door. I have no idea how this summer is going to go—if this new version of my mom's beloved restaurant will resonate with people, if Omar and I will do half as good a job running this place together as she did, if this town will welcome me back with open arms or recognize me as someone who didn't realize how special it was until it was too late. And I have no idea if I'll ever see Lina again.

But as I give James the green light to roll up the garage-style window to The Jetty, I can't help but feel a flicker of hope. It's a new summer, after all. Anything can happen.

Chapter 36

Now
Lina

A few hours later, I'm sitting in the passenger seat of David's car while he drives us toward the beach.

Though *drive* is a generous term for what he's doing—the traffic is so bad, we're barely moving.

When a Range Rover with New York plates attempts to cut him off, David lays on his horn.

He rolls down the window and flips the other driver off. "Better luck with that shit in the Hamptons, asshole!"

I glance at the back seat through the rearview mirror. Maren stifles a laugh. Henry rubs his temples, eyes closed.

"His road rage is almost as bad as his kitchen rage," Henry groans.

"I told you guys I should have just biked," I say.

"In those shoes?" Maren scoffs, genuinely offended by the suggestion.

After we'd filled the guys in over breakfast, I'd let the three of them collaborate on my look. The dress I'm wearing is from an Italian designer Maren works with that I've never heard of. It's a skintight white linen midi with spaghetti straps and slits on both sides that reach a little too high on my thighs. It hugs me in all the right places—and probably costs more than I'd make freelancing for a month. The shoes are vintage Jimmy Choo sandals that Maren scored at an estate sale in Knightsbridge. I'd styled my hair in loose waves, brushed my eyebrows into submission and swiped on mascara, blush and lip gloss. Like the mice in Cinderella, my three friends awed with approval.

I am way overdressed—but I have to admit, I look pretty damn good.

"Uh, guys?" Henry says, leaning forward. "I think this is as far as we're going to get."

We've made it to Ocean Avenue, but the entrance is blocked off, and two police officers are directing beach traffic to an overflow lot a few blocks north—in the direction opposite of where we need to go.

David squeezes the steering wheel. "*Fuuuuck.*"

I glance at the dashboard clock. It's already 11:57. I kick off my shoes and grab them with one hand, then open the door with the other.

David throws the gearshift in park. "What are you *doing*?"

I shut the door, leaning in through the window until I can see all three of them. "Thanks for the ride. I'll meet you guys there!"

And then I run.

The boardwalk is mobbed. I shouldn't be surprised: Weatherwise, it's forecasted to be a stunning Memorial Day weekend. I mutter apologies as I weave through bikers and joggers and power walkers and kids with boogie boards, the wooden planks hot against my bare feet. I thank myself for applying an extra layer of deodorant before we left and pray that the material of this dress can handle a little sweat.

As I cross Tenth Street, the first thing I notice is the line for The Jetty. People are wrapped around the gazebo and halfway up the block. I smile, because Sebastian was right, and so was I: Revamping the snack bar was a good idea.

I slow down to catch my breath as I approach the outdoor hostess stand for the main restaurant. Bubba herself is manning it. I duck out of view to jam my burning feet into my—Maren's—shoes.

Bubba notices me anyway and calls out, "Clocking in?"

I take a deep breath.

"Actually," I say, straightening, "I was hoping to speak to the manager."

Her lips curl into a smirk. She tips her head, gesturing inside. "If you see a headless chicken running around, that's him. You should be able to catch him after the welcome."

I thank her and start toward the threshold, then think better of it, double back and fold her into a hug. She squeezes me back, and I just have this feeling she knows why I'm here. Approves. It's all the reassurance I need.

Inside, I scan the dining room for Sebastian, my heart racing. The tables have already started filling up. Everything looks the same, aside from one section near the windows, where a few of the usual four-tops have been replaced by a Bruce Springsteen tribute band. I've heard this band play at various festivals and small concert venues over the years: They're sort of local legends, and they're actually pretty good.

If Sebastian had arranged this I'd be impressed. But honestly? It has Bubba written all over it.

As the band plays the first notes of "Rosalita," I duck into the kitchen. No sign of Sebastian there, either, but I do see Omar jostling one of the fry baskets while scanning the first round of order tickets. I want to say hi, but I don't want to interrupt him while he's in the zone. I'm about to turn around when he spots me.

I wave and mouth, *Congratulations.*

He winks at me. And then he glances toward the swinging

door that used to lead to the snack bar. I know exactly what he's trying to tell me.

Tentatively, I push it open far enough to peer inside, half expecting to slam into Kevin or Tina. What's on the other side stops me in my tracks.

It's still a small space, but it's transformed. The concrete floor has been covered with black and white tiles. The back wall still connects to the kitchen via a window, but the counter in between is lined with elegant pastries, fancy breakfast sandwiches and glasses of iced coffee instead of baskets of burgers and French fries. A humongous silver espresso machine gleams along one of the shorter walls, expertly operated by a thirtysomething man in a clean-cut polo, khakis and an apron. I recognize the similarly dressed teens who are manning the registers as Parker and Wade. The line is long, but it's almost constantly moving, and no one seems frustrated. I have nothing to do with this, of course, but I feel a swell of pride anyway.

"Can I help you with something, miss?" The barista has noticed me. His tone is cordial, accommodating, but I'm not so far removed from restaurant work to miss the hint of alarm of his eyes. He thinks I'm a customer gone rogue.

"I'm so sorry," I say, hands up. Translation: *I come in peace.* "I was just looking for Sebastian. Do you know where he is?"

"He was here a minute ago," he shouts over the sound of the milk steamer. Now that he's pegged me as friend or family, he drops the formal tone. "Dining room, maybe? Or he could have run out—ice machine is broken and we're almost through all the backup bags in the freezer."

"Thanks," I say, turning—and slamming into someone.

"Oh my God, sorry!" I yelp as the tall, red-haired woman I crashed into adjusts the crate she's carrying.

The same red-haired woman I saw surfing with Sebastian last August. My stomach plummets.

"You're fine, hon! James, mind giving me a hand?"

The barista rushes past me and takes the crate from her. I stop running through the worst-case scenarios my brain can conjure up long enough to notice that it's filled with rows and rows of brown paper bags and smells like coffee.

And that the woman is wearing a baseball cap that reads SQUAN ROASTERY.

I rewind through the last full conversation I had with Sebastian and a lightbulb goes off.

On Mondays I've been working on plans for the café . . . casually meeting with potential vendors.

Surfer Girl is Sebastian's coffee bean supplier?

"Thanks, Gina," James says. "I can't believe we already ran through what we ordered for today."

I duck into the dining room. The band is taking a break, and a longtime customer named Mr. Gerstein has taken the mic for a toast. Still no sign of Sebastian. Defeated, I decide to grab a table while I curse myself for being such a jealous idiot and plot my next move.

I remember Mr. Gerstein's wife passed the summer before my junior year. He's telling the story of how Bubba hand-delivered him a week's worth of food, then organized a spaghetti dinner fundraiser for a breast cancer charity in her honor. But her kindness didn't stop there: She came by to check on him every week or so, always with a tray of food in hand, long after other visitors stopped.

"That's the kind of woman Bubba is," Mr. Gerstein says. "Someone who never stops showing up for her people."

After a round of applause, he hands the mic off to a young man who looks to be college age. He introduces himself as JJ, and he thanks Omar for taking him under his wing last year. With Omar's guidance, he applied for and received a scholarship to culinary school this fall.

The toasts continue like this for a little while. They're informal—memories and words of gratitude shared above the din of clanging silverware and whispered lunch orders—but they're a reminder of the role this place has played in Brantley Beach for so many years.

Before I can convince myself otherwise, I'm standing. I smooth my dress, walk over to the makeshift stage and accept the mic from a regular who I remembered always ordered eggs Benedict with the hollandaise on the side and a black coffee.

I clear my throat. Is it me, or does the audience suddenly seem rapt? I still don't see Sebastian, though I do spot Theo, Hana, baby Esther and Andre at a table in the back. Andre's eyeing me curiously and pulling his phone out. Maybe it's better to not know if Sebastian's listening or not. I take a breath.

"Um." *Good start, Lina.* "Hi, everyone. Some of you may remember me, but some of you may not know me at all. My name is Angelina Mariano. I worked here while I was in high school. Bubba's was my very first job. And honestly? It was probably my favorite."

I glance toward a slight commotion by the entrance. My friends have finally arrived, out of breath. David and Maren are exchanging words, and I'm not sure who looks more annoyed. I silently thank myself for not waiting with them to find parking. Henry spots me and shushes them both. David and Maren immediately drop their tiff and grab on to each other in excitement. Bubba watches them, her expression one of amusement, then focuses her attention on me, too.

I speak this next part right to her. "These days not many people are willing to hire teenagers. I get it, honestly. Giving a fourteen-year-old—or even an eighteen-year-old—a shot seems risky when it's your livelihood on the line. But I'm so glad Bubba Nikolaou wasn't one of those people. Because this first job taught me more than I could have ever imagined."

I turn back to the dining room. "For me, Bubba's isn't just a restaurant. It's the place where I learned real responsibility. It's the place where I first experienced the satisfaction of coming home exhausted from a full day of hard work. It's where I learned how to work as a team. How to not mind getting my hands dirty. How to start managing my time and money. How to treat people with care and respect."

My attention is drawn toward movement in the back left corner of the dining room. It's not a customer headed for the restroom: It's Sebastian, emerging from the door to the parking lot. He locks eyes with me, and something in his expression tells me he hasn't just started listening. He shuts the door quietly behind him and crosses his arms.

"It's also where I experienced my first love," I say, "and my first heartbreak. It's . . ." I look at my fancy sandals, searching for the right words. "It's where I grew up. And I guess I just want to wrap this up by saying, I'm glad it isn't going anywhere." I'm looking directly at Sebastian now. "When you have something this special—something that's always been there for you, helped shape you into who you are—it's easy to take it for granted. I wish it didn't take almost having to say goodbye for me to realize that. But I realize it now. And I can't imagine letting it go again. So, yeah. I'll stop talking now. Thanks."

I click off the microphone and return it to the stand. I don't move for a moment, looking at Sebastian across the room while he looks back at me. It occurs to me that I should probably feel awkward, talking about my feelings in front of all these people. But honestly? I don't feel awkward at all. Because these people—whether I've officially met them or not—are part of my home. Why should I hide who I am from them?

And then he's in front of me. So close I can see the rise and fall of his chest. Breathe in his familiar scent: salt water and sweat and coffee beans.

"You came back," he says.

I shake my head. "*You* came back. I never really left, remember?" I smile so he knows that, for once, I don't mean this in a self-deprecating way. "The café looks incredible, by the way. Great name."

His mouth curls into a brief smirk, then flattens again.

"I thought you never wanted to see me again," he says. "I wouldn't have blamed you."

"Honestly, I think Maren was angrier at you than I was."

"She was just trying to protect you. I get it," he says. "I only spent a month in Santa Barbara. I felt like I owed it to my job to quit in person, and I needed to pack up my life out there anyway. Once I was back in Brantley Beach I almost came by your apartment so many times, but my mom told me you didn't even want to talk about me." He smiles sadly. "She told me you're crushing freelance life, by the way. I'm so proud of you."

Around us, the lunchtime sounds have resumed. A few curious customers are still glancing our way, but most have returned to their own conversations. I take a step closer to Sebastian, tipping my head back so I can look up at him.

"What happened with Diamond Group?" I have so many questions, starting with this one.

"Oh, you were right," Sebastian says. "They were totally bullshitting me. Andre helped us get out of the contract. I honestly didn't know what we were going to do at that point, but then one night Omar and my mom and I were talking about the options for the millionth time, and Omar finally admitted that he didn't want to let the restaurant go. We came up with a whole new business plan that night and made the paperwork official the next day."

"In this case, I'm definitely glad I was right." My smile quivers. "I do wish you were more honest with me last summer. But I also understand where you were coming from. You had a lot to figure out, and so did I. I shouldn't have taken it so personally."

I almost add, *and assumed you were sneaking around with your coffee supplier*, but think better of it.

"You're right, I did have a lot to figure out." He reaches a hand out to cup the side of my face, brushing his thumb over my cheek. "But the funny thing is, Mariano, the one thing I *was* certain about was you. I wish I'd said that a lot sooner."

"Well," I say, "lucky for you, I'm a very patient person."

He laughs and says, "I promise to make it worth the wait." Then he braces my back with the other hand, pulling me closer, and presses his lips to mine.

I lean into the kiss, forgetting we're far from alone, until someone starts to clap, and then the whole dining room breaks out in applause. I'm slightly embarrassed now, but not enough to stop kissing him, and apparently he feels the same, because now he's lifting me off my feet. I tighten my arms around his neck to steady myself, but relax once I realize I don't really need to.

He's not going to let me go this time.

Epilogue

One Year Later

"Okay. Which earrings?" I ask Maren, holding up my trusty gold hoops and the dressier pearls I reserve for weddings and holidays (if I actually remember I have them).

"Pearls for sure." Maren smiles gleefully. She got into town two nights ago and has been acting strange ever since. "Put them on and let's go. You're gonna be late for your own party."

"It's Sebastian and Omar's party, too," I remind her.

When we get to Bubba's, we find Parker and Wade outside, wrestling with the finishing touches on a massive balloon arch. In place of the hostess stand is an easel with a book open to a full-bleed photo spread: On the left, a six-year-old Bubba stands with her parents in front of the restaurant the day it first opened in 1965, and on the right is a photo from last year of Bubba, Sebastian and Omar standing outside The Jetty. I'd spent hours interviewing Bubba for this chapter, mostly while seated with Sebastian at her dining room table, flipping through faded photo albums and scrapbooks.

Maren gives my hand a squeeze and says, "I'm so proud of you, Leens."

Life really does have a funny way of coming full circle. Last summer, my old boss from *Ever After* had come across my article on Atlantic City's original saltwater taffy shop and DM'd it to a friend, who just so happened to be an agent who mostly reps culinary travel guides. The agent read more of my clips and reached out to see if I would be interested in putting together a proposal for the book publisher Rizzoli. Officially, the restaurant is closed tonight for a private party for the one-year anniversary of the grand opening of The Jetty and the new-and-improved Bubba's. Unofficially, we're also celebrating the launch of my new coffee-table book, *Beach Bites: A Culinary History of the Jersey Shore.*

In the dining room, we find my parents and the Murphys already halfway through a round of cocktails. They throw their arms around us and congratulate me, and then I'm shuffled toward more of my favorite people: Omar, Andre, David and Henry, Theo and Hana and Esther.

Thirty minutes fly by and I realize I still haven't seen Sebastian. I'm chatting with Mr. Gerstein and his middle-aged daughter when I feel a broad hand graze my back.

"Mind if I steal her for a minute?" Sebastian asks.

The Gersteins head for the appetizer spread and I whirl to face Sebastian, my heart rate quickening. We've been officially dating for a year now, but his presence still momentarily knocks me off my axis.

"Congratulations," I say, linking my arms around his neck as he wraps his around my waist.

"Right back at you." He smiles, but there's a heaviness in his eyes that—along with the tribute on the wall behind him—reminds me how bittersweet this occasion is.

In September, Bubba stopped responding to treatments, and she passed just before the holidays. Sebastian was devastated—

we all were. But there's a peace in knowing she got to experience one final season, and a pretty epic one at that. No one can replace Bubba, but in just one summer Sebastian and Omar proved they are more than capable of carrying her legacy into a new chapter.

We spend the evening with our friends and family, sharing memories of Bubba and summers past. I referee good-natured debates between Omar and Sebastian about new menu ideas and whether or not The Jetty is worth trying to air-condition (Wade pipes up strongly in favor). We catch up on everyone's news, their goals and worries and accomplishments big and small, and it feels like Bubba is here with us, listening.

Then again, maybe the point was always to give us a space to listen to each other.

The festivities wrap up around ten o'clock, and only Omar, Sebastian and I are left.

"Just like old times," Omar teases when he passes me stacking the chairs.

"At least I get to wear cuter shoes now." I wiggle one of my sandaled feet.

"You should get some rest, Omar," Sebastian says, jangling the keys. "Lina and I will finish closing up."

I hug Omar goodbye, congratulating him again, and then he claps Sebastian on the shoulder and heads out the back door.

Once Sebastian and I finish up in the dining room, we do a final round to make sure all of the equipment and lights are off. Then Sebastian locks the doors and we head to the parking lot.

"My place tonight?" Sebastian asks as we head toward his Jeep. Both of our cars are here, but I'll ride to work with Sebastian in the morning to grab mine. That's the only way I'll get up early enough to try The Jetty's new seasonal cold-brew flavor before it sells out.

"Definitely," I say. "Maren tore through my closet to pick

out my outfit. My room looks like it threw up young millennial."

"You know, my offer to solve all this back-and-forth still stands," he says as we climb in.

"And my answer still stands, too," I say, pulling him across the console for a kiss so he knows I'm not being ungrateful.

Before his mom passed, Sebastian had gotten her blessing to sell the house and start fresh, but it needs a bit of work before it's ready to go on the market. He's made it clear I'm more than welcome to move in with him in the meantime, but I'm not ready to let go of my apartment yet. By next year my savings will be solid, and maybe we could buy something together. It's important to me that we feel like equal partners.

We spend the short drive exchanging stories from the party, filling each other in on conversations the other person missed.

"Did you notice Maren actually laughed at one of Andre's jokes?" Sebastian asks as he turns the key to his house.

"Yes! But she's honestly been so giddy this week, so who knows if that means anything. She had me wondering for a second if you were planning to—" I stop short when Sebastian steps inside and I gain a view of the dining room table, which is covered in photographs. "Whoa. What are all those?"

"See for yourself," he says, pulling the door closed and gesturing toward the table.

I pick up the first photograph that catches my eye. It's a blurred selfie of Sebastian and me in our Bubba's T-shirts. I'm making a duck face, and he's holding up a peace sign. I place the photo back on the table and pick up another one, of Chris and Ravi pretending to be in a sword fight with a mop and broom. There are so many candids, too, mostly of either Sebastian or me, and even some of Bubba in her office or behind the hostess stand and Omar in the kitchen.

"I completely forgot about these," I say, in awe.

"Maren had come by one day with that old film camera," Sebastian says.

I nod, skimming the prints with my fingers. "Someone had brought it to the thrift store, and she immediately took it for me."

"You were obsessed with it that whole week." He comes up behind me, hands skimming my shoulders.

I laugh. "Until it ran out of film and I realized I had no idea how to develop it, or where to get more."

As the words leave my mouth, the realization hits.

"You kept these all this time?" I ask, turning to him.

"I held on to the film, and then my freshman year roommate at UCSB was a film major and he figured out how to develop it. I thought about mailing the pictures to you so many times—along with an apology—but I never figured out what to say."

We're silent for a moment, and then I say, "They're incredible, Sebastian. Thank you."

"Lina," he says, green eyes glimmering, "I know that I haven't always said the right things at the right times, but I want you to know that I always saw you."

He presses his forehead to mine, and then he reaches into his pocket and pulls out something sparkly.

"Don't worry," he says with a smirk, "I'm not proposing—or at least, not exactly. This was my mom's favorite ring. Not the one my dad gave her. It was originally my grandmother's, and I want you to have it now. I know that you're the person I want to marry, Lina, but I'm not asking you to marry me anytime soon if you don't want to. What I *am* proposing is whatever we decide to do next, we do it together. We can save up for a huge Bonnie and Amelia–style wedding one day, or if you're still sick of weddings we can have a little one, or we can just be together and do nothing celebratory at all. I love you, Lina Mariano, and I don't want to let another summer go by without you feeling that in your bones."

He slides the delicate gold ring onto my finger, and I manage to blurt out a combination of words that I hope resembles "I love you, too."

I stretch up on my tiptoes and pull his body against mine, craving as much contact as humanly possible. His embrace feels like being wrapped in the fluffiest beach towel after hours in the ocean: warm, dry and safe from the waves.

And as we hold each other I let myself picture past, present and future Lina not as three separate women, each with her own beginning and end, but one real, concurrent whole. Insecure and confident, naive and experienced, loving and beloved. All of it—all of me—right here, at once.

Author's Note

At some point in middle or high school I came up with what now feels like an arbitrary goal: Write a book by age thirty. I spent my twenties in editorial jobs, working my way up the masthead at national outlets, and all the while that goal simmered in the back of my mind. I wrote and edited for a living, but I missed writing creatively. I wanted to write a story that felt truly mine. Of course, wanting to write a book and actually doing it are two very different things! What I really needed was an idea.

The idea I'd been waiting for hit me in 2022, when my husband and I were applying for our marriage license at the city clerk's office. It reminded me of being at the DMV—not exactly romantic—and I felt sort of rushed through all the paperwork, including the part where a friend of ours served as our witness. My husband picked up the documents when they were ready. *Did you double-check everything?* I asked, like I do when we order takeout. He nodded a little too quickly (like *he* does when we order takeout). I opened the envelope myself later, and lo and behold, they'd missed a letter in my last name.

We caught the mistake in time to fix it for the wedding, but that hiccup got me thinking. What if a silly paperwork mistake like that had made our whole wedding void? How often do mix-ups like that happen? And are they ever more egregious—not just a typo, say, but the wrong name altogether?

The thought made me laugh and cringe at the same time. It reminded me of something out of a rom-com. Which got me thinking about the particular brand of rom-coms I've always loved: *27 Dresses*, *The Wedding Planner*, *Father of the Bride*. I realized they had something obvious in common: They were all about weddings.

At the time, weddings were starting to become a big part of my life. I was in the trenches planning my own, and every inch of my fridge was covered in "save the dates." Friends began joking that my fiancé and I were professional wedding guests. A few of my editorial friends had worked for wedding magazines, and I'd written some articles about wedding trends and registry ideas myself. I began to imagine a character: a burnt-out wedding writer. She's desperate to move on from the wedding beat, but she has to nail one last story—and the wedding of the season just so happens to be that of the boy she had a huge crush on in high school.

I didn't start writing right away. I had a lot going on at the time. I switched jobs. My husband and I got married. We moved. We went to more weddings. It was a happy and chaotic and stressful time. But by the summer of 2023 the dust had settled, and I found myself still thinking about that silly little idea. So I sat down and started typing.

The setting came to me next. The phrase "write what you know" sounds so clichéd, but once I decided to set this book on the Jersey Shore it became my guiding principle. Since college I'd been living in North Jersey and commuting to New York City, but in the summer I spent as much time as possible back home in Monmouth County, where I grew up. My parents still live in the same town-house development in Ocean Township where they raised me, about a ten-minute drive from the beach and boardwalk made famous by Bruce Springsteen's debut studio album, *Greetings from Asbury Park, N.J.*

Like Lina, I started high school in 2009. A show called *Jersey Shore* debuted on MTV that winter and became an instant hit. My friends and I rolled our eyes at what we considered a harmless, if very unrelatable representation of our slice of

Jersey. In college and afterward, whenever someone brought up the association, I'd lament that the show wasn't even about locals—most of the cast was from New York!

I wanted to write about the Jersey Shore I know and love, because it's nothing like what everyone saw on MTV. It's funnel cake on the boardwalk and fireworks over the beach and Springsteen on the speakers. It's claiming a spot on the sand with your friends and hoping you'll spot your crush a few towels away. It's saving up the cash you earned every high school summer as a lifeguard or a waitress while dreaming of big-city jobs in Manhattan, just an hour and a half away on the train. I wanted to truly capture the backdrop of my childhood and teenage years—charm, angst, hope and all.

Brantley Beach is fictional, but it's a conglomeration of several very real Monmouth and Ocean County towns that mean a lot to me. Long Branch, where I spent three summers working restaurant jobs on the Pier Village boardwalk. Manasquan, Belmar and Avon-by-the-Sea, where my friends and I snuck past the badge checkers and spent long days swimming, tanning and ogling the surfers. (Fun fact: On one occasion I did slip on a jetty and land in the hospital with a knee full of stitches. Sadly, no handsome crush materialized to save me, but a middle-aged fisherman kindly carried me to shore.) Point Pleasant, where I spent sunny days mini golfing and rainy ones at the aquarium (and where my nephews now do the same). Asbury Park, where my husband and I take our dog to the beach and where my hometown friends converge the second we're back in town. This book is a love letter to them all.

I also drew on my own career path while crafting Lina's. Her stint at the fictional bridal magazine *Ever After* is inspired by my own *The Devil Wears Prada*–esque years at Hearst's *Food Network Magazine*, where I started as an editorial assistant after college and fell in love with writing about food. To devise Lina's job at Shore Life, I reached even further back, to my internship at a New Jersey newspaper called the *Asbury Park Press.* I'd spent a college summer driving up and down the Shore, covering everything from vehicle crashes to lighter news, like where to watch Fourth of July fireworks and the best coffeehouses on Long Beach Island. Channeling my own real-life career experiences, anxieties and triumphs working in the editorial world wound up becoming a huge element of Lina's character development. Not to mention, it's a fun nod to some of my other favorite rom-coms that center around magazine or newspaper editors, like *The Holiday*, *How to Lose a Guy in 10 Days* and *13 Going on 30.*

Jersey food culture was a big source of inspiration for me, too. Say what you want about people from Jersey, but we'll keep you well fed. We take our food—whether it's coffee, pizza, bagels or boardwalk specialties—very seriously. Though Bubba's is a fictional restaurant, many of my favorite real-life Jersey Shore businesses appear in the book, including Rook Coffee and Kane Brewing Company. Throughout *HAGS*, many different characters use food as a way to connect and express their care for one another, whether that's by sharing cookies at a sleepover, gossiping during office lunch breaks or sacrificing the better cup of coffee.

When I started developing Lina and Sebastian's dynamic, I wanted to capture what it feels like to have a massive crush. But about halfway through the manuscript I had a realization. When I tried to think back on the crushes I had in school, the clearest memories were about discussing those crushes with my girlfriends. The way we analyzed brief interactions, dissected text messages and masterminded run-ins made me wonder: Was it ever really about those boys at all—or was it more about having something to obsess over with my best friends? That's where Maren came in.

Most romance novels and rom-coms include a best friend character, but I knew from the second I started writing Maren that she was destined to be much more than a sidekick. I'm fortunate to have many dear female friends, some going back twenty-plus years. My closest friendships have survived breakups and career changes and family drama and cross-continent moves. We've navigated life milestones side by side. Whenever I've struggled with confidence or self-acceptance, my girlfriends were there to remind me of my worth. And sometimes, a girlfriend was the only person willing to tell me a truth I didn't want to hear. I hope everyone reading can see a glimpse of their best friend in Maren. Her and Lina's friendship is a love story, too.

I finished this manuscript in August of 2024, three months before my thirtieth birthday, and I'm feeling all the feelings now that it's out in the world. Though Lina's story differs from my own in many ways, the emotions behind it are nothing but true. I wrote *HAGS* with so much love and nostalgia. I hope reading it transports you back to your own version of Brantley Beach, whether that's a place, a community or a specific person. A place that's witnessed the entirety of who you are and wouldn't change a thing.

Acknowledgments

It takes a village to publish a book, and this one wouldn't be in your hands without the support, encouragement and expertise of many people.

Thank you to the very first person to believe Lina's story was worth telling: my incredible agent, Alexander Slater. Publishing is a wild world, and I'm so grateful that you're the one guiding me through it every step of the way. Here's to many more books (and Gracie Abrams–heavy playlists) together. Thanks also to Hannah Strouth for your early feedback on the manuscript, and to the rest of the Sanford J. Greenburger Associates family, for believing in this book and in me as an author. I'm honored to be on your roster.

From the moment Elizabeth Trout said she grew up going to the Jersey Shore, I knew she was meant to be my editor. Thank you, Elizabeth, for your thoughtful questions and insightful edits and for laughing at all of my millennial jokes. You "got" this story from day one, and you somehow helped me understand my own characters even better. I love this book infinitely more because of the developmental edits we made together.

Thank you to the entire team at Kensington for taking a chance on me and bringing this book into the world, including Vida Engstrand for your early enthusiasm and publicity expertise and Lou Malcangi for the beautiful cover design.

I grew up with parents who always had books in their hands, and I feel so lucky that they never made me feel like my dream of becoming a writer was far-fetched or impractical. Dad, thank you for reading me the fables and for always prioritizing my education. You're still the best storyteller in the family, but I hope I'm a close second. My mom graduated college at forty years old (I was there, in my stroller), and after waitressing for twenty-five years she became a teacher. Mom, thank you for showing me how to not give up on a big dream, and for being the reason I fell in love with learning. Our daily phone calls are still the highlight of my day. Love you, darlin'.

I emailed my sister Natalie a partial draft of this book back in 2023. She read it at warp speed and demanded more pages. Natt, your immediate investment in these characters gave me the confidence to keep going right when I needed it. Thank you for being the person I can always trust to read my earliest drafts. (P.S. Who would have thought the third grader who wrote and illustrated a "book" about how mad she was at you for leaving for college would become a real author one day? I'm so lucky to be your little sister.) Thank you also to Dan, Louis and Theo for always letting Auntie crash your beach days and Jenks trips while writing this book.

Lina's name is an homage to my grandmothers. My mom's mother, Angelina (Maceo) Andrich, passed away before I was born, but I've always felt her presence with me. My dad's mother, Lucille (Mariano) Cocchi, showed me how to tell a good story and is still doing just that at ninety-seven. I fell in love with words during all those days we spent playing Scrabble and watching *Lingo* together. I love you, Gram.

Thank you to my big, loud Italian-American family all across New Jersey and beyond, who have been counting the days until this book came out. Thank you also to Charisse, Mark and Lindsay, for their love, support and encouragement; I hit the in-law jackpot with all of you.

Having a small circle is great, but mine is big and I love it that way. Thank you to my many dear friends across New Jersey, New York and Illinois who didn't look at me like I had twelve heads when I said I was writing a book, and who sent texts to check in for updates along the way. I promise we can talk about something else now.

Ellen: Thank you for being the S to my B, and the M to my L, even when we had an ocean between us. (But thank God we don't anymore.) Love you, Sis. Sarah: When I think back on every life milestone since middle school, you're right there with me. Thank you for making sure we have dinner on the calendar every single month, a tradition I plan to continue for the rest of our lives. Laur: For being my first editorial mentor turned dear friend, and for letting me monopolize our post-barre chats with book updates for an entire year. I'm so glad we're chosen cousins. Erin: For being one of my very first readers, cheering me on and teaching me how to use TikTok. Remember, we're the funny ones. Steven: For a friendship that transcended the job where we met, and for telling everyone who sets foot on the Shore about this book. Lauren and Devin, aka My Loves: For the monthly FaceTimes and texts of encouragement.

I'm so grateful to several people who took time out of their busy schedules to offer me publishing advice and contacts, including Jeff Walker, Peter Ginna and Andrew Gerber. Kelly Vaughan: Thank you for your early feedback and all the coffee-fueled vent sessions while I was querying and on submission. Britnee Meiser: Thank you for always being a text away when I need author advice, and for reminding me to keep writing.

Thank you to the teachers and professors at Communications High School, Villanova University and New York University's Summer Publishing Institute who encouraged me to pursue my dream of becoming a writer, including Andi Mulshine, Alan Drew, Mary Beth Simmons, Jeff Silverman and Andrea Chambers.

Thank you to all of the talented people I've worked with at Hearst Magazines and NBC's *TODAY*. You've made me a better writer, editor and storyteller.

I wrote the majority of this book on my couch between the

hours of 8:00 p.m. and 10:00 p.m. Huge thanks to my dog, Stevie, for the emotional support cuddles, and for forcing me to touch grass every day.

My husband, Matt, was the first person to read a word of this manuscript. I was so embarrassed that I locked myself in a separate room while he did it. Matt: Thank you for saying the words "keep going," and for talking about this book like it was a real thing way before you had any business doing so. For never once complaining when I spent hours writing after work every day. For proudly reading romance books on the bus so you could give me good feedback. For seeing my hometown through fresh eyes and helping me fall in love with it all over again. For being the foundation of our little family and making me feel secure enough to take a leap. And, finally, for setting an impossibly high standard; the fictional men I write will likely never measure up (but I'll keep trying). Ours will always be my favorite love story.

A READING GROUP GUIDE

HAVE A GREAT SUMMER

Francesca Cocchi

ABOUT THIS GUIDE

The suggested questions are included to enhance your group's reading of Francesca Cocchi's *Have a Great Summer.*

Discussion Questions

1. The book alternates between two timelines, fifteen years apart. How does getting to know Lina as a teenager influence the way you view her as an adult? Did any specific scenes from the past timeline help you better understand her feelings or decisions in the present?

2. At the start of the book, Lina feels stuck in many aspects of her life, from dating to her career. Why do you think she struggles to get out of this rut?

3. What did you think of Lina and Maren's friendship? How does it evolve from their teenage years to when they're adults?

4. Lina and Sebastian become close while working together as teenagers, even though they're in different grades and social circles. What do you think draws them to each other?

5. Food plays an important role in the book. What are some ways the characters connect through food? Was there a particular dish or drink you'd most want to try?

6. In the present timeline, David encourages Lina's second-chance romance with Sebastian, while Maren expresses wariness. Why do you think Lina's two closest friends react so differently?

7. Boardwalk Night is a turning point in Sebastian and Lina's teenage friendship, but the details aren't revealed right away. What did you initially think of the incident that caused their falling out? Did Lina's reaction feel warranted? Did your opinion change at all once you learned the context behind Sebastian's behavior that night?

8. Lina initially feels betrayed by Maren's phone call with Sebastian after the London trip. Did you empathize with Maren's decision? If not, how would you have handled that phone call?

9. Most of the book is told through Lina's point of view. What did you think of the author's decision to include one chapter from Sebastian's perspective toward the end? Are there any other scenes you'd have wanted to see through his eyes?

10. Lina had big-city dreams and feels some shame around the fact that she never made it out of her hometown. How do her feelings about Brantley Beach change by the end of the book?

11. While in London, Maren tells Lina, "It's easier to take a leap when you have people to catch you." Discuss the role that community plays in the book. Which characters contribute most to the Brantley Beach community, and what lessons do they teach Lina in the past and present?

12. According to Lina, "Sebastian wasn't a bad guy back then, and he isn't now. We just can never seem to get the timing right." Do you think timing is everything, when it comes to romantic relationships? What are some circumstances that stand in the way of Lina and Sebastian's relationship throughout the book, and how do they overcome them in the end?